Rotherwood

A PREQUEL TO IVANHOE

CHRIS
THORNDYCROFT

Rotherwood: A Prequel to Ivanhoe
By Chris Thorndycroft

2021 by Copyright © Chris Thorndycroft

https://christhorndycroft.wordpress.com/

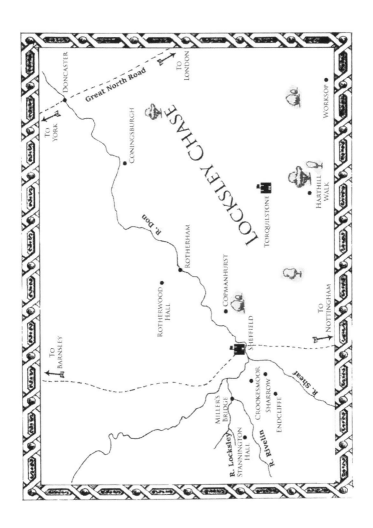

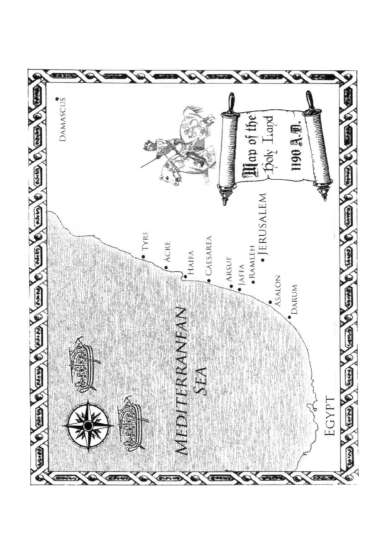

DAMASCUS

Map of the Holy Land
1190 A.D.

TYRE
ACRE
HAIFA
CAESAREA
ARSUF
JAFFA
RAMLEH
JERUSALEM
ASALON
DARUM

MEDITERRANEAN SEA

EGYPT

CHAPTER I

Rotherwood Hall, April 1190

The road north was little more than a trackway as it passed through the densely wooded portion of Locksley Chase that lay between Sheffield and Doncaster. The splayed branches of ancient elms and oaks formed a canopy overhead and, through the dense greenery on either side, occasional splashes of colour could be seen in patches of bluebells and cowslip. It was warm for that time of year and the woods hummed with life.

Wilfred Cedricsson breathed the woodland air deeply, the old familiar smells of home returning to him like happy memories. These were the woods of his youth in which his father had taught him to ride. His thoughts darkened somewhat as he remembered those carefree days, now so distant to him. Four years had passed since he had left his father's hall to join the service of the knight, Roger of Hambleton.

London had thrilled him for his previous experience of big cities had been limited to York. It was truly a world away from all he had known. The noise and colour of the crowded streets was drowning and the houses were so jammed together that they even clustered on the very bridges that spanned the sluggish waters of the Thames.

As all good pages in the service of English knights, Wilfred had learnt the pursuits and customs of the fine Norman houses such as hawking, dancing and playing backgammon. He learnt how to serve his master, to pour his wine and to cut meat. He also improved his martial skills and learnt how to tilt; a pursuit he found that he excelled at and had made quite a name for himself in the lists, earning the attention of the king himself.

He returned home now to celebrate Hocktide with his father, perhaps for the last time. He passed the familiar old sunken cross that stood at the meeting point of four roads. The road to the left led to Sheffield and the one to the far right, to Doncaster. Wilfred followed one of the smaller trackways that continued north to Rotherham and beyond, to his childhood home.

As he approached the village, he became aware of several figures up ahead, partially screened by the foliage, as if hiding from the road. There had been an increase in outlaws turning to banditry in the years before Wilfred had entered the service of Roger of Hambleton, but had things got so bad in his absence that robbers would dare waylay travellers on Rotherham's very doorstep?

The bushes up ahead wavered. He heard low voices whispering excitedly and a sterner one hushing them to silence. Somebody was giggling. *Giggling?*

Wilfred's hand dropped to the hilt of his sword in preparation to draw cold steel on anybody who thought to assail him. As the group of figures emerged from the greenery he realised that violence would not be necessary. They were women, about a dozen in number, dressed in bright linen with spring flowers in their veils and in chains around their necks. They swarmed Wilfred with much laughter and soft gestures to assure his horse that they meant no harm.

Wilfred couldn't help but smile as he was gently lifted down from his charger and blindfolded. He should have known better than to ride into Rotherham on the Monday of the second week after Easter. Hock Monday was marked by a ritual that saw rural women capture any men they encountered and hold them for ransom, donating the money they extracted to the parish church. This group had evidently lain in wait for unsuspecting travellers heading into Rotherham.

"Bind him!" cried one of the women in a voice familiar to Wilfred's ears. He felt sure that he would recognise at least half of his assailants had he been able to see through the strip of cloth that was quickly fastened over his eyes, for these were his father's people; ones he had known all his life.

His arms were secured to his sides by a length of rope that was wound and tied, not too tightly, around him. Then, the women began to spin him around, gently at first, but increasing in speed to make him thoroughly disorientated.

"Now, girls," said a mature voice in the tones of one in authority. "I believe our prisoner is quite giddy enough."

Soft hands were placed on Wilfred's shoulders to steady him although his head still spun.

"Knight errant," spoke another voice. "Though you travel with no squire or servants, it is easy to see by your sword and tunic that you are no pauper. Your ransom shall be high, we fear." The voice was that of a young maiden, sweet as music but laced with mischief.

"True, I am no pauper," said Wilfred. "But the pennies in my purse amount only to a few shillings."

"Then a few shillings it must be."

"And if I refuse to pay?"

"Then we must tie you to a tree and leave you as an example to others."

Wilfred grinned. "Spare me that fate, kind maiden. Had I a hand free, I would gladly reach for my purse."

"Unbind him!" the young voice commanded, "so that he may pay his ransom."

The rope was loosened but the blindfold was not removed. Wilfred reached for the purse at his belt and opened it. He drew out a fistful of silver pennies and held his palm out so that his captors could count the coinage.

"Two shillings, nine pence," said the young woman. "I suppose that will have to do. Remove his blindfold."

Dainty hands tugged at the cloth that obscured his vision and, as it was pulled away, he found himself staring into the blue eyes of an exceptionally pretty maiden. Her golden hair hung in two plaits on either side of pale cheeks that were lightly dusted with freckles. She wore a yellow dress and looked the very picture of a pagan spring goddess.

"Rowena," he said, the name of his childhood companion escaping his lips almost as a gasp.

Her eyes lit up as she took in his features, recognising him at the same time as he did her. "Wilfred! I hoped it might be you but I wasn't sure for the other girls were so quick to blindfold you. And your clothes and sword! You are much changed since your last visit."

"Much *has* changed," agreed Wilfred.

"It's Wilfred, son of Cedric!" chorused several of the other girls and there was much whispering and giggling.

"The hour grows late, girls," spoke a tall woman in a wimple Cedric recognised as Maud Lapsley, a figure of some authority in the parish and the owner of the stern voice he had heard. "We had best head back to the village and join the festivities."

It was only a short walk into Rotherham yet Wilfred was pelted with questions all the way. He led his horse by the bridle and walked with Rowena and Elgitha, her most trusted handmaiden, while the other ladies asked him about life at court, his service to the knight, Roger of Hambleton, and if he had met England's new king. When he replied that he had, the intensity of the questioning and eagerness for detail increased, especially as to a physical description of the monarch.

"He is tall," said Wilfred, "taller than I, and stronger too, I shouldn't doubt. He has coppery hair like his father but he is much more refined. He only wears the finest silks."

"Is he handsome?" one of the younger women asked, eliciting much mirth from the others.

"I suppose so," Wilfred replied, colouring a little. "Although he is past thirty."

"And what of his temper?" asked another. "Is it really as ferocious as they say?"

"No more or less than any other of the Angevin men, I suppose," said Wilfred. "But really, I only met him the once, not long after his coronation. He is currently in Normandy making preparations for his journey to the Holy Land."

"When is he to depart?"

"His English fleet assembles at Dartmouth as we speak."

"A soldier of God!" gasped one of the women in admiration. "May he be blessed with victory over the infidels!"

The village of Rotherham was a scattering of heavy thatched roofs frowning over limewashed cob walls. A patch of waste close to the road leading into the ramshackle collection of dwellings played host to the festival and villagers danced to the harps and flutes while ale was poured liberally from a great cask the alewife had brewed specially for the occasion.

"It's good to be home," said Wilfred, as he gazed on the festivities with fondness.

"Surely you don't tire of life at court?" Rowena asked him. "Rotherham's meagre amusements must pale in comparison to the merrymaking of knights and barons at Westminster and London."

"The extravagances of court have to be seen to be believed, it is true, but they are not as pleasantly familiar to me as this. I have missed these simple pleasures almost as much as I have missed you. And I wish to savour every moment while I am here for I do not know when I will be able to return home again."

Rowena detected the melancholy in his voice and turned to him, poised to ask him what was on his mind but the mood was broken by shrieks of mirth and delight as Rowena's companions swarmed a grey-haired old man who made a valiant but futile effort at escape. It was Maud Lapsley who led the assault, brandishing the rope herself and moving with a speed that defied her size and years.

"Anketil Lapsley has been captured at last!" said Rowena with a giggle. "He is notoriously tight with money and was up with the lark this morning to evade his wife."

"His ransom will be all the heavier for his efforts, I think," said Wilfred with some sympathy as old Anketil was bound and dragged into the centre of the festivities much to the amusement of the villagers.

"That it will," Rowena agreed. "Maud is most keen on raising money for the parish. She organises the ladies every year but I think she sees it as her duty to accompany us to allay the Church's fears of inappropriate behaviour. Hocking is often an excuse for flirting between men and women."

"I'm shocked!" said Wilfred, with mock severity.

Anketil, hands bound to his sides, was summarily relieved of his purse, the contents of which his wife joyfully counted out and added to the bag the ladies carried between them.

"I'll have double the ransom from you on the morrow, my good wife!" Anketil cried. "Do not forget that Hock Tuesday follows Hock Monday and the roles are reversed!"

"Now that's a thought!" said Wilfred, glancing at Rowena. "I had forgotten it is the man's right to extort money from the lady tomorrow just as it is her right to extort it from him today. Perhaps I will have my two shillings nine pence back from you!"

Rowena laughed. "You'll have to get up early to catch me. I go with the other ladies to St. John's church to clean the floors and distribute fresh rushes."

"Then I must accost you on the way, like a common hobhood."

"And you will receive Maud Lapsley's cudgel alongside your ear," said Rowena, "for she rides with us to hand over the Hock Monday takings to the church warden."

Wilfred pretended to stifle his frustration. "Then I will never see my two shillings nine pence again, for even a knight of King Richard dares not tangle with Maud Lapsley."

Rowena's eyes widened at his words. "A knight?" she said but there was no opportunity for Wilfred to answer as the musicians had struck up a lively tune to mark the penultimate ransoming of Anketil Lapsley and the villagers had taken up a carole. As the circle dance enveloped them, Wilfred and Rowena had no choice but to hold hands and join the dance which, fuelled by the ale in the dancers' bellies, began to spin with dizzying speed.

When the carole ended and the circle broke apart amid much laughter and clapping, Wilfred kept a hold of Rowena's hand and gently pulled her away from the crowd and behind one of the houses. There, screened by the wall and in the shadow of the overhanging thatch, he kissed her on the lips. Her hands went up to his head and they held the kiss for as long as they dared.

"I've missed you, Wilfred," she said.

"And I you, Rowena."

"Is it true? You are a knight?"

"Yes."

"Oh, Wilfred, I am so proud of you!"

"I have something for you."

"A gift?"

Wilfred took a thin gold chain from around his neck from which dangled a small locket held closed with a clasp. He gave it to Rowena. She took it and carefully opened it. It contained a small scrap of discoloured cloth held in place by a glass lens.

"It is reliquary," said Wilfred, "containing a scrap of Thomas Becket's robe which he wore when he was martyred at the altar."

"Oh, Wilfred! To think that you have visited the tomb of that sainted man and now I may carry a piece of his essence around with me always!"

"There's more. I did not come home merely to celebrate Hocktide with my father. I came to ask him to give you to me in marriage."

Rowena covered her mouth with her hand, unable to speak.

"We have loved each other since we were children. In fact, I believe that I fell in love with you the day my father brought you to Rotherwood Hall when you were nine years old, newly orphaned. I have never stopped loving you and I mean to make you my wife. My father can't refuse me, not now I have been knighted and given a fief besides."

"A fief?"

"Aye, the fief of Ivanhoe. It is my payment for my knight's service. I am to go with King Richard to Outremer and help him reclaim the holy city from the Saracens. I'll bring you back another reliquary containing a fragment of rock from Calvary. Jerusalem should fall within the year. Saladin's ragtag army will cower before King Richard and his army."

All previous joy fell from Rowena's face at this. *Outremer.* The Land Beyond the Sea. "You came here to say goodbye, didn't you?"

"For now, my love, only for now. Once we are victorious, I shall return and we shall be married. I will have an estate and tenants with rent and we shall not want for anything. Even my father could not baulk at that."

"You do not know how bitter your father has become since you went away, Wilfred," said Rowena. "He despises the Norman barons with more vehemence every day. It might not be so easy to persuade him to give me to you in marriage. You remember Athelstan of Coningsburgh?"

"Athelstan? I could not forget my fat fool of a cousin for he and I were playmates in our youth. How is he?"

"Fatter and duller than he ever was. Your father has invited him to Rotherwood for Hocktide. I fear he hopes for a union between us. You know how he values Athelstan's descent from the old Saxon kings just as he does mine. He harbours a dream to see our two lines reunited and a stronger Saxon family born as a result."

"Ha!" said Wilfred. "Always it's Normans and Saxons with my father! He grieves for a people slighted long ago by those who are now dead. He pines for a world he himself never knew."

"He speaks a half truth," said Rowena. "The transgressions of those such as Front-de-Boeuf keep that old wound open as much as your father's romantic longing does. More so, in fact. The memory of the Battle of Hastings burns all the more painfully every time a man of Norman stock takes land or a castle that belonged to one of the old families."

"Do not say that my father has twisted your mind too!" said Wilfred. "Reginald Front-de-Boeuf is a robber and a knave. There have always been such men in positions of power long ere Hastings. And as for 'Norman blood', to speak of it as if it were a foreign malady must surely border on treason. Do not forget that the king I serve claims direct descent from the very man my father calls 'bastard tyrant'. Old families? Ha! My father may be content to while away his time seeking out pedigrees that lack foreign blood but I tell you there are few enough of those these days. To be English is to be Norman and until my father comes to terms with that, he will continue to be a laughing stock of better families than ours."

"Is that the way of it in Westminster?" Rowena asked, looking hurt by Wilfred's words. "That Cedric of Rotherwood is a laughing stock?"

"Few in Westminster have heard his name but those closer to home call him 'Cedric the Saxon', a term I am sure he would wear with pride if he did not know that it was used with derision. His obsession with the past and an age that probably never was mark him out as a harmless eccentric."

Rowena looked deeply upset at the thought of her guardian's name being used as a byword for ridicule but she seemed to push her melancholy away from her. "Oh, let us not speak of Saxons and Normans, for I fear we will hear enough of that at table tonight. Come, we must re-join the festivities before we are missed."

As they left the shade of the thatch and rounded the corner of the building, Elgitha hurried over to them. "My lady, I thought I had lost you!"

"Never fear, Elgitha," said Rowena. "My brave Percival is here to protect me."

Elgitha glanced at Wilfred, not sure if she was missing a joke.

"You look upon the knight, Wilfred of Ivanhoe," Rowena explained. "And now, my knight, I believe it is time we retired to Rotherwood Hall where I am sure the tables are being laid with dishes and the mead is being poured as we speak."

Rotherwood Hall stood less than five miles north of Rotherham, surrounded on all sides by trees. It was a hall in the old Saxon style, preserved as best its owner could out of stubbornness and defiance for all that had changed in England since the Battle of Hastings over a century ago. The main hall, low and thatched, was surrounded by a spiked palisade and a moat. A drawbridge spanned the channel of water and led into the main compound. As Wilfred led his horse across the bridge, he spied Wamba, his father's fool, and his inseparable companion, Gurth the swineherd, idling by the kennels.

"Don't you two ever work?" he enquired, causing them both to leap to their feet, fearing some reprisal for their laziness.

"A warm spring wind blows last year's leaves in through Cedric of Rotherwood's doors," said Wamba in his usual poetic patois. "But these can't be autumn's leaves for they are as bright and vibrant as spring's. Who is this warrior of noble rank in a scandalously short cloak who carries such a resemblance to our lord Cedric's wayward son?"

"Hello, Wamba," said Wilfred. "And Gurth. How goes it?"

"Master Wilfred, it gladdens my heart to see you again," said Gurth. "Rotherwood hasn't been the same since you left."

Brutus, Gurth's aging wolfhound, crept cautiously forward to sniff at Wilfred, recognising the familiar scent of a friend.

"Brutus is getting too old to be of much use to me," said Gurth. "He is nearing the end of his days but a bitch has just whelped over Rawmarsh way and I am promised one of its pups. Brutus's last job will be to help me train him."

"And a fine tutor he will make," said Wilfred.

They entered the main building and Elgitha accompanied Rowena to her chamber to help her dress for dinner. Wilfred was met in the antechamber by Hundebert, his father's steward, who looked just as surprised by his appearance as Wamba and Gurth had been.

"Master Wilfred," said Hundebert, bowing low. "Welcome home. Your father was unaware that you would be joining us for Hocktide."

"I will not be staying long, Hundebert," said Wilfred. "And it is good to see you, old friend."

"And you, young master. This hall has darkened somewhat since you left us."

The interior of Cedric's Great Hall matched its exterior in terms of simplicity. The floor was hard-packed earth mixed with lime and the walls and beams were of rough-hewn logs. Long ago, Cedric had hired the finest artisans to carve the pillars into curling serpents in the oldest Saxon style but now both pillars and beams were blackened by woodsmoke. Cedric considered the modern stone fireplaces and chimneys a damnable Norman custom and favoured the open cooking fires of his ancestors. Hearth fires blazed at either end of the hall and one of Gurth's fattest hogs cracked and spat as the cooks turned it over the flames of the furthermost one.

Upon a raised dais before the roasting hog, was the high table at which sat Cedric of Rotherwood. He hadn't changed much since Wilfred had seen him last, perhaps a few more strands of his flaxen hair had turned to grey but he was still the ruddy-faced, short-bearded man as before, just as stout and hale as Wilfred remembered. He wore a green tunic trimmed with grey fur and short breeches that left the leg below the knee covered by grey stockings cross bound with cloth strips. His clothes were of an outdated fashion, just as his hall was a relic of a bygone age.

While Oswald, Cedric's cupbearer, refilled his horn with mead from an earthenware jug, Cedric was busy making conversation to a tubby man sitting next to him. The man was a little older than Wilfred and wore far better clothes than Cedric did. He appeared to be more interested in the meat pasty he was helping himself to than whatever words Cedric was speaking into his ear and Wilfred recognised him as his cousin, Athelstan. To one side of him sat Athelstan's mother, Edith.

Cedric looked up and saw Wilfred across the shimmering heat of the fire and, even at that distance, Wilfred could see the sudden recognition replaced with disgust at his returned son.

"So, our noble Norman courtier returns to us, dressed in the gaudy fashion of his new masters!" said Cedric, and Wilfred could immediately tell that Oswald had not neglected his duty for mead had already done its work on the aging man's temper. "Come to shame us all with your superior manners and customs?"

"I have come to spend Hocktide with my father," said Wilfred.

"Come to lord it over me, more like! And I a true lord, native to this land, at that! Very well, take a seat and help yourself to our meagre victuals. I'm sure your palette has grown accustomed to richer fare in the company of our king."

Wilfred sighed and took his seat at the table. A basin of rose water was passed to him so he washed and dried his hands before accepting a trencher while an empty horn was filled with mead. He helped himself to the dishes on the table as conversation was struck up once more.

The man to his left – Wat of Flanderwell, Wilfred recalled – was most interested in hearing about Wilfred's life at court, in particular his distinctions that had seen him knighted. Wilfred explained that it had mostly been his prowess in combat, both on horse with lance and on foot in the melee that had earned him his spurs. With the king's expedition to Outremer approaching, men with skill of arms were in popular demand.

It was as Wilfred was describing the tactic of unhorsing a charging knight that Rowena entered the hall followed by Elgitha. Hundebert the steward called for a place to be set at the table as she crossed the dais. Admiring eyes were cast in her direction. She had changed into a kirtle of green under a crimson robe. Her hair had been newly braided and fell in ringlets from beneath her veil which she wore back over her head, revealing her face. Around her neck, Wilfred was pleased to see the reliquary he had given her. He couldn't tear his eyes away from her beauty.

"Is she not beautiful?" Cedric asked, although the question was directed specifically at Athelstan.

The younger man was more preoccupied with his meat than the object of the hall's attention as she took her place on the other side of Cedric. Athelstan seemed to suddenly realise that some form of compliment was required on his part for he wiped his mouth with a soft piece of bread and nodded a polite greeting to Rowena. "My compliments, Cedric, your ward grows more beautiful every time I see her."

"Worthy of her name," agreed Cedric. "Her parents, God rest their souls, did well to name her after Hengest's daughter. Rowena here would give that ancient beauty a run for her money and would have bewitched all the British nobles had she been there at the founding of our nation. You have heard me say, I am sure, that her family is of the line of Alfred, the mightiest of Saxon kings?"

"You have indeed mentioned it," said Athelstan, supping from his mead horn.

"A fine match for a man also of royal pedigree. Would that those of Saxon blood still ruled England!"

Perhaps fearing another melancholy monologue, Wamba the fool, who had taken his position on a stool behind Cedric, spoke up; "Do not begrudge Vortigern for succumbing to the beauty of the Rowena of yore, sire, for his weakness was Hengest's gain. The fall of the Britons was the rise of the Saxons. Perhaps the beauty of Rowena might be put to use in our own time? By bewitching a Norman lord, might we not see a second rise of our people? A second Night of the Long Knives, even?"

"Rowena marry a Norman?" said Cedric testily, as he took a meat bone from his trencher and tossed it beneath the table for Balder, his favourite hound, to chew on. "Be careful you do not overreach yourself, fool. My ward is a Saxon jewel that shall be cherished by a Saxon and no other."

Wilfred, who could bear no more talk of Rowena as if she were a polished gemstone to be bartered with, rose from his seat. "It is the matter of Rowena's betrothal that forms part of my purpose in coming here this Hocktide, Father," he said.

Cedric glared at him dangerously. The hall had fallen silent. Wilfred had intended to broach the matter with his father in private but the opportunity, and the sight of Rowena's shamed face as her guardian discussed her future happiness, had galvanised him into action.

"It is no secret that I love Rowena and she loves me," said Wilfred, "for we have become as kin since she was brought into this household long ago. But our love is no longer the love of childhood companions. We love each other in the truest, purest sense of the word and I would make her my wife with your blessing."

"You, Wilfred?" Cedric snapped. "My own son marry this most precious of Saxon treasures?"

"A Saxon treasure so precious you would give her to somebody other than your own son who loves her more than life itself?"

"It is true," said Rowena, rising from her own seat. "Wilfred and I have confessed our love for one another. I would have no man but him for my husband."

"Love?" Cedric sneered. "A childish notion borne of Norman romances! I would not throw away the hopes of a nation on your infantile infatuation. Rowena will marry a man of royal Saxon pedigree. Her bloodline will fuse with another to form a mighty Saxon dynasty. I will hear no more of this foolishness!"

"Are we not," said Wilfred, "as you have so often reminded me, descended from Hereward the Wake, that Saxon rebel who was such a thorn in the sides of the Normans?"

"Aye, ours is a noble family brought low by Norman oppression," said Cedric. "I am a mere Franklin with a fraction of the lands that would have been mine had Hereward or, indeed King Harold, been successful in their enterprises. And you, son of mine, are even less than me. Do you really think a Saxon who plays squire to a Norman knight, with no lands or wealth of his own is a suitable match for fair Rowena?"

"I have been made a knight, Father. And given the fief of Ivanhoe for my sustenance."

"Given? Given by your new Norman friends, no doubt! And who was the poor Saxon who originally held that land before it was stripped from him by the butchers of the bastard tyrant William? I cannot remember, it has been so long that we have lived under the boot of foreign oppression since Harold's fall at Hastings."

"Father, when will you let go of old quarrels that do not concern us? None of us here had our lands stripped from us by William and his kin. And no baron of Norman blood alive today was there when Harold was slain at Hastings."

"There!" cried Cedric. "My own son, not content to wear the clothes and affect the customs of our oppressors, defends them in the very hall of his father! And with the lady Rowena present and Torquilstone Castle not three leagues away to remind him! Do you forget, Wilfred, how your childhood companion's family were slaughtered and her left an orphan to my care? Do you forget how that knave Front-de-Boeuf and his father butchered my good friend Torquil and his whole family and took his castle?"

"These crimes I have not forgotten, Father," said Wilfred. "And had I the means and opportunity to avenge the lady Rowena and good Torquil against the likes of Front-de-Boeuf, I would do so in a heartbeat. But I do not extend my feelings of revenge to all who happen to bear a Norman name."

"Then you are perhaps as much a fool as Wamba here," his father snapped. "A wise man does not ponder which of the ravening wolves has good intentions."

"And what of our king?" Wilfred asked. "Do you bear him the same ill will you bear Front-de-Boeuf? Is he also a 'ravening wolf'?"

"Do not seek to trick me into speaking against our king," his father said. "He and he alone I forgive his Norman ancestry."

Wilfred smiled. Even his father's hatred for the Normans stopped short of outright treason. "I am glad, Father. For I would hate to think you bore me ill will for entering our king's service."

"Service? What service?"

"In exchange for my knighthood, I owe King Richard my knight's service, as is the custom."

Cedric regarded him in silence.

"I am to go to the Holy Land, Father," Wilfred explained. "To aid our king in the reclaiming of Jerusalem from the infidels."

"Ha! A fool's errand!"

"You are content to let Saladin and his Muslim hordes occupy the holiest city on earth?"

"It is not the desired result I sneer at but the feeble attempt. Jerusalem is too far from here to be of any import. Let others die trying to capture a dream. Your duty should lie in defending your family and the names of your proud ancestors here in England, not with a foreign king and his desire for glory in distant lands!"

"Had my ancestors not Christian hearts?" answered Wilfred. "And is it not my father who shames them rather than I for sitting in his hall and thinking on the past instead of dedicating himself to the present? Our king fights for God and I would be ashamed not to follow him. Any other father would be proud of his son and see in him a fit husband for any ward of his."

Cedric slammed his fist down on the table in a rage. "The sun will bleach your bones in the sands of Outremer before I let you marry Rowena!"

Wilfred rose slowly, rage boiling inside his gut. "You may get your wish, Father, for the road ahead of me will be long and treacherous. I do not know when I shall return, if ever. But if I should, then I hope the distance and time between us will have cooled your temper and given you opportunity to reassess your opinion of me." He glanced at Rowena who looked on the verge of tears at the heated exchange. The rest of the hall had fallen into an embarrassed silence. It was time for him to leave. He turned from the table.

"If you leave Rotherwood to depart on this mad expedition," his father said, "if you choose the wishes of our Norman king over your own father's then I will make it known far and wide that I have no son!"

This drew an intake of breath from the assembled hall. Rowena covered her mouth with her hand, appalled by her guardian's harsh words.

"I have already made my decision," said Wilfred. "I would be a craven and a dishonourable knight if I were to go back on my pledge now. Goodbye, Father. I hope I will see you again one day."

"Then I have no son!" Cedric roared, rising in a sudden bout of rage. His horn was overturned, spilling mead across the board. He seized it and hurled it in Wilfred's direction. It clattered harmlessly across the earthen floor, spattering Wilfred's boots with its remaining droplets.

"So much for the great Saxon race," said Wilfred bitterly. "Reduced to a drunken old man raving in a barn."

In a rage-filled motion, Cedric drew the sword at his belt and made to hurry around the table. Terrified that the old man would do something unforgivable in the eyes of both the law and God, his servants grabbed at him, Oswald seizing his sword arm and Wamba pulling at his tunic to keep him back. Balder leapt up and began to bark, not knowing what was happening but sure that his service was required. Sapped of his strength by mead, Cedric fell back on top of Wamba, the sword slipping from his grasp with a clatter.

"Get out!" he roared at his son. "You are welcome in my hall no longer! Get out, you traitorous whelp! I disinherit you!"

Wilfred paid a last glance to Rowena, his heart aching at the sight of tears streaming down her cheeks, before turning and leaving the hall.

He refused to spend the night at Rotherwood. All he wanted was to head to Dartmouth, board a ship and begin his journey to Outremer.

It was three hundred miles to Dartmouth and took Wilfred the best part of a week to get there. The meagre coin he had to his name meant that he spent most nights sleeping in barns and haylofts, only affording himself the occasional meal at an inn. Things would be different, he kept telling himself, when he returned from Outremer with exotic treasures in his saddlebags and an estate in England to spend them on. Before he went to sleep each night, he imagined taking Rowena to Ivanhoe for the first time as his wife. He imagined introducing her to the servants and telling her how she would be in charge of governing the household. They would drink wine by the hearth – a proper Norman fireplace, not one of his father's damnable firepits – and they would be happy.

But first, Outremer awaited and all the hardships it held for him. It was to be his rite of passage. He would leave England a youth and return a man; a man worthy of all who doubted him.

The town of Dartmouth wasn't large but it overlooked a tidal inlet in the estuary of the River Dart that was deep and wide enough to harbour over a hundred ships. It had been the main embarking point of the previous crusade and, as Wilfred came within sight of the town, he could see from a distance that it was full to bursting.

Tents and pavilions blanketed the green fields that surrounded the town and told Wilfred that he hadn't a chance of finding lodgings in the town itself. Smoke from hundreds of hearths and forges hung over the thatched rooftops and people swarmed its cobbled streets, all dressed in the liveries and colours of a thousand households.

The inlet to the south of the town was bristling with the masts of clinker-built cogs and busses that gently strained at their moorings with the tide. They were packed so closely together that it was possible to step from one to another in many cases and gangplanks had been laid across the gunwales for the conveyance of supplies. All about was activity. Men shouted to one another as they carried sacks of grain, barrels of salted meat, tuns of wine and water, horse fodder and siege equipment down into the holds. On the vessels closest to the shore, horses were being loaded where they would be secured below decks with canvas slings beneath their bellies.

Wilfred found a cluster of trestle tables where clerks were documenting the cargos and passengers in ledgers. He wanted to seek out Roger of Hambleton so that they might travel together as he didn't know a soul from Adam in this bustling, busy town. But things looked to be moving fast and Wilfred didn't want to end up not getting a spot on a vessel so he strode up to one of the trestle tables and addressed the clerk who sat there in Norman French.

"How many horses?" said the clerk.

"Just the one," Wilfred replied.

"Squires?"

"None."

"Servants of any kind?"

"No."

The clerk looked Wilfred up and down as if not convinced he was a real knight. "You travel light."

"I do indeed. I just need a stall for my horse and a place I can rest my head at night."

"There's still space abord the *Greyhound*. Your horse will have to be loaded today."

"When do we sail?"

The clerk shrugged. "Depends on the wind, I suppose. I'm just a clerk, not a sailor. What's your name?"

Wilfred was silent. His eyes watched a drop of ink form on the nib of the clerk's quill. The clerk looked up, confused by his hesitation.

All his life he had been known as Wilfred Cedricsson but that was a name that stuck in his throat now. His father had stripped him of it as a king might hack off a knight's spurs. After a moment's further hesitation, he glanced at the clerk and gave him the only name he had left to him.

"Wilfred de Ivanhoe."

CHAPTER II

Acre, July 1191

The tower had fallen when most of the camp had been breaking their fast. It wasn't so much unexpected but alarmingly premature. King Richard had ordered his sappers to dig a mine under the walls of the besieged city of Acre and weaken them by setting light to the support timbers. The plan had worked surprisingly well, far surpassing previous attempts, and the tower's fall had caught the Christians completely unaware.

Cries of alarm at the cascading masonry and rising dust cloud quickly changed to elated cheers in the Christian camp as the besiegers realised what had happened. The walls were breached! Now was their chance! But they were far from ready. Most hadn't yet roused themselves and those men who were in their armour were far from Richard's position on errands in other parts of the sprawling camp.

The king pressed on nevertheless, even demanding that he be carried out on a stretcher so he might command the assault from his sick bed. He ordered the pile of rubble to be cleared and, true to his usual disregard for cost, promised two gold bezants for every block of masonry removed.

The price of stone was raised to three bezants per block as arrows began to sail down on the eager Christians who charged the breach, killing some and making the rest exercise extreme caution. All available archers and crossbowmen were mustered to cover the excavations and even the king in his fevered state lent a few arrows to the effort from a gilded crossbow which he shot while reclining on silken cushions.

Wilfred had been one of the few knights on hand to join in the assault on the breach. Most of the other men who charged alongside him were Pisans who had pledged their support to Richard upon his arrival at Acre.

To begin with, the Saracens contented themselves with raining death down on the Christians from their positions on the shattered walls but the continuing barrage of the English mangonels and the heavy crossbow fire forced them to take shelter, only occasionally daring to break cover to cast jars of Greek fire at the attackers.

These incendiary weapons were every crusader's nightmare. Earthenware pots filled with a highly flammable substance, the exact recipe of which was a closely guarded secret, exploded in billowing clouds of flame as they shattered on the rocks, engulfing any poor soul who was too close in an agonising and fiery death.

The morning sun already provided an uncomfortable level of heat for the Christians in their padded gambesons and heavy mail but the additional blasts of heat from the exploding jars of fire made the air around them a hot, shimmering hell.

Wilfred and his squire, Leonard, were carrying a large stone between them. Wilfred knew the attack was coming. Missile fire had ceased and there had not been an attempt to hurl any more pots of Greek fire at them for a while. Some of it still burned where it stuck to the broken masonry and the bodies of the men who had been slain by it blazed merrily, the bodyfat bubbling and crackling.

Wilfred dropped his end of the stone and drew his sword. He crept up the pile, away from where the Pisans and other men-at-arms were still heaving away chunks of masonry. Through the thick dust that hung over the destroyed wall like a mist, he caught his first glimpse of the city of Acre that cowered behind its fortifications, the gateway to the East that had defied the Christians for nearly two years.

The helmed heads of the Saracens rose before him like phantoms as they crested the mound, the sunlight glinting on their swords. Wilfred turned his head and barked at the men behind him; "Fall back! Fall back!"

Then, they were upon him.

He parried a swipe from a sword and lashed out with his foot, knocking his attacker off balance. Then, with a downwards chop, he felled him, opening him up between the shoulder and the neck.

The Christians who were unarmed scurried back towards the English lines, some even carrying a few last chunks of masonry with them, still keen for some of the king's gold. Every other man with a blade hurried to join Wilfred at the top of the mound.

Wilfred glanced to his right and smiled as Leonard appeared at his side, sword gripped in his shaking fists as more and more of the enemy crested the mound. His squire's loyalty was second to none.

As the Saracens hurried to meet them, Wilfred realised it was hopeless. He and a handful of soldiers were all that stood in the breach and soon they would be overwhelmed.

The Saracens fenced them in in a semicircle, stretching from one end of the shattered wall to another, blocking the entrance to their city. But entry to the city was no longer the objective of the few Christians who stood atop the mound. They had to cut a fighting retreat back to English lines until a more concerted assault could be organised.

And the Saracens weren't going to let them escape if they could help it, not now they outnumbered a small group of the cursed infidels. They would redden their blades in Christian blood while they had the chance. One by one, the Christians fell, slipping and sliding in their own blood that splashed the stones beneath their feet, turning the white masonry crimson.

"Get the wounded out of here!" Wilfred bellowed.

Several of the men-at-arms, all too happy for an excuse to leave the fight, attended to the fallen, carrying them out of harm's way. The few fighters who remained blocked the way bravely.

Leonard cried out as a blade nicked his arm. Wilfred saw the danger and cut in at his attacker before he could finish the job, knocking his faithful squire out of the way as he did so. Steel clanged as the Saracen defended himself but his swordsmanship was inferior to Wilfred's and he split his skull with a downwards chop that clove the helm.

The battle was lost. Only Wilfred remained standing, with the wounded Leonard at his side and half a dozen men-at-arms further down the mound who were still struggling with the wounded.

Outnumbered they may have been but the blades of the Christians had taken their toll and the other side of the mound was littered with the Saracen dead. The enemy were being more cautious now and there were a lot fewer of them. Wilfred took his chance to escort Leonard down the mound. His arm was bleeding badly but the brave Pisan was holding up admirably.

"I will be alright, sire," said Leonard. "Help another in more dire need. I am not so wounded that I cannot walk unaided."

Wilfred patted him on the back and bent down to help a man who had a nasty gash in his head that seemed to have dashed some of the sense out of him for he was unable to stand. As he was helping the man to his feet, he heard several of the men around him cry out in alarm. Wilfred glanced up at the top of the mound and could see a Saracen silhouetted against the dust cloud, holding one of the dreaded pots of Greek fire by its long fuse.

As the man crouched down to light the fuse with flint and knife, Wilfred knew that in moments, the whole mound would be up in flames, and the Christians – healthy and wounded alike – with it.

Wilfred left the man he was helping and dashed back up the mound. The Saracen had the fuse lit now and was holding the jar above his head. The distance was too great for Wilfred to reach him in time and even if he could, what would he have done? The moment that jar shattered on the rocks, it would be the death of them both.

There was only one thing Wilfred could think of. It was a poor move, not encouraged in those who learned the art of the sword but it was not considered unchivalrous in the heat of battle when one's life sometimes depended on the crudest of efforts. He wrapped his index finger around the cross guard of his sword and rested the flat of the blade on his palm. Then, drawing his arm back, he launched his sword as if it were a javelin.

It whickered through the air and pierced the Saracen in the neck, a foot of the blade's length sinking into the flesh and thrusting out the other side. The Saracen gargled a cry of defeat, his eyes wide in shock as he was knocked backwards by the weight of the blade. The jar tumbled from his grip and smashed on the rocks at his feet.

The sound of the substance igniting was as a bolt of lightning. The Saracen went up in a billowing cloud of flame and Wilfred shielded his eyes as the heatwave rolled over him, almost knocking him back as a physical force. The heat scorched his mouth and he choked as the foul fumes of the burning concoction entered his lungs. Liquid fire ran down the mound towards him like the contents of a volcano's belly. He knew he had to get out of its way and fast.

Barely seeing where he was going, he stumbled back down the mound to where the last of the wounded were being carried away. Men from the English lines had run forward to help drag the wounded out of harm's way and Wilfred felt a pair of heavy hands grasp him under the armpits and drag him forward, away from the walls of Acre and the burning death that consumed the small breach they had so very briefly occupied.

As the seriously wounded were taken to the infirmary set up by the Knights Hospitaller, Wilfred was given a skin of water which he swigged from gratefully, soothing his parched lips. His gallantry had not gone unnoticed and there were many hearty slaps on the back from other knights and men-at-arms. By now, most of the English camp had roused itself and were gearing up for battle although their chance at storming the breach had long since passed.

The Christian camp was more of a blockade that surrounded the port city of Acre in a semicircle of earthworks, spiked palisades and trenches. The line of tents, workshops, hospitals and stables was home to around thirty-thousand Christian warriors and stretched for miles. The stink of the latrines, the noise of livestock, the blows of hammer on anvil and the cries of hawkers and whores selling their wares made the place feel like a bustling town back home, albeit a very international one. A myriad of different tongues – French, German, Latin, Italian, English – rang in the air and put Wilfred in mind of the Tower of Babel.

It was a double siege in a way, as Saladin had gathered an army from all corners of the Muslim world and besieged the besiegers, camping in the hills to the east and regularly attacking the Christian barricades. Although he was unable to break through the crusader lines and relieve Acre's beleaguered garrison, Saladin was able to put a chokehold on supplies into the Christian camp resulting in famine and disease.

King Richard and his host of English and Norman followers had been in Outremer a mere month but the siege of Acre had been going on for nearly two years. Saladin, unable to break through the Christian blockade, seemed content to simply wait it out and distract them in their efforts to take the city, while the Christians alternated attacks between the city and the Muslim camp, unable to decide which was the more important target. The dithering and indecision that had been going on infuriated Wilfred who had begun to lose patience before they even landed in Outremer.

It had been a year since Wilfred had stormed out of Rotherwood, leaving England, his father and his beloved Rowena behind. Far from taking Jerusalem before Christmas of 1190 as he had hoped, the journey to Outremer had been painfully slow due to King Richard having to untangle a couple of sticky political situations en route. First, they stopped in Sicily where Richard's younger sister, Joan, was queen. They arrived to find Joan recently widowed and the crown of Sicily usurped by Tancred, a distant cousin of Joan's late husband. Joan had been placed under house arrest while her husband's crown and her dower lands had been stolen by Tancred.

Outraged by this treatment of his little sister, Richard had stormed the port town of Messina and raised his standard on its walls, letting his men run riot in the streets. Tancred was forced to return Joan's dowry and was allowed to keep his crown if he agreed to marry his daughter to Arthur of Brittany, Richard's three-year-old nephew. This was a surprising move on Richard's part as it was bound to upset Heinrich of Germany, the new ruler of a collection of kingdoms, principalities and bishoprics known as the Holy Roman Empire. Emperor Heinrich had a claim to Sicily through his wife, Constance, and would strongly resent King Richard's support of the usurper Tancred. By the time the negotiations concluded, winter was upon them and further sea voyages were put on hold.

King Philip of France also wintered in Sicily with his army and, in addition to his alarm at Richard's boisterous and aggressive ways, soon found another bone to pick with his crusading ally. Richard was betrothed to Philip's sister, Alys, but some doubt was cast on the marriage plans by the arrival of Richard's mother, the formidable Eleanor of Aquitaine. In Eleanor's charge was Berengaria, the beautiful eldest daughter of King Sancho of Navarre. Her presence in Sicily was suspicious to say the least and Philip had a fair idea as to what was brewing in the minds of his Angevin neighbours. Not only was Berengaria of the same Provençal culture as Richard and his meddling mother, but she came with a hefty dowry and an alliance with Navarre would protect the southern borders of Aquitaine.

In the spring, Eleanor returned to England and the Christian fleet finally set sail for Outremer. A storm blew them off course and scattered the ships, with some forced to anchor on the island of Cyprus, which was ruled by Isaac Komnenos, a cruel tyrant with a nasty sadistic streak. When Richard caught up

with his wayward ships, he found Joan and Berengaria
cowering in the face of Isaac's troops who had a mind
to take them prisoner. Richard's wrath swept the
island and within fifteen days, Isaac was in chains and
Cyprus was his. It was a tale worthy of the
troubadours. One who did not celebrate in its telling
was King Philip of France whose suspicions had not
been unfounded for Richard and Berengaria were
soon married in the Chapel of St. George at Limassol
and Berengaria crowned Queen of England.

It had been a long and complex journey and now
there were finally here to break Acre and storm the
lands beyond. Wilfred was aware of somebody hailing
him. He turned and saw one of the king's retainers
riding towards him on a brown destrier. "The king will
see you now, Ivanhoe."

Wilfred nodded and, after taking a last gulp of
water, passed the skin to a nearby man-at-arms. He
followed the knight through the camp to the royal
pavilion. It was a massive thing of gold and scarlet
with fluttering pennons. Inside, at least twenty men
were gathered, all in armour and talking excitedly.
They hushed as Wilfred was admitted and he felt
himself propelled to the far end of the tent where the
king lay on a bed strewn with silks and cushions.

King Richard looked terrible. His pallor was pale
beneath the tan and sweat stood out on his brow. It
was hot inside the tent, no doubt about it, but the
English king looked like he was burning up on the
inside. A servant was spooning him fruit and ice from
a large bronze basin. Upon seeing Wilfred, Richard
waved his attendant aside.

"Ah, the hero of the hour!" Richard said in a voice that still carried some of its confident bluster, weakened though it was by sickness. "Approach, good knight. Ivanhoe, isn't it?"

"Yes, sire," said Wilfred, getting down on one knee.

"I seem to recall you were squire to Roger de Hambleton."

"I was, sire. You knighted me yourself."

"Yes, and I appear to have done well by it. Hambleton would no doubt be proud too, were he here."

Wilfred said nothing. As far as he knew, his former master was languishing in a dungeon in Damascus after Saladin captured him and many other knights in one of their first engagements with the enemy.

"I saw you lead the charge when the infidels filled the breach," the king continued. "That was bravely done. You showed them what my English followers are made of! I only wish we had been more prepared and that I wasn't incapacitated by this damnable fever. We might have taken the city! But no matter, they've been breached before and they'll be breached again and they know it. What's more, so does Saladin. He sent me this bowl of ice and fruit, you know? I think our mangonels and brave English knights might be warming him up to the idea of parlay! He refused to meet me once, let us see if he will still refuse when my banner is flying from the walls of Acre and its garrison is in my custody!"

The king's enthusiasm at this prospect incapacitated him with a bout of coughing. His attendants fluttered around him, helping him move into a better position and holding a cup of wine to his lips. He drank deeply and was able to regain control of his breathing. "A cup for Ivanhoe, too!" he demanded.

Wilfred accepted the cup of wine and Richard toasted him. "To Ivanhoe! Would that I had a hundred men of his quality under my banner!"

"To Ivanhoe!" spoke every man in the tent and Wilfred tried to hide his colouring cheeks as he drank from his cup.

"I heard that you lost your sword," said the king, "and that it remains embedded in a Saracen's neck. Well, let it stay there, I say, but a knight of mine needs a blade. Henry! Bring me that sword I kept from that insolent German who thought he could match me on horseback."

A young, handsome knight Wilfred recognised as the Count of Champagne, the king's nephew, went over to a carved chest and brought out a sword in a red scabbard. He handed it to the king who then presented it to Wilfred.

It was a fine blade, one of the finest Wilfred had ever seen. It was longer than average – at least forty inches – and its pommel had three points in the modern style, resembling an apple wedge with two bites taken out of it. Its hilt was bound in red leather which matched the scabbard and an inscription of 'Benedictus' ran along the blade.

"Thank you, sire!" Wilfred said, sliding the blade back into its scabbard. "It is a magnificent weapon."

"Far more suited to your hand than its previous owner's," said the king. "You'll soon rechristen it in infidel blood, even if Acre falls without any further resistance. We're still a long march from Jerusalem."

As it happened, Acre did fall without further resistance and the following day, its garrison sued for peace. They were utterly broken, having lived through famine, disease and relentless assault for far too long. The fall of the Cursed Tower was the final straw. They no longer had faith in Saladin's ability to save them and they wanted out, whether their great sultan gave them permission or not.

The negotiations took place in King Philip's pavilion with the leaders of the Christian army on one side and Acre's governors on the other. A quiet lull borne of trepidation hung over the camp all morning while the talks continued. They seemed to go on forever and everybody was on tenterhooks wondering how long it took to hand over a damned city.

At last, the emirs left the pavilion, mounted their horses without a word and rode back towards the city. The Christian kings emerged looking very pleased with themselves and the call was given out that the siege was over. Acre was theirs. The cry swept the camp like a fresh spring breeze and was taken up by one voice after another until the whole camp was cheering uproariously. After two years of hard fighting, it was done.

Acre was given over to the Christians along with two-hundred-thousand bezants to be divided up between them. Additionally, two-thousand Christian prisoners were to be released along with the piece of the true cross which had been seized by the Muslims at the battle of Hattin four years ago. That both the prisoners and the piece of the true cross were in the custody of Saladin, who was not at the negotiations, was a problem for another day. Until then, the city's garrison would remain hostages to be released upon fulfilment of the terms.

The gates of Acre were flung open and the Christians marched in, triumphantly announcing themselves with a cacophony of drums, trumpets and songs of victory. The city's denizens shuttered their windows and cowered within their homes, fearing the celebrations of a conquering army.

King Richard took up residence in the citadel while Philip followed the Templars down to the southwest corner of the city where they were keen to salvage what was left of their great headquarters, denied them for too long. The rest of the Christians found lodgings where they could and the city's Muslim population either found new dwellings in the poorer residential district or left the city entirely and headed for Saladin's camp in the hills.

Its walls may have been crumbling, many of its buildings may have been smashed by constant bombardment, but Acre was, if anything, resilient. Its new masters had barely lodged themselves in their quarters before market stalls began springing up again, wine shops opened and brothels began plying their trade, everybody keen to make the best of the situation. For the war-weary Christians, the city opened up to them like an oyster, offering pearls and flesh in equal measure.

As Wilfred wandered the streets that first night, he marvelled at how war could transform such a fabulous and beautiful city into such a shattered fleshpot of sin. Beautiful courtyards with marble benches and mosaics lay in ruins. Drunken soldiers sang and brawled in idyllic gardens that were scented with exotic flowers and fruit trees, their raucous voices drowning out the trickle of sculpted fountains. They danced and vomited in the streets between the flat-topped buildings where lanterns burned and canvas awnings shaded the cobbles which were still warm after the day's sun.

Leonard walked with him, his arm in a sling, as they went in search of a wine shop that wasn't heaving with drunken soldiers. Wilfred had gone to see his squire as soon as he had been dismissed from the king's presence. The wound was not serious and required only cleaning and stitching, much to Wilfred's relief. Leonard was a good squire and had a stout heart.

His previous master, a Pisan knight of rather greater means than Wilfred, had been slain in the same battle that had seen Roger of Hambleton captured and Leonard had struggled to find a new master. Much as Wilfred needed a squire, he was short of funds and it troubled him to pay so little for a desperate lad like Leonard but truly, the Pisan seemed glad of the companionship as much as the coin. Not once did he ever show shame at serving a young, poor knight like Wilfred when he had clearly been used to a grander station and the two of them got along well.

They found a wine shop that wasn't too rowdy and took a table and a flagon of wine to share. A group of English knights were well into their drinking on the other side of the room and were paying a young woman to sing a bawdy song about an alewife and a village priest. Wilfred recognised Harry of Leicester in their company and nodded a greeting.

Harry was an older knight who came from a good family despite being something of a rowdy, coarse brawler. Wilfred had encountered him on the stormy voyage from Messina and found himself taken under the older man's wing. There was little else to do but talk and boast as they sat in the hold among the stores and horses for days on end as the cog pitched and rolled on the waves.

"Wilfred!" Harry cried, stumbling over to them, rosy cheeked and swaying slightly. "Where have you found lodgings?"

"Up at the citadel with the king and your good self," said Wilfred, trying to keep the pride out of his voice. The king had demanded his presence at the citadel, still pleased with his efforts the day the Cursed Tower fell.

"Riding the winds of favour, I see!" said Harry, slapping Wilfred on the shoulder. "I heard how you held that breach against a score of Saracens!"

"I hardly held it alone," said Wilfred. "And it was more like a dozen than a score."

"Who cares? Your name is spoken with admiration from tavern to brothel."

"I'm flattered."

"It's a good thing if us lot stick together," said Harry, leaning forward and giving Wilfred a big, conspiratorial wink he probably thought was subtle. "There's trouble brewing among the victors already. Richard and Philip are at each other's throats again by all accounts."

"Really? What have you heard?"

"Well, it's this business of who gets to be king once we take Jerusalem. Guy or Conrad? Doesn't make much difference to us for one is about as useless as the other, but Richard supports Guy so that's the camp we find ourselves in."

Wilfred nodded slowly. The rivalry between Guy de Lusignan and Conrad de Montferrat was almost as bitter as the rivalry between Christian and Saracen. Before the fall of Jerusalem, Guy had married Sibylla, the sister of its leprous King Baldwin. When Baldwin had died of his disease, quickly followed by his infant nephew, Guy had found himself the de facto King of Jerusalem; a position he almost immediately disgraced at the disastrous Battle of Hattin.

That dark day was spoken of with shame throughout Christendom. It had been Guy's decision to march Jerusalem's army across the dry plains and fight Saladin's army in the open. That was exactly what Saladin had wanted and, weakened by thirst and exhaustion, Jerusalem's army was resoundingly defeated at the horns of Hattin, leaving the way to the holy city open to the infidels. Guy had been captured and eventually released but was now a king without a kingdom.

It had been Guy who had rallied a Christian army and marched on Acre which had fallen to the Saracens after their victory at Hattin. That had been two years ago and in the interim, disease had claimed the lives of Queen Sibylla and their two daughters, further weakening Guy's claim to the crown of Jerusalem. That was all Conrad de Montferrat needed to push his own claim. He was the brother of Sibylla's first husband, and, after the death of Queen Sibylla, he married her sister, Isabella, claiming that he was now King of Jerusalem.

Guy or Conrad? Guy was a vassal of King Richard for his lands in Poitou, while Conrad was cousin to King Philip of France. Lines in the sand were drawn and the great Christian army began to resemble a political nest of vipers. Wilfred wondered why war was so complicated.

"We might as well get comfortable," said Harry, calling for more wine. "We could be here for a while. Saladin won't like the terms made on his behalf and we can hardly continue on to Jerusalem until all these hostages are handed over. Still," he took a deep draught from his cup, "not a bad place to put our feet up, eh? If we don't all start killing each other instead of the Saracens!"

The days that followed were ones of great industry. Now that they had the most important port on the coast and with it, control of the caravan trails to the east, the Christians were keen to fortify Acre and restore it to its former glory. Crosses were replaced on churches which were cleared of all vestiges of Muslim worship. King Richard set his men to work rebuilding the walls and emptying the moat of corpses and rubble. The markets began to flourish once more with the smells of cinnamon, cloves and nutmeg. Fruits and delicacies that Wilfred had never heard of glistened on the stalls: figs, dates, pomegranates and those strangely curved yellow fruits known to the locals as 'apples of paradise'.

Beyond the city walls, the fortifications that had been home to the Christian besiegers for two years remained in place and under guard. There wasn't enough room in the city to accommodate everybody and, in any case, Saladin's wolves still prowled the hills on the other side of the siege camp.

There was naturally some grumbling from those who remained in the half-deserted camp wondering when it would be their turn to enjoy the fruits of the conquered city but it was the jealousy and pride of those of higher rank which indicated the inevitable trouble in paradise.

Duke Leopold of Austria had arrived at the citadel in a hot temper and demanded an audience with King Richard, who was in a private chamber discussing the rebuilding of the southern wall. As Duke Leopold strode down the length of the Great Hall, Wilfred watched him coolly from his window seat where he was enjoying a pomegranate he had purchased from a vendor.

The duke was a little man who made up for any shortcomings he imagined this entailed by dressing ostentatiously and putting on an air of bluster and bravado that outranked his station as a mere duke. He was a prideful man who had already butted heads with Richard over his handling of Isaac Komnenos who happened to be the cousin of Leopold's mother. Now he apparently had another axe to grind and, after he had been admitted into the king's presence, the raised voices of both Richard and the duke could be heard from behind the closed door.

"Any idea what's the ruckus is?" Wilfred asked Harry, who was giving a pair of Queen Berengaria's ladies-in-waiting some pointers on chess strategy.

"That Austrian blowhard will be pressing his claim to more loot, I don't doubt," said Harry, not looking up from the board as he contemplated taking a bishop. "He thinks he has a right to some of those two-hundred-thousand bezants Richard and Philip squeezed out of the negotiations but if you ask me he's barking up the wrong date palm. Damn!" The expletive was the result of his queen being taken by the ladies-in-waiting who giggled at their victory.

"That money has yet to be forthcoming," said Wilfred. "And the kings might not see any of it if Saladin does not hold up his end of the bargain."

"A bargain he had no hand in," Harry reminded Wilfred. "And what's more, Duke Leopold played no part in taking Acre. He barely left his tent."

"That hasn't stopped him from flying his banner from the city walls."

"So I've seen. The gall of that man!"

There was a clatter from behind the door that sounded very much like a table being hurled over, sending its cargo of plates and goblets rattling across the floor. After his heavy bout with fever, Richard's strength and infamous Angevin temper had returned in full force.

The door swung open and a red-faced Duke Leopold strode from the room, uttering oaths in German. His attendants hurried to follow him and kept out of the way of King Richard as he emerged like a raging bull, singeing the air with foul language.

"Whatever is the matter, Richard?" Queen Berengaria said, as she swept across the floor to cool the temper of her new husband.

"The matter?" Richard snapped. "That cursed duke is the matter! He's been after table scraps as soon as we set foot in Acre, even flying his own bloody banner alongside Philip's and mine! He seems to think it's unfair that the lion's share of the ransom we are asking for Acre's garrison goes to Philip and myself. I told him in no uncertain terms that those who were instrumental in this city's fall deserve the fruits of their labour without sharing them with hangers-on like himself."

"Richard, you didn't!" said Berengaria, covering her mouth with her hand. "What did he say?"

"Nothing suitable for your sweet ears, my lady, but he didn't take it well, I can assure you. Well, I've got another unpleasant surprise for him." He glanced at Wilfred and Harry and the few other knights who were watching the conversation with quiet uncertainty. "You fellows! Make yourselves useful! Get up onto the walls and take down Leopold's banner for me. We'll see how he likes that!"

"Husband, please be careful," said Berengaria. "Would that not be a gross insult to the duke?"

"It will and the man deserves no less! I should have cast down his banner as soon as he put it up but I was in a generous mood that day. Now, enough is enough. Only those who fought for this city may fly their banners from its walls and enjoy the spoils of its conquest!"

The queen still seemed worried but that was not a matter Wilfred and the other knights had to concern themselves with. They had their orders and hastened to carry them out. They left the Great Hall and passed out into the courtyards and gardens that surrounded it, blinded by the brightness of the mid-afternoon sun.

They climbed the stretch of broken wall from where Duke Leopold's banner fluttered. Only one guard stood there, looking idly out over the azure sea. He turned to face them as they scrambled up the ladder, one by one. He uttered something in German which they ignored and made for the banner.

It was Harry who got to it first and, rather than reeling it gently in, he seized the cloth in both fists and tore it from its fastenings. The Austrian guard cried out in horror and tried to interfere but was shoved roughly back by one of the English knights. Wilfred glanced at Harry who, before Wilfred could advise caution, flung the banner from the walls.

They watched in silence as it fluttered away, caught by the wind and carried far from the walls, down into the moat which still had not been fully cleared of the dead. The men who were working down there glanced up, confusion written on their faces as the banner settled atop a particularly rotten corpse.

"That was a stupid thing to do," Wilfred reprimanded Harry. "The duke will be up in arms."

"Let him!" said Harry. "What can he do about it? He is only a duke, after all, and the king did tell us to take down his banner."

"But not to toss it into the bloody moat!"

"Oh, he'll see the funny side."

King Richard did, as it turned out, see the funny side and he roared with laughter at table that evening. The duke had demanded another audience but Richard had turned him away, saying that he refused to waste any more time on such an insignificant popinjay. As the king and his followers continued to find merriment in the duke's impotent rage, Wilfred couldn't help but feel as if they were making needless enemies. Saladin was still out there at the head of a massive army. Surely it was folly for allies to bait and insult each other when Jerusalem was still far from recaptured.

The ugly incident was not an isolated event and was indicative of the souring mood in Acre. Despite the victory there was a growing feeling of resentment, especially in the lower ranks, concerning the nature of it. Acre had ultimately been handed to them by a garrison too worn down to keep up the city's defence. The common soldiers had wanted a resounding conquest; a storming of the city that would result in a wholesale looting spree, not this limp conclusion to a two-year-long siege in which the spoils of war were divided up between kings with very little trickling down to the lower ranks.

There was also the sticky matter of appointing a new Grand Master of the Templars; a business that caused even more friction among the conquerors of Acre. The previous Grand Master – Gerard de Ridefort – had been largely to blame for the disaster at the Battle of Hattin, having been the one who had convinced King Guy of Jerusalem to cross the arid plains in high summer rather than wait for Saladin to come to them. Gerard had been captured along with King Guy but eventually released. He had commanded what was left of the Templar order in the early stages of the siege of Acre, only to be captured once again. Saladin was less magnanimous this time and had Gerard beheaded.

As well as being homeless, the Templars had officially been leaderless for two years with various men filling the role on a temporary basis. Now that the Templars had moved back into their old quarter in Acre, the time had come for something more permanent to be arranged. A keen candidate was Lucas de Beaumanoir, an elderly yet fierce figure in the order. His age presented a problem for many who believed that the Grand Master of an order of warrior monks should be a competent warrior himself and Beaumanoir's battlefield days were long behind him. What's more, Beaumanoir had made a name for himself as a joy-hating tyrant who despised sin in all its forms and was too puritan for many stomachs, even for a Templar. King Richard had provided his own nominee in the form of Robert de Sablé, a rugged old veteran from Anjou who had been commander of Richard's fleet on the voyage to Outremer.

Politics, as ever, had reared its ugly head in the choosing of a new Grand Master. Lucas de Beaumanoir favoured Conrad of Montferrat's claim to the crown of Jerusalem, while Robert de Sablé, as a vassal of Richard, naturally supported Guy de Lusignan. That automatically put King Philip in Beaumanoir's camp, as if enough love had not been lost between him and Richard. As discussions grew ever more heated, Philip had even relocated to the city of Tyre which was ruled by Conrad, taking his portion of the hostages with him.

Robert de Sablé was not even a member of the Templar order, a matter that was quickly rectified by Richard who pushed de Sablé to take his vows and become a Knight Templar quickly after the taking of Acre. The Templars in Beaumanoir's camp tried to block his initiation but were overruled. Nevertheless, bad blood continued to grow between all factions and Richard found himself yet another enemy in the form of a Templar splinter group represented by its most orthodox members.

In an effort to clear the air a tournament was arranged. These informal martial contests were rough, violent affairs but often gave people at odds a chance to air their grievances in the form of brutal combat. Sometimes it could be a way of nullifying quarrels and settling disputes but more often than not it only deepened them and occasionally created new ones. Richard, who had begun to tire of all the administrative and logistical tasks involved in repairing and running Acre, was keen to take part in the tournament himself and took the part of the challenger, handpicking his own allies.

"Robert de Beaumont here shall be my champion," said the king, clapping his hand on the Earl of Leicester's shoulder. "A finer horseman I could not ask for. I have also requested de Turnham's younger brother, Edwin, as a favour to me, along with Thomas de Moulton and Fulk d'Oilly. We shall be challenging all comers and one does not need to be clairvoyant to know that the Templars in Beaumanoir's camp will be sending their best against me. Brian de Bois-Guilbert has thrown his lot in with them, I hear, and he is one of the finest knights in the order. We can expect his lance against us."

"With Beaumont and Turnham, not to mention yourself, sire," said an aging knight called Gerard de Furnival, "Even Bois-Guilbert will get knocked on his arse."

Richard chuckled. "True, no doubt, but I want to give those Templars something that will put the wind up them and make them second-guess us." He turned to Wilfred. "I want young Ivanhoe here as my sixth man."

There were surprised glances at this. "Ivanhoe?" the Earl of Leicester asked. "Isn't he a little inexperienced?"

"Nonsense," Richard replied. "This is the man who nearly stormed Acre single-handedly. If you had seen him holding that breach against the infidels, you wouldn't question his ability in battle."

"On foot perhaps, sire but …"

"But nothing! Ivanhoe has also made something of a name for himself in the saddle too if the reports I hear from London are correct. Did you not unseat William de Fosse at the tournament at Cheapside last year?"

"I did, sire," said Wilfred. "And I thank you for your confidence in me. I will do all that I can to see that it is not unfounded."

The event was a welcome distraction from all the negotiations, administrative headaches and petty squabbling that had soured the mood in Acre and nearly the whole city turned out to enjoy the spectacle. The pavilions and the lists were set up north of the city where the salty breeze from the sea made the coloured banners flutter and the smells of cooked food from the hawkers' stalls drift over the heads of the swarming spectators.

Tournaments had become more civilised affairs in recent years as they moved away from the more informal *bohort* which was akin to a gladiatorial fight in which anything went. In an effort to appease the clergy who widely condemned these violent competitions, organisers of tournaments had tried to introduce at least a few rules. Each knight would be allowed a maximum of five lances and the goal was to unhorse an opponent, after which he would be considered defeated and out of the competition. Although still dangerous, tournaments provided an excellent opportunity for less well-off knights like Wilfred to win huge prizes as a defeated knight had to buy back his horse and armour from his vanquisher.

King Richard and his fellow challengers set up their pavilions at the southern entrance to the lists, with their shields erected on poles, displaying their coats of arms. Guy de Lusignan was chosen as the tournament's judge and sat with the more high-profile spectators including King Richard's wife and sister, on a raised gallery richly decorated with banners. It was his honour to decide which knight was the tournament's winner and award him the prize of a tun of Gascon wine and a horse King Richard had donated from his own stable.

Even in a friendly tournament, the choice of judge was seen as a political statement and King Philip and Conrad de Montferrat refused to attend an event that recognised Guy's authority over Conrad's. This was King Richard's tournament, there was no doubting that. The Templars who supported Conrad's claim could not refuse, however, for they saw it as paramount that they defend Conrad's honour by accepting the challenge thrown down by Richard and his knights. Lucas de Beaumanoir sat in the gallery directly facing Guy's position as if the lists between them were a battlefield that would decide the fate of nations rather than a sporting ground.

The sun beat down on the lists as Wilfred and the other knights stood outside their pavilions with their squires, watching the spectators fill up the seats. Once Guy had decided that the time was right for the tournament to begin, he lifted a sceptre that had been polished to reflect every possible ray of sunlight and held it high for all to see. The northern barrier to the lists was removed and six knights, selected from the all-comers at random, entered the lists amid much cheering and trumpeting from the heralds.

Wilfred watched as the knights rode towards them, lances held high, the sun glinting off polished helms. They drew up at the pavilions of the challengers and each touched a shield with the butt of his lance to signify the challenger he wished to oppose. Then, they rode back to the northern gate to line themselves up and await the response of the challengers.

A Genoese knight by the name of Guglielmo da Caschifellone had rapped his lance on Wilfred's shield and, as Wilfred turned to mount his horse, Leonard said to him, "If you send that pompous Genoan reeling from his saddle, I would consider it a personal favour, master."

Wilfred tried to muster a smile. "I'll do my best, Leonard. Do you know anything of him?"

His squire shook his head. "Only that he is one of my people's rivals. A blow against them would please many Pisans."

Wilfred put on his helm and fastened the straps. Being a knight of little significance and means, he had only a round iron cap with a nasal by way of protecting his skull and his eyes were particularly vulnerable when charging another knight head on. He accepted his lance from Leonard and tried to control the shaking fear that seemed to ripple through his body. He hoped it wasn't visible for he would hate to shame himself in front of the others and the king most of all.

He had fought in tournaments before and, through God's favour, had come out unscathed apart from a few minor cuts and bruises, but the fear before the initial charge never seemed to lessen. His gut churned and he fought down the urge to vomit. He asked Leonard for a wineskin. When it was passed to him, he guzzled a little, hoping it would settle his stomach and relax his jumping nerves at least a bit.

King Richard led them out with a bellow of confidence that Wilfred barely registered. He urged his horse on and followed the others out to their positions opposite the arrayed knights. A deathly silence of anticipation fell over the lists. All that could be heard was the chomping of the horses at the bit, the sea breeze rippling the banners, and the occasional nervous cough.

Wilfred stared at his opponent astride his massive black charger. The bucket helm obscured his face and made him look like a demon out of hell come to claim Wilfred's soul. Wilfred gripped his lance tightly and rotated his shoulder in its socket, preparing it for the blow that was to come. In the corner of his vision, he could see Guy de Lusignan standing, his sceptre held high. Then, with a sudden movement, the glittering ornament swung down. A blast of trumpets signalled the advance and they were off.

Wilfred dug his heels in and spurred his mount forward. The other English knights were already outpacing him and he knew he had to reach a decent speed if he was to have the desired impact on his opponent.

The gap between them grew closer and Wilfred stared into those black slits in the bucket helm of the Genoese knight. He lifted his shield to protect his chest and left flank. Both lances lowered and then, like a thunderclap, they made contact.

Da Caschifellone's lance shattered on Wilfred's shield but the blow nearly cleared Wilfred from his saddle. Struggling to remain upright, feeling the weight of his mail hauberk pulling him backwards, Wilfred barely registered the damage his own lance had done on his opponent. It had been a good blow, he knew that, sliding over the top of da Caschifellone's shield and catching him on the shoulder. It was only when Wilfred wheeled his mount around that he realised he had unhorsed him.

The cheers of the crowd filled his ears and he looked around to see that his companions had also fared just as well. The king and the others were still in their saddles, some holding shattered lances, while their six opponents sat or lay on the ground, clutching bruised limbs and ringing heads. Chants praising the skill of Richard and the English knights were taken up by the crowd but a distinct silence hung over Lucas de Beaumanoir and his followers. Of the six vanquished opponents, four had been Templars.

Richard led them back to their pavilions where their squires rushed to attend them, carrying away their broken lances and replacing them with fresh ones. Wine was passed around to refresh themselves and quickly toast the first victories of the day.

"Congratulations, master," said Leonard, as he checked Wilfred's lance for signs of fractures. "I knew you'd easily overcome that oaf."

"Oaf he was," said Wilfred. "For his aim was clumsy. I might not fare as well against somebody more skilled."

Leonard seemed about to say something dismissive of his master's modesty but fell silent as the next round of opponents approached. Two of them wore the white tabards and red cross emblems of the Templars and one of them rode directly to Wilfred's mounted shield and rapped on it with the butt of his lance.

"Your early victory has earned you some recognition, Ivanhoe," said the king with a grin.

"The Templars have it in for us, and no mistake," Wilfred replied in what he hoped was a jovial tone.

He saddled up and they rode out again to meet the oncomers. This time, Wilfred's lance glanced off his opponent's shield and snapped in two while the Templar's lance shattered against his own. The blow nearly laid Wilfred flat across his horse's rump but, with every muscle in his back screaming in protest, he was able to remain in the saddle and pull himself back up into a sitting position.

The Templar galloped around and headed back to the north gate where his squire was waiting with his second lance. Several of Wilfred's companions were still engaged with their own foes so, he skirted the chaos in the centre of the lists, picked up a fresh lance from Leonard, and prepared to charge the Templar once again.

This time his aim was true and caught the Templar under the chin and carried him from his saddle like a rag doll. The weight of man and mail weighed down the tip of Wilfred's lance until it snapped and the Templar tumbled to the ground.

The crowd went wild at this and Wilfred raised his broken lance in appreciation. It was turning out to be a good day for him. Richard and the other English knights were also doing well and, once again, had cast down all of their opponents. Thomas de Moulton appeared to be badly wounded, however. A large splinter of his opponent's lance was embedded in his right shoulder, the force of the blow having wedged it through mail, gambeson and flesh.

"How are we doing?" Wilfred asked, as he rode over to the king and the others.

"I'm down to my last lance, curse those Templar bastards," said the king. "And Moulton here is out of action, I fear."

"No, sire," said Moulton, grimacing through the pain. "A minor flesh wound. I can still lift a lance."

"Get that bit of wood out of your shoulder and have it bound before telling me that. How many lances have the rest of you?"

The Earl of Leicester had two, Fulk d'Oilly and Edwin de Turnham had one each. Wilfred had four.

"This may be our last bout," said the king. "We've done well so far, so let's go out in a blaze of glory."

They barely had time to prepare themselves before the next set of opponents approached. This time they were led by a Templar on one of the finest chargers Wilfred had ever seen. The gleaming white tabard with its blood-red cross fitted a tall figure whose head was encased in a bucket helm with a raven's wing feathers affixed on either side.

"By Christ," said Fulk d'Oilly. "Brian de Bois-Guilbert is having a crack at us at last."

The famous Templar rode up to the posts and then, removed his helm and glared down at Wilfred.

Wilfred looked up into a black-bearded face that was not uncomely. His features were strong and his eyes a cool blue.

"Ivanhoe?" said Bois-Guilbert.

"I am," Wilfred replied.

"The only place I have heard of by that name lies in the West Riding of Yorkshire. I have a friend with lands that border it."

"Indeed? I am lord of that Ivanhoe, although I have yet to visit it. I was newly knighted before we left England and Ivanhoe is my fee. Who is your friend?"

"Reginald Front-de-Boeuf. You have heard of him, I am sure."

"I have." Wilfred said no more out of politeness, for if this Templar was a friend of Front de Boeuf, then it spoke volumes about his character and had little good to say about it.

The Templar looked Wilfred up and down, his mouth curling slightly at the inferior appearance of the knight before him. "The last lord of Ivanhoe died childless, or so I am told. Who is your father?"

"Cedric of Rotherwood." Wilfred kept his voice steady and free of any emotion. He was merely stating a fact. Speaking of his father was not something he had made a habit of lately.

"Ah, yes," said the Templar, smiling slightly. "Cedric the Saxon or so he is called. Not a man from one of the great families of England. How is it that his son, and he barely a man at that, is able to unhorse one of my Templar brethren?"

"I may be young, but I have been trained well. By Roger de Hambleton. You have heard of him, I am sure."

"I have. And his capture by the infidels is a great loss to the Christian cause. I pray that he will soon be restored to us. He has trained you well but the Templar you knocked to the ground was Aimon de Ais, a dear friend of mine. My brethren are some of the most pious of God's children, but if there is one sin that we dance a little too closely with, then it is Pride. The defeat of a Templar of Ais's stature by a common youth newly knighted is not something that can go unanswered. Make your prayers, Ivanhoe."

He placed the extraordinary helm back upon his head and then slammed the butt of his lance against Wilfred's shield with resounding force before riding away.

Wilfred glanced at his companions who stared at him, agape. Even the king seemed to have a look of sympathy on his face.

"You've got your work cut out for you there, and no mistake," said the Earl of Leicester. "Bois-Guilbert is one of the finest knights in his order."

"Young Ivanhoe isn't expected to unseat the bugger," said the king. "Just hold out long enough until your four lances are used up. Then you can exit the tournament with honour. We all can."

It was a generous vote of confidence that Wilfred was grateful for, but he could see that the king knew how hopeless it was. *Four lances against Bois-Guilbert?* He'd be lucky to survive one bout against that devil.

"Good luck, master," said Leonard glumly, as they saddled up and prepared to head out once more. "Try to break your lances quickly. Don't give him more opportunities to unseat you than he needs."

Wilfred said nothing as he took his lance from Leonard and rode out to join the others. He couldn't dispel the sense that this was all a little unfair. Aimon de Ais had chosen him for an opponent and had been defeated fairly. To have to face a knight as renowned as Brian de Bois-Guilbert just because the Templars took his lucky victory as a personal slight, was not particularly sporting in Wilfred's mind. But there was nothing for it. He was determined to finish this tournament as honourably as he could.

The trumpets blared for the third time that day and Wilfred kicked his mount into a gallop. Bois-Guilbert came up fast as a thunderbolt and they both broke their lances on each other's shields with simultaneous cracks that echoed across the lists, much to the crowd's approval.

It was too much to hope for that Bois-Guilbert had been unhorsed by the blow and, as Wilfred turned his mount, the Templar galloped past on his way to claim his second lance from his squire. Wilfred rode over to Leonard and took a new lance for himself. He saw that the king was out of the tournament, having unhorsed his opponent with his last lance which had shattered in the effort. He seemed frustrated to be done for the day but brightened to see Wilfred was still in the saddle.

"Give that bastard hellfire, Ivanhoe!" he called.

Wilfred nodded in gratitude and set off to meet his opponent who was already preparing to charge.

This time, Bois-Guilbert's lance did not shatter on Wilfred's shield but it struck it with such a force that Wilfred reeled backwards. He gripped his stallion's sides with his legs as hard as he could and was able to regain his posture. His own lance had snapped in half and he discarded it, glad that he only had two more to go.

He was baking hot inside his gambeson and mail hauberk. The sun was unmerciful at its full height in the sky and the sweat poured down his face, stinging his eyes. Fulk d'Oilly and Edwin de Turnham had broken their last lances and were being stripped of their armour by their squires. The Earl of Leicester was down to his last one and had just unseated a Pisan knight to a roar of applause. The king beamed. The English knights had been outstanding that day and had defeated every man who rode against them.

Now only Wilfred and Bois-Guilbert remained. Wilfred took his second to last lance and, cheers of encouragement ringing in his ears, rode out to meet the Templar once more.

Wilfred refused to aim for the shield and hope for an easy break. Instead he aimed for the Templar's neck as a good knight should. Bois-Guilbert raised his shield in the final moment and Wilfred's lance slid over the rim and glanced off the Templar's bucket helm, tearing off one of the raven's wings as it did so. Bois-Guilbert's own lance slammed against Wilfred's shield which, due to the angle, slid off it.

Wilfred cursed inwardly. His lance was unbroken. His luck was not bound to hold out and sooner or later he knew he would be sent crashing to the ground by the Templar's lance.

Wheeling around, the two knights charged each other once again. As before, Wilfred aimed for the deadly point between helm and chest. He knew that Bois-Guilbert would raise his shield just a little at the last moment, as he had done before, and so overcompensated just a tad with his aim.

The shield came up, Wilfred's lance scraped past its rim just as the Templar's lance slammed into his own shield. As Wilfred was knocked sideways by the blow, the tip of his lance caught his opponent in the right breast. The lance shattered at last, but not before the majority of its force had been spent on sending the Templar tumbling from his saddle in a shower of splinters.

Wilfred dropped his broken lance and seized the reins of his horse as he kept on riding. The roar of the crowd was deafening but he wasn't sure how much of it was the blood singing in his ears. He couldn't believe what had just happened. He had unhorsed Brian de Bois-Guilbert; his second Templar Knight of the day.

The king and the other English knights were jumping wildly and roaring themselves hoarse as

Wilfred rode back to them. He slid off his horse onto shaky legs, still not quite believing what had occurred.

"God's legs, Ivanhoe!" the king roared, nearly felling him with a thump on his back. "You've got some skills in the saddle! Those Templars don't know what's hit them! Brian de Bois-Guilbert on his arse, by Christ!"

It was not just his own companions who were impressed by Wilfred's performance. Guy de Lusignan proclaimed Wilfred the winner of the tournament and crowned him with a laurel of thin gold plate. He was presented with the warhorse, which was a fine Spanish destrier named Jago, and the tun of Gascon wine. All Acre, it seemed, cheered and praised him.

But Wilfred knew that there were some out there who were not so pleased with his victory. Once Bois-Guilbert had been helped to his tent by his squires, Lucas de Beaumanoir and those Templars who supported him silently left the lists, their faces like thunder. It sullied the whole affair in Wilfred's heart. He had conducted himself with honour and prowess that day but so had all of Richard's knights. His unhorsing of the Templar champion and one of Lucas de Beaumanoir's staunchest supporters had evidently pleased Guy de Lusignan and played no small part in his decision to crown Wilfred as the day's champion. Although Wilfred was proud of his victory, it had the stink of politics all over it.

They celebrated back at the citadel that night and Wilfred was the toast of the festivities. The squires of the knights Wilfred had defeated came to the citadel bringing the armour and horses of their masters for him to either keep or ransom as was the custom.

Wilfred was keen to replace his poor nasal helm with a fine bucket helm that would give his face much more protection and there was good mail and spurs to be had too, but it did not sit well with him to wear the armour that had been made for another. Instead, he took the ransom money and found himself nearly a hundred pounds richer. It was a fabulous amount of wealth for a new knight of lowly stature who had left England a year ago with barely a shilling to his name.

On the morrow he would go to the armourers and order a new helm with a brass reinforced cross, a blue surcoat and a kite shield of the same colour. With the fine sword the king had given him and the magnificent destrier he had won at the tournament, he would be a knight more than fit to ride in the company of the King of England.

If only Rowena could see me now, he thought as he glanced around at the hall and all its merrymaking in his honour. And then, in a darker streak of thought, *if only my father could see me now*. When he returned to England, he would prove himself to the both of them. Jerusalem had to be recaptured first, of course, and God alone knew how long that would take, but with his newfound wealth and status, he at least felt ready to face whatever stood against them on the road to glory.

The celebrations lasted long after the ladies had retired for the night. The men, knowing that war would soon be calling them from the comforts of Acre, were keen to exploit the occasion of the day to its fullest. When it was all over, Wilfred, drunk on wine, slept deeply and dreamt as he often did, of Rowena's golden hair, dappled in the sunlight that shone through the green boughs of Rotherwood.

Not long after the tournament, Robert de Sablé was voted the new Grand Master of the Templars. Lucas de Beaumanoir was forced to accept this decision but was reluctant to give up any of the authority he had curried in the past two years. He still railed against the sin and debauchery that ran rampant in the streets of Acre and even King Richard was forced to agree that he had a point. The army was stagnating amid the fleshpots and taverns of Acre while they waited for Saladin to pay the ransom for the release of Acre's garrison.

To make things worse, news emerged that King Philip intended to return to France pleading ill-health. King Richard accused him of cowardice and vain glory-seeking; accusations that did nothing for his relationship with the French. Philip's departure would sorely weaken the crusade but with him gone, Conrad de Montferrat would have a hard time pressing his claim to the crown of Jerusalem, which was one small blessing as far as Richard was concerned.

A council was held and it was decided that Guy de Lusignan would be recognised as King of Jerusalem for the rest of his life while Conrad and his wife, Isabella, would be his heirs and retain control of Tyre, Sidon and Beirut. At the same time, Richard sold Cyprus to the Templars who placed Lucas de

Beaumanoir in charge of the island. "That ought to keep the joyless old bastard from stirring up trouble in Outremer," Richard had commented.

Feeling that he had done all he could for Conrad, King Philip sailed for Europe and left his men under the command of Duke Hugh of Burgundy and his share of the hostages with Conrad at Tyre. Duke Leopold of Austria also returned home and the entire crusade seemed to be crumbling apart.

Several weeks had passed since the fall of Acre and there seemed to be little haste or eagerness on the part of Saladin to cooperate with the bargain struck on his behalf. Communications passed back and forth and the sultan seemed to be playing for time. Was he busy raking together the two-hundred bezants? Was he bringing the Christian prisoners from where they were held at Damascus? Or was he waiting for reinforcements, calling in favours and planning his own siege of Acre?

It was a frightening prospect and King Richard grew increasingly frustrated by the delay. "Damn that infidel!" he cursed. "While he dithers and puts us off, we must sit here awaiting his pleasure for I dare not continue on to Jerusalem, not with so few men to guard so many prisoners."

It had already been agreed that Joan and Berengaria would remain in Acre while Richard and his army embarked on the next phase of the crusade, and the thought of leaving them in a city with nearly three-thousand prisoners and a minimal guard was out of the question. The hostages had to be successfully ransomed before Richard left Acre.

By late August, Richard's patience had run out. He was chomping at the bit to be on his way and could feel the crusade stalling beyond repair. Another council was held to discuss what was to be done with the prisoners.

Little was known about the council's decision as the prisons were opened on the morning of the 20th of August. The hostages were led out, their hands bound before them, to be marshalled beyond the city walls where King Richard's army waited. They were to travel to a hill called Tell al-Ayyadiyya, the purpose of which, Wilfred assumed, was to hand the prisoners over to Saladin. At least, he hoped that was their purpose. Perhaps a deal had been struck at last? But the ominous silence and sombre faces of those in the king's closest circle made Wilfred worry that there was some ulterior motive.

As they accompanied the long train of prisoners through the scorching heat of the plains, Wilfred sidled up to Harry of Leicester. "Have you heard anything about a prisoner handover?" he asked him. "Has Saladin finally agreed to pay up?"

"It's a possibility," said Harry. "But no, I haven't heard any words to that effect."

"But surely that must be the reason for all this. Why else march these wretches out into the middle of nowhere?"

Harry said nothing and kept his eyes on the wavering heat that obscured the hills ahead. Wilfred did not draw much comfort from the more experienced knight's expression.

When they got to Tell al-Ayyadiyya, Wilfred's hopes sank even further. There was no Saracen camp to greet them. The hill was a bare, barren place that seemed to have no particular purpose or significance. On a similar hill in the distance, the pennons and tents of a large camp could be seen.

"The Saracens have moved to Tell Kaysan," said Henry of Champagne, riding over to them. "The king has ordered that we form battle lines."

"Surely we have not marched out here to do battle with them?" Wilfred asked.

The Count of Champagne shrugged. "We are vulnerable out here in the open. Saladin would relish the opportunity to attack us."

"Why would he attack when we have all these hostages?" Wilfred asked Harry, as the Count of Champagne rode off. Harry did not answer and Wilfred's darkest suspicions as to the reason for this excursion were realised.

The army arrayed itself in a long line with the men-at-arms in front of the mounted knights. Orders were given for the mass of prisoners to be lined up before them like chattel at market. There were signs of movement on the hill of Tell Kaysan. The Saracens had noticed that something was up. Dust clouds were kicked up by the hooves of many horses as they descended the hill and rode across the plain to get a closer look at what these mad Christians were up to.

King Richard, gleaming in his mail and open-faced helm, rode between the men-at-arms and the prisoners, his sword drawn. He was shouting something which Wilfred couldn't make out, but the intention was clear. The line of footmen moved forward as one, swords, axes, spears and falchions, at the ready.

Wilfred felt the contents of his gut rise up in revulsion as the slaughter began. The prisoners, their hands still bound, cried out in terror, offering their prayers to God as the blades of the Christians descended. It was an awful cacophony of anguish and butchery. The Christians, driven to a frenzy by the violence they were called upon to do, banished every scrap of humanity as they avenged every comrade they had lost over the past two years to Saracen blades and arrows. They waded in with a bloodlust that clouded their senses like a heady wine. The terror-stricken Saracens, driven mad with the desperate, primal desire to live against all odds, tried to run in all directions. Some tried to flee and were cut down. Others turned to face their butchers and ran towards them, cries to Allah on their lips.

The lines began to fall apart. The men-at-arms couldn't keep them back and the mounted knights found scores of blood-soaked, livid-eyed Saracens charging at them, spooking their horses which reared and sidestepped nervously.

"Cut them down!" cried Harry, drawing his sword. "Don't let any through!"

Wilfred was momentarily frozen. This all felt like some horrible nightmare. The men that pawed at them with bloody, bound hands were infidels, it was true, but they were unarmed and begging for mercy. Everything Wilfred had learnt about being a knight screamed against this dishonour.

And yet, was it dishonourable? This hill. This scene of brutality within sight of Saladin's army. It had been planned. It was a display. Saladin was not honouring the deal. Why take hostages if you were not prepared for this to be the end result? Saladin had been given every chance to save these men; these men who had held Acre against the crusaders for two years. These men who had taken their share of Christian lives in the name of a false prophet. Would the situation have been any different had it been Saracens with Christian prisoners?

Wilfred felt his hand going to the hilt of his sword and didn't remember ordering it to do so. Almost as if in a dream, he drew his blade and swung it down on the head of the Saracen that grasped at Jago's flanks.

The blade split the unprotected skull like a melon and the man sank to his knees. Wilfred yanked it free just in time to raise it at another desperate figure who ran towards him, apparently unaware that mercy was a forgotten word that day.

The Saracens from the camp on Tell Kaysan had charged as soon as the massacre had begun. By the time they reached the Christian lines, it was almost over. The few prisoners who were still left standing were caught between two armies and either flung themselves flat or were knocked down by the charging lines as the two armies met.

It was little more than a light skirmish. Not all the Saracens from Tell Kaysan had attacked meaning that the charge had probably been an uncontrolled gut impulse on the part of the Saracens who were forced to watch the massacre of their comrades from afar.

Outnumbered by the Christians, they eventually turned tail and fled back to their masters who watched from across the plain, indecisive in their outrage at what had occurred.

Wilfred felt numb as they rode back to Acre. Blood soiled his blue surcoat. It spattered the newly cleaned and oiled mail, and the sword King Richard had given him was sticky with gore and matted hair. Even Jago, the powerful warhorse, trained by the very best Spain had to offer, seemed skittish, as if he knew the stench of blood in his nostrils was not the blood of those slain fairly on the battlefield. *The beast knows this was wrong*, thought Wilfred. *As do I. As do we all. So why then, has this been allowed to happen?*

He recalled his own thoughts from mere moments ago, as he had tried to justify what they had done, and felt ashamed. They had been false justifications. They had been the words he needed to tell himself in order to physically draw his sword and partake in the barbarity.

Nobody spoke as they rode in through the gates of Acre. The city welcomed them silently, as if accepting of what they had done but refusing to comment on it. The mood was much the same in the citadel. The ladies retired hurriedly to their chambers upon the sight of the king and his bloodstained knights dismounting in the courtyard. An ugly business had been taken care of, that was all. Tomorrow, the crusade could get back on track.

But tomorrow could never just be another day, not after what they had done. A messenger arrived with news that enraged everybody but was wholly expected by Wilfred. Saladin, in reprisal for the massacre at Tell al-Ayyadiyya, had beheaded the Christian prisoners in his custody.

CHAPTER III

Rotherwood Hall, October 1191

The girl had been out gathering blackberries in the woods that surrounded the manor hall. The sky was overcast and the rain clouds that had loomed so threateningly all morning had not yet burst. She had not wandered far. She never did, always keeping the plume of smoke from the chimney of the hall in sight through the bare branches of the trees.

It was the approach of the horses that frightened her. The jingle-jangle of the harnesses and the snorting breath steaming on the chill air made her jump and she turned to see them pass through the trees towards the manor hall's eastern side. She stood stock still as she looked at the towering men in mail and nasal helms with their great kite shields painted in colours so vivid, they looked like fresh blood on snow.

They hadn't seen her and the way they kept their voices low, murmuring to each other as they rode past, made her feel very glad that they had not. She didn't know how many there were, only that there were a lot of them. As a rider passed close to her position she ducked behind an oak tree and pressed her back against its rough bark, the basket of blackberries tumbling from her hands to land at her feet. She held her breath so no wisp of steam from behind the oak would give her away. She squeezed her eyes shut and waited for the riders to pass.

When she was sure they were gone, she peeped around the trunk of the tree. There was no sign of them. Creeping out from her hiding place, she hurried towards home, the basket of blackberries forgotten, her small feet hurried by desperate urgency.

When she reached the precinct wall that surrounded the manor hall and its outbuildings, she knew that something terrible was happening. The mounted men were moving between the buildings with their swords drawn, booting open doors and dragging people out. The big door to the Great Hall stood open and from within could be heard shouting and the clang of blades.

The girl watched in terror as her father's servants were rounded up, dragged from the stables and bakehouse and away from the vegetable patches, then herded towards the hall as several soldiers exited it, wiping blood from their blades. There were no more sounds coming from within. The terrified servants were pushed into the building and the great door was bolted. Flaming torches were shoved under the shingled roof and thrust in through the windows.

Screaming began as the hall started to burn. The girl lay face down on the other side of the precinct wall and covered her ears from the awful sound. She didn't know how long she lay there but the cold ground grew damp beneath her face from her tears. Eventually, she removed her hands from her ears and could hear nothing but the crackle of burning timbers. She dared herself to get up onto her knees and peep over the wall.

The manor hall – the only home she knew – blazed against the cruel, grey sky. There was no sign of the men who had done this and all that remained of their passing was the inferno and the mud churned up by the hooves of their horses.

The girl scrambled over the wall and wandered through the wreckage of what had been her entire world. A deathly silence hung over the place. The doors to the outbuildings stood ajar. Storehouses had been looted, grain from the silos had been stolen and the stables were empty of horses.

She approached the blazing building until she was so close the heat stung her face and she could go no closer. She wanted to run into that inferno and be with her mother and father and all the servants that had treated her with kindness in her short life but she could not summon the courage to do so. She couldn't cry, she was too numb, too disorientated. Instead, she stood there in the scorching heat and watched her whole childhood go up in smoke.

The memories of that day often came back to Rowena in her lonelier moments. She didn't remember leaving the burning hall but she had been found in the local church by the parish priest. She supposed she had headed for the only safe place she could think of, though she remembered nothing of how she had got there. Once word got out that she had survived the calamity that had engulfed Caythorpe Hall, Cedric of Rotherwood immediately agreed to take her in. He had known her parents and held them in very high regard due to their lineage from the distant King Alfred, greatest of all the Saxon kings.

Cedric was convinced that Rowena's heritage had been part of the reason for the attack on Caythorpe Hall. Even back in those days, he had been inordinately opposed to the Norman blood that ran through the ruling families of England. Torquilstone Castle had recently fallen to the elder Reginald Front de-Boeuf and Cedric saw the slaughtering of Rowena's parents as another Norman attempt to erase yet more of England's old Saxon stock.

It was unknown who had ordered the attack and however much they questioned Rowena, she could recall no detail that might identify the mounted brigands. There was one suspect, although it could never be proved. Walter of Grantham had been in negotiations with Rowena's father to marry her when she came of age. He no doubt had his eye on Caythorpe's rich fishponds and had been most offended when Rowena's father had backed out of the negotiations. If the attack was his form of vengeance, then it was an abominably cruel one.

Ten years had passed and now, once again, Rowena found herself the subject of another round of marital negotiations. She supposed she should be grateful that Cedric had allowed her to reach womanhood before marrying her off. Even more mercifully, Athelstan of Coningsburgh seemed to show little to no interest in marrying her, for reasons best known to himself, causing the negotiations to stall indefinitely. Cedric had no intention of giving up but Rowena counted every day that passed as a blessing for it brought her one day closer to seeing Wilfred again.

If he still lives.

No.

She refused to think like that. News had come from Outremer that King Richard had taken the coastal city of Acre and was poised to strike at Jerusalem. If the very worst had happened and Wilfred had fallen, surely they would have received word of it? She relied on this logic to keep her spirits up but it wasn't easy. She had felt so very lonely since Wilfred had left. She had been lonely before, when he had gone to London to become a page for Roger of Hambleton, but now it was worse, knowing that he was on the other side of the world, fighting for his life against unknown odds.

Some distraction at least was to be found in tonight's feast. Thankfully, it was not another visit from Athelstan whom Rowena was convinced only came for the food and ale and tolerated Cedric's attempts at renewing the betrothal negotiations as merely a price to be paid for a good feast. Tonight, they were to be visited by Geoffrey of Stannington with his wife and three sons.

Geoffrey was yet another of Cedric's circle of noblemen who had some trace of Saxon blood. In Geoffrey's case, it came from Earl Waltheof, the last of the Saxon earls who had met the headsman's axe after leading a revolt against King William. Rowena didn't much care for Geoffrey or his haughty sons but was glad of a chance to busy herself in preparation for the feast.

Hundebert, Cedric's steward, was barking orders in the Great Hall while servants moved trestle tables about and spread fresh rushes on the floor. Rowena made herself useful and instructed the servants in the changing of a tapestry on the eastern wall. Cedric had requested that, in honour of his guest, the tapestry depicting Waltheof's rebellion against King William be displayed.

There were three panels to it and Rowena had forgotten that the first one showed the Saxon chieftains Hengest and Horsa before the tyrant Vortigern. Hengest's daughter – and Rowena's namesake – stood between Saxon and Briton, a jug of mead in her hand while Vortigern held his cup out. Rowena's seduction of King Vortigern, which had led to Hengest's triumph over the Britons at the Night of the Long Knives, was a tale often told in the households of the old families for it was considered England's foundation myth. Households with more Norman ancestry preferred the stories of King Arthur, the Briton who had waged war on the Saxons after Vortigern's death.

As the servants carefully rolled up the other tapestry and carried it away, Rowena gazed upon the Rowena of legend. The stories depicted her as a canny seductress, a sorceress even, who eventually poisoned Vortigern's eldest son before vanishing from history. Rowena wondered how much of that was an accurate portrayal of a girl who could not have been much older than she was when she was married off to a tyrant. Had she gone willingly? Had she agreed to her father's plan to unite two powerful families through her marriage? *Perhaps she had merely done her duty while her heart belonged to somebody else …*

"Where is that blasted Oswald?" Hundebert bellowed. "I sent him to take stock in the buttery an age ago! Somebody go and fetch him. Lord Cedric wants the best mead for the table tonight."

"I'll go," said Rowena. She suddenly felt the need for some fresh air as well as the desire to hide the tears that had quickly welled up in her eyes.

The buttery was a thatched pit house a few yards from the Great Hall where the ale and mead was stored, its sunken floor providing a cool, dark cellar. Rowena found the door unlocked and when she opened it, she found Wamba the fool and Gurth the swineherd sitting on a cask, enjoying a cup of ale. They both leapt to attention as she stepped down through the doorway. They tried to hide the evidence of their crime by pushing the cup behind their backs but only succeeding in knocking it to the floor, spilling some ale which soaked into the hard-packed earth.

Rowena smiled. "You're lucky it was me who found you here and not Hundebert or you would both be whipped. Who gave you the key anyway?"

"Oswald, my lady," said Wamba. "May God bless him for his Christian charity, for I am welcome no other place in Rotherwood."

Wamba was currently in disgrace after upsetting Cedric with some well-meaning remark. Cedric had banished him from his sight, uttering oaths that he would suffer horribly if he should anger him once more so Wamba had made himself scarce over the past few days.

"I had best be about my business," said Gurth, hurrying past Rowena. Once he was outside, he called for Fang, his new hound who had replaced old Brutus and the pair of them hurried off to see to the pigs.

"My lady, I am ashamed," said Wamba, looking thoroughly miserable and his speech slurred. Rowena guessed that he had partaken in more than one cup of ale. "When I am denied my purpose, I find an eviller one. My family were right to wash their hands of me, for I can't even make a good fool. My ailment robbed me even of that."

"Pull yourself together, Wamba," said Rowena. "You're drunk and feeling sorry for yourself. Cedric will forgive you. He always does."

Wamba was only a little older than Rowena and had been a childhood companion to her and Wilfred. He had been destined for the Church and had been well-educated in letters and Latin but also in music and song in accordance with Cedric's demands. Cedric had a mind to make him both cleric and *scop* in the old Saxon tradition but a brain fever in Wamba's youth had cut that path short leaving him deprived of many of his wits. That did not make him *witless* however, and Cedric had found that Wamba was an amusing fellow, alternating between idiocy and occasional wisdom. So, instead of playing the harp at the mead benches, Wamba donned a motley tunic and belled cap and the role of fool with it.

Wamba rose, a little unsteadily, and slapped his cheeks with his hands. "Right you are, Lady Rowena," he said. "Such a queen you have become, wise and stern. I remember the day Cedric brought you to Rotherwood. You were as meek as a kitten. Wilfred pretended that you held no interest for him but I could see that he was smitten by you, even at that age."

"That'll do, Wamba," said Rowena. "Be off with you. I only came here to find Oswald. Where is he?"

"How should I know?" said Wamba with a smile. "He gave me the key and flitted away like a sparrow." He hiccupped and swayed out of the buttery, leaving Rowena shaking her head.

Geoffrey of Stannington and his entourage arrived a little before noon. He wasn't a tall man, but he was stout, much in the way that Cedric was, except that his hair was dark rather than flaxen. His sons were admittedly handsome, even if they were a little boorish. The eldest, Robert, was tall and dark and considered himself a better huntsman than most and liked to remark upon it as often as he could. The middle brother, Hugh, hung on every word Robert said and seemed to have little personality to call his own. As for the youngest brother, Simon, perhaps the less said about him the better, except to say that he shared his elder siblings' haughtiness if not their seriousness. Everything seemed either a joke or a bore to him.

Rowena dressed for dinner and could hear the feast beginning downstairs as Elgitha finished braiding her hair and fixing her veil. When she went down to join them in the Great Hall, she found that the conversation had predictably turned to recent political events.

"In my opinion," Geoffrey was saying, "our king was just asking for trouble when he gave his brother control of so many counties but denied him the castles themselves. How else was John to react? It was a clear indication of the king's lack of confidence in his younger brother. An insult even."

"Surely you do not side with the Count of Mortain against our king, Father?" asked his youngest son, Simon, a half-smile playing on his lips.

"Certainly not," said Geoffrey rather huffily at such a prospect. "I only wish the king had shown a little more diplomacy in dealing with his own family members. Then we wouldn't be in the situation we are now."

It had been a troubled year. Before King Richard had embarked on his crusade, he had appointed William de Longchamp the Bishop of Ely and Hugh de Puiset the Bishop of Durham, as England's joint Chief Justiciars. To appease his younger brother, John, who clearly felt a little put out that he had not been made regent in Richard's absence, he made him Count of Mortain and gave him extensive territories in England. Richard did, however, retain control of key castles in those territories making it clear to all that he did not trust his own brother not to steal the kingdom from him in his absence.

Longchamp and Puiset were a bad match from the beginning and their working relationship soon broke down. Longchamp ousted Puiset and became England's sole justiciar but he was generally disliked due to his extravagance and his nasty habit of replacing sheriffs and castellans with his own friends. When he tried to replace the Sheriff of Lincolnshire, who was an ally of John, John took the opportunity to seize Tickhill and Nottingham, two of the castles in his own territories that had been denied him, and began making his move to step in as an alternative regent.

Word of this reached the king, who had only got as far as Sicily, and in response, he sent Walter de Coutances, the Archbishop of Rouen, to try and cool things down between John and Longchamp. A peace was brokered and John gave back the castles he had taken while Longchamp agreed to recognise his authority north of the River Humber. But, with two such men in charge of England, it was a peace destined to be broken before long.

"You have heard the latest news from London, I suppose?" said Geoffrey, as he held his cup out to be refilled.

"I rarely concern myself with the goings on south of the River Trent," said Cedric in a tired tone. "But I assume you refer to Longchamp's newest outrage, in that he imprisoned the Archbishop of York, your namesake. Yes, I had heard that."

"If that is the latest you have heard, then you are sorely behind," said Geoffrey, evidently pleased to be more informed than his host. "My namesake, as you so graciously put it, was forcibly dragged from the sanctuary of a priory by Longchamp's agents. An archbishop, no less, hauled from the holy altar by common soldiers! It is enough to invoke the memories of Thomas Becket's murder and Count John was quite rightly infuriated."

"Why should John care about the Archbishop of York?" Cedric asked. "He is, after all, his bastard half-brother. All the king's family hated him except his father. The whole reason he was forced into the Church was to eliminate another rival for the throne in a family that already had too many rivals."

"John's outrage is feigned, no doubt, but it has presented him with the perfect opportunity to end Longchamp for good. Everyone in London is up in arms about the archbishop's treatment and earlier this month Longchamp was summoned to a council. He did not attend and has now been excommunicated. As we speak, he is barricaded inside the Tower of London; the only property he still controls. He may have to leave the country and many of the barons are looking to John now, particularly here in the north."

"John or Longchamp?" said Cedric with a sigh. "There is little to choose between them. This is a Norman problem for Norman lords."

"It could be civil war when the king returns, if indeed he does return. Then it will be everybody's problem."

Rowena felt as if a cold blade had pricked her heart at these words and she wondered how anyone could speak so casually of the king's crusade when the lives of so many good men hung in the balance.

Geoffrey, failing to notice the pain his words had caused her, continued; "John is surely thinking this too for he is certainly consolidating his position. He hands out parcels of land to his allies as if they were treats at Yuletide. I understand he has even handed the fief of your absent son to that beast, Front-de-Boeuf."

A silence fell over the table at this, a silence Rowena could not help but break. "John has given the fief of Ivanhoe to Front-de-Boeuf?" she exclaimed.

"The very fief the king gave to Wilfred in exchange for him accompanying him on the holy crusade? Can he do that?"

Geoffrey looked surprised at her outburst. "I think it is being made abundantly clear that the king's brother can do whatever he jolly well pleases."

Cedric, who had fixed his eyes on Geoffrey, said; "I do not permit the mentioning of the wretch who used to be my son in this hall. And it does not surprise me in the slightest that Ivanhoe is stolen as soon as it is gifted. These Normans would steal the very air we breathe and then seek to sell it back to us."

Geoffrey had coloured a little, sensing that he had made some sort of faux-pas and hurriedly tried to steer the conversation onwards. "Perhaps we should turn to matters closer to home. My eldest son, Robert here, is ripe for marrying and I have my heart set on a very particular bride."

"Oh?" asked Cedric, showing some interest in the conversation at last. "And who is the lucky lady you have in mind for this strapping young lad?"

"Maud de Lovetot."

"The great heiress?" said Cedric. "Who is fourteen and yet unmarried. Surely her guardian has refused a great many suitors."

"I have already entered negotiations with Philip de Malvoisin," said Geoffrey proudly. "He is entertaining the idea but, as you rightly surmise, I am far from his only consideration. In fact, I had thought to ask you a favour in that regard. I desperately need some help in tipping the scales."

"A favour from me?" Cedric asked, astonished. "I have no business with Malvoisin, any more than I do with his friend, Front-de-Boeuf. They are both devils cut from the same cloth."

"I quite agree. Malvoisin is an ogre but in marrying Robert to the heiress, my family will then rule Locksley Chase and the manors of Hallam, Sheffield and Attercliffe, just as we did in the old days. Think of it, Cedric! My family, who are descended from the Saxon earls of Huntingdon, would reclaim the land taken by Norman lords when Waltheof was slain. We would be neighbours! And if you marry the fair Rowena here to Athelstan of Coningsburgh, thus fusing their noble lines, a wide swathe of the West Riding would no longer be ruled by Normans, but by the descendants of Waltheof, Hereward, Alfred *and* Edward! Think what we could begin here!"

Rowena nearly rolled her eyes. Geoffrey knew how to play Cedric like a harp. By appealing to his romantic sense of Saxon pride, he could convince Cedric into any scheme no matter how mad. Robert of Stannington marry Maud de Lovetot? She was surprised Philip de Malvoisin hadn't laughed old Geoffrey out of Sheffield Castle for bringing such a proposal to him. Besides, Malvoisin was only Maud's guardian and an heiress of such means couldn't be married until the king returned.

"A marvellous thought," said Cedric a little wistfully. "But how might I play a role in bringing it to fruition?"

"As it happens," Geoffrey said, "young Maud has found herself a little lonely of late. After all, it's not much of a life for a child to be cooped up in a castle with no family or real friends. Philip de Malvoisin, beast though he is, has always seen fit to provide the young girl with the companionship of several ladies-in-waiting. Of course, it is hard to have any her age without them being a burden themselves but he has tried to employ unwed girls below the age of twenty. The last one I fear, was dismissed recently for some indiscretion and Malvoisin is looking to fill the vacancy. If we could place a young girl sympathetic to our cause within Sheffield Castle, she might be able to steer Malvoisin's opinion in favour of Robert."

Geoffrey smiled at Cedric and waited for his point to sink in. Cedric still seemed confused as to what all this had to do with him but Rowena saw the picture clearly enough.

"The lady Rowena here is young enough to make an admirable companion for the heiress," Geoffrey prompted at last.

"Rowena?" Cedric exclaimed. "I have already lost my son to a Norman lord; do you really think I would allow my ward to vanish from me also?"

"She wouldn't be lost from you," said Geoffrey. "A year at the most, and she would be close enough. Sheffield lies nearer to Rotherwood than Stannington."

"Close enough but at a Norman's hearth," said Cedric. "Learning Norman customs and manners, just as my son did."

"As I understand it, she would be called upon to set an example to the young Maud, not the other way around. And Malvoisin will hardly be spending much time with the ladies of his charge. Rowena may even teach the Norman heiress a few Saxon customs."

The last was said in jest but it seemed to have some effect on Cedric for he sat deep in thought as he considered Geffrey's words. "I had hoped to conclude the betrothal negotiations with Athelstan before Yule," he mused. "So that they might be married after Lent."

"A minor postponement," said Geoffrey. "But our victory will be all the greater if there are *two* wedding feasts to arrange come Easter!"

"Yes ..." said Cedric.

Rowena waited patiently in case anybody thought to ask her own opinion on these matters but she knew it was a false hope. If Cedric would marry her off without consulting her then he certainly wouldn't think twice of sending her to babysit a young girl at Sheffield Castle if he thought to benefit from it. Besides, the proposal wasn't so terrible to her mind. Her loneliness always increased with the onset of winter. It might be rather comforting to be around other young girls through the dark months. And of course, if it meant postponing her marriage to that oaf Athelstan ...

"Very well," said Cedric. "I give my blessing but convincing Malvoisin to take Rowena on may be another matter entirely. He isn't exactly fond of his Saxon neighbour."

"You are not presenting yourself as a potential lady-in-waiting, but the fair Rowena here. And who could ask for a more charming, beautiful and virtuous example for a young girl?"

"My lord is too flattering," said Rowena.

"And besides, there are few enough noble ladies yet unwed in these parts. Malvoisin will jump at the chance to employ Rowena and be done with the task."

"And you, Rowena," Cedric asked, turning to gaze at her. "Does such a duty sit well with you?"

"Sire, in truth I would enjoy some female company. I am very happy here at Rotherwood but since ... well, I *have* grown lonelier of late."

"And what about the interruption in your betrothal negotiations?"

"If Athelstan truly wishes to marry me, then he will wait until next year."

"You are right, of course," said Cedric. "Very well. I will send a message to Malvoisin in the morning. Now, let us drink to our plans, Geoffrey."

There was little more to be said on the matter and the rest of the afternoon was given over to drinking heavily and celebrating dreams of future reprisal against their Norman overlords. Geoffrey and his sons took every advantage of their host's hospitality, young Simon in particular, who had taken a shine to Gunhild, one of the serving girls. He amused himself by winking at her whenever she poured him some mead, which was often as the youngest Stannington drained his cup twice as fast as his brothers. Before night had fallen, the men were roaring drunk and Rowena grew tired of it all and excused herself.

Geoffrey and his family were given lodgings for the night and bedded down in the guest chambers in the eastern aisle of the hall which was screened by walls of whitewashed wattle and daub. It was as

Rowena climbed the short series of timber steps from the antechamber from which doors led to the various apartments, that she was startled by movement in the shadows. Evidently someone had not yet been ready to retire to their bed.

By the light of the candles which the servants had not yet extinguished, she could see two figures in the corner of the chamber, one with his back to her. She realised with a start that the man's hose was around his ankles and his tunic bunched up around his waist for the candlelight illuminated a pair of white buttocks that seemed to be moving back and forth.

The top of a woman's head could be seen over his shoulder and Rowena recognised the serving girl, Gunhild, her face screwed up into a tight grimace of pleasure as the man nuzzled her neck and thrust harder and faster with his hips. Her hands ran across his back, scooping up fistfuls of his tunic as if attempting to rip it off him.

Rowena couldn't tear her eyes away. Strange feelings had been awoken in her; feelings of both revulsion and fascination. She had vague ideas of what married men and women got up to and indeed she often dreamt of being held intimately by Wilfred, kissed by him, even, but *that*?

The man gasped suddenly, making Rowena jump. A shiver seemed to ripple through him and his shoulders sagged as if his whole body had suddenly relaxed. He pulled away from Gunhild and stooped down to pull up his hose. As the candlelight caught his face, Rowena realised that it was Simon of Stannington.

Not wishing to be seen by either Simon or Gunhild, Rowena climbed the steps to her chamber as quickly and as noiselessly as she could.

Cedric's messenger was received by Philip de Malvoisin and the arrangements were made. Before November began, Rowena was summoned to Sheffield Castle. She was to undergo a probationary period and, if Maud de Lovetot and, more importantly, Philip de Malvoisin took to her, then she would stay on indefinitely.

Elgitha was nearly sobbing as she helped Rowena pack for her journey and, in truth, Rowena was a little tearful at leaving. Her faithful handmaid had been a friend to her since childhood and had become her only confidant since Wilfred had left. Now that Sheffield beckoned with its promises of a higher class of company, Rowena found that she had grown very fond of Elgitha and wanted to cling to her in the shadow of the advancing unknown.

"Oh, I'll be back, Elgitha," she told her handmaid, summoning some courage for the both of them. "And I won't be far away. Sheffield is hardly Jerusalem."

That brought Elgitha up short. "I apologise, my lady. Here I am making a fuss about your leaving when you miss Wilfred so dreadfully."

"I did not mean it like that, Elgitha. I do miss him and I will miss you too. But we must both be brave. It won't be long, God willing, before the three of us are reunited here at Rotherwood."

"You truly believe that, my lady?"

"I must," said Rowena. "My faith is all I have left."

Cedric had arranged a mounted guard to take Rowena to Sheffield and she left the Great Hall to find her horse saddled and waiting for her. Cedric was there too, along with Wamba who had at last worked himself back into Cedric's favour.

"Be safe, my girl," said Cedric, as he kissed her goodbye. "Rotherwood has been your home since you were a child and it always will be. But now you are a woman and you must begin to take your steps into the wide world. But never forget who you are and what blood flows in your veins. You will see many fine things and new customs in the company of Malvoisin's people but always remember that you are a Saxon lady, and one of the last."

"I will, Cedric. Don't worry about me. I know where I belong and it is not at a Norman's hearth. I will return to you when I am able."

"I am glad to hear it. And if you do find some opportunity to pour a little honey into Malvoisin's ear regarding young Robert of Stannington, then do what you can, but never put yourself in danger by doing so."

Rowena said nothing. She kept forgetting that her mission was not just to befriend a young girl but something of a more nefarious nature. She promised herself that she would at least try. Cedric and Geoffrey had placed their trust in her and she hated the thought of letting anybody down.

CHAPTER IV

Locksley Chase, November, 1191

Simon of Stannington drew the bowstring back to his ear so that the arrow's fletching brushed his cheek. He took careful aim as the partridge rose from the patch of fern and flapped its way into the iron grey sky. He loosed and the arrow streaked away from his bow, climbing into the air and keeping perfect pace with the bird. Simon grinned with satisfaction as it struck its mark and the partridge tumbled from the sky, a few feathers knocked loose from the impact of the arrow.

"Go on, Balthazar!" Simon said to the spaniel at his heels. "Fetch it!"

The small but eager dog rocketed forward and vanished into the deep ferns, a path of rippling leaves showing his passage. He promptly returned proudly carrying the partridge between his teeth.

"Good dog!" said John of Hathersage, stooping forward to collect the bird and ruffle Balthazar's ears. John was a short but stocky retainer who had become something of a companion to Simon despite being one of his father's servants. He had previously been a hunter in the service of William de Lovetot before the old lord's death.

John and Simon often went hunting on the uplands beyond the northern boundaries of Locksley Chase. It was the peace of mind that pleased Simon and the chance of getting away from Stannington Hall.

He breathed the cold, autumn air deeply and smiled. He was starting to recover from the dreadful hangover he had woken with. Last night had been a heavy one on account of a visit from Gilbert of Tankersley, steward of the manor of Hallam, and his bailiff, a burly thug by the name of Osbert. Not that Gilbert of Tankersley was a particularly merry fellow, in fact Simon despised the man, but he always found the best way to get through a tiresome meal was to get as drunk as possible and that is exactly what he had done.

He had disgraced himself, of course. As usual. It had been the steward's fault. He was a rotund man with a sweaty face that always seemed to be on the verge of a sneer. The man was so haughty that he gave Simon's older brothers a run for their money and one could tell that he despised the Stanningtons and their pretentions. Simon could hardly blame him for that, for in truth, he despised his own family on that account. This rotten business of trying to marry his older brother, Robert, to the Lovetot heiress? And then that sordid plan of sending Rowena of Rotherwood to play the part of spy at Sheffield castle? It made him sick with shame to be associated with it all.

And Simon hated to see his father bow and scrape to such a loathsome man as the steward of Hallam who only graced them with his presence because he needed a comfortable place to stay for the night. He was touring the manor with his bailiff and was due at Sheffield in a few days to meet Yorkshire's new sheriff. It was on this point that Simon had insulted him.

"Hugh de Bardulf will restore some order to this shire, I have no doubt," Gilbert had said. "He has been sheriff of Cornwall, Wiltshire and Somerset previously and has been a justice of Eyre for many years. A better sheriff we could not ask for."

"And friendly to the king's brother to boot," Simon had interjected over the rim of his wine cup. "Just as Malvoisin is."

Gilbert squinted at him, sensing some hidden criticism in his words. "Indeed. But it is prudent to be friends with Count John, now that he is the sole justiciar of England."

"After William de Longchamp was forced to flee London for France dressed as a woman, or so it is said," Simon replied, glancing down the table to see if anybody else found this as amusing as he did. None did.

"And good riddance," said Gilbert. "Longchamp was a foreigner and a poor choice for regent. The king's brother is far better suited and is doing a fine job of appointing competent men to positions of authority."

"Men like Bardulf."

"Quite."

"Who aided in John's removal of Longchamp. Was it not Longchamp's brother, Osbert, whom Bardulf has replaced as Sheriff of Yorkshire?"

"You know very well it was," said his father testily.

"No doubt John wished to reward Bardulf for aiding in his coup."

"Coup?" Gilbert said.

"One has to wonder," Simon continued, "what favours Malvoisin has done for our new regent. Or what he promises to do."

"I'm not sure I like your tone, boy," Gilbert warned. "Lord Malvoisin is a powerful man."

"Yes, Count John seems to draw powerful men to him, those who agree with him that is. He exiles those who don't."

The steward's face was in full snarl now while his bailiff glared at Simon with a dangerous glint in his eye. Simon looked from them to the faces of his family. The warning glare from his father. The sour looks of disapproval from his brothers, Hugh and Robert. The usual look of distress from his mother. They all seemed to be waiting for him to say something further. *Oh well, in for a penny, in for a pound.*

"Still, every man has his price, I suppose," said Simon. "I wonder what yours was, steward, for the hall at Hallam Head did not belong to your father."

"Damn your impudence!" Gilbert roared. "I'm no man to be bought! Hallam Head was given to me by Malvoisin when he made me steward!"

"My apologies, sire," said Simon's father desperately. "As you can see, my son is overly fond of wine. Or anything else that muddles his wits, few as they are. Please ignore him."

The steward did his best to ignore Simon and the conversation quickly turned to other topics. Simon descended into sullen silence and drank until it was time to retire to bed, a point in the evening he did not fully remember.

"Well, master," said John, as he tied the partridge to Simon's saddle where two hung already. "Are we to fill your father's larder with game birds or is it time to head back?"

"I think I've shot enough birds for one day, John," said Simon. "This Yorkshire air has cleared my head. So much in fact, that I might manage a tankard of ale at the Cross and Cup. Hair of the dog, so to speak. What do you say?"

John grinned. "I say we might manage a few hairs."

The Cross and Cup was a low thatched hall with a stable that jutted off at a right angle to form an 'L' shaped building. As well as providing food and lodging for travellers on the road from Stannington to Sheffield, it was a popular haunt for locals keen to quench their thirst after a day's labour. Simon often frequented it as he found its unpretentious atmosphere far preferable to his father's hall. Many a night he had diced, danced and sung with the very salt of the earth – farmers and craftsmen from Locksley Chase mostly – and now had many acquaintances among the common folk he had come to call friends.

It was still early and not much noise could be heard as Simon and John rode up. They stabled their horses and, Simon taking his bow and valuable game birds with him, rounded the building to the front entrance. Balthazar trotted along beside them, hopeful of a scrap of meat.

There were a few travellers inside, supping on fresh ale and eating with their long knives. Hamar the innkeeper hailed them as they entered and Simon tossed him a partridge. "See what meat you can get off that, Hamar, and bring us two tankards of ale and whatever grub you've given these fellows."

Simon and John sat down at the end of a trestle table, nodding politely to the travellers who occupied its far end. Hamar hurried over with their ale and a board of bread and cheese. "A good hunt, sire?" he asked.

"Best time of year for it, Hamar," said Simon. "The trees are bare and the birds are easily spotted but these ones looked a bit starved for so late in the year."

"It's been a hard year for all," said Hamar, almost under his breath as he left them.

Simon and John drank deep and smacked their lips, glad of the warmth the ale and hearth brought them after their morning on the uplands. Harold of Studley, who was a hooper by trade, came in with his fifteen-year-old son, William, and sat down with them.

"How goes it, Harold?" Simon asked. "Business brisk?"

"Brisker than some," Harold replied.

Hamar returned with ale for Harold and William and a plate of innards he had just cut from the partridge. This he set down for Balthazar who began gobbling them up.

A beggar woman entered the inn and began to move down the hall, bowl held out tentatively and hood pulled down to cover as much of her shame as she could. A few locals dropped some pennies in her bowl while the travellers peered at her with distaste. Simon shared their sentiment. It was most unlike

Hamar to allow beggars to pester his customers. *The old fool must be getting soft*, he thought.

When the beggar woman drew near, Simon made to shoo her away irritably, but he caught a glimpse of the face under the hood. It was young, pretty and above all, known to him as the daughter of Thomas the miller, a regular drinker at the Cross and Cup.

"Judith!" he exclaimed. "What in heaven's name are you doing begging for alms?"

A small gasp of anguish escaped Judith's lips and she turned her face from him, even more ashamed than she had been previously. She moved quickly for the door. Simon rose to call after her but caught the look on Hamar's face and said nothing.

"Her family's fallen on hard times," said the innkeeper once Judith had scuttled out and made her way off down the road. "Thomas the miller was fined heavily at the last manorial court. They don't have two pennies to rub together, let alone pay a fine of six shillings."

"Six shillings!" Simon exclaimed. "What did Thomas do to deserve that?"

"It's that bastard steward," said Harold. "He's always had a dislike for Thomas. You remember how he was always the miller for the manor?"

Simon nodded.

"Well, the price of using his lordship's mill has crept up of late; too high for the likes of Thomas to afford. I reckon it was a way for Gilbert of Tankersley to push him out and make room for a miller of his own choice. Poor Thomas took to private enterprise with his own quern stone. I took my grain to him, as did many in the manor, for Thomas was one of our own, a Locksley man; not like that new fellow from Tankersley way. Anyway, word got back to Gilbert and he dragged Thomas before the court, fined him and confiscated his quern stone."

"What Thomas is to do now is anyone's guess," said Hamar. "He's a miller by trade and if he can't afford to use the manor mill or mill in his own house then he's no way of making a living."

"And no way of paying that fine," Harold agreed. "He and his family will be out on their ears come spring."

"But this cannot be allowed to pass!" said Simon. He was outraged for he had spent many a drunken evening with the burly, jovial Thomas and had taken quite a fancy to his daughter Judith.

"Well, it's already done," said Harold. "Not all in the manor are so lucky in our birth as you, Simon."

"What is that supposed to mean?"

"Nothing much. But many poor folk in the Chase will go hungry this winter. We can't mill our own grain for the rents are too high, and we can't hunt for all game in the Chase belongs to Malvoisin."

"There's always partridge to be had on the uplands," said Simon weakly. "Nobody owns them."

"Most don't have the horses or the time to take off from our regular employments," said Harold. "We are bound to the Chase as we are to our stations in life and neither offer us much by way of coin or food. But I'm wrong to complain to you. I'm sure the folk of Stannington Hall have their own problems and no time for the complaints of poor folk." He drained his tankard and, clapping young William on the shoulder, made to leave.

Simon didn't know if there had been an intentional barb in Harold's words but he felt its sting nonetheless. How long had it been since the last manorial court? He hadn't even known that Thomas the miller was in such dire straits, but everybody else apparently did. Harold had made his point abundantly clear; there was a world of difference between life at Stannington Hall and the hardship of living in the Chase. And for the first time in his life, Simon was painfully aware of it.

He had no more stomach for ale and they made ready to ride back to Stannington Hall. He thought back on all the cheerful evenings he had spent at the Cross and Cup, surrounded by people he had felt a kinship with, despite their differences in class. Had he been deluded? Had all the jovial banter and fellowship been nothing but common folk humouring the local nobleman's son?

"Have I been blind, John?" he asked his servant, as they mounted their horses. "To not see the suffering of those I call friends?"

"You are noble-born, sire," said John. "It is not for you to worry about the struggles of villeins and freemen."

"But Thomas is a friend. Had I known that his family faces such doom, I would have done something."

Exactly what he could have done was unknown to him. He may have been noble-born but he had no real coin to call his own, certainly not six shillings.

Everything he needed came from the hall, paid for by his father. "Well, I'm *going* to do something," he said, his voice filled with resolve. "We'll see what my father has to say about Steward Gilbert's justice."

Stannington Hall occupied a hill between the River Locksley and the River Rivelin. It was not a large house like some of the big manor halls, but it was a comfortable residence for a family of some means.

When Simon put the case of Thomas the miller before his father at table that night, he was met with cold indifference.

"Thomas, good man though he is, broke the rules," his father said. "And, as such, must pay the fine. Everybody knows that all grain must be milled at Miller's Bridge."

"But how can he pay the fine when he doesn't have any employment?" Simon protested. "He stands to lose everything just because he couldn't afford the new rates for using the mill."

"Why do you care, anyway?" his brother Hugh asked. "Why does a poor miller's fate sit so ill with you?"

"Because that 'poor miller' is one of his friends," said Robert, lounging in his seat, cup of wine in hand. "Don't you know our little brother is given to roistering with peasants?"

"Your brothers do have a point," said their father. "Not only is it unbecoming for a nobleman's son to carouse in ale houses with the commoners, but it is far from your business to object to our steward's judgement of them. Concern yourself with other things more suited to your station, Simon."

"I see," said Simon. "I should look to my noble pursuits while a friend of mine is cast out with his whole family just as the nights are drawing in." His face felt hot with anger. What he had learned about himself today and Harold's barbed words had raised a previously unfelt sense of outrage at the cruelty of the world. "I do not seek to interfere with the steward's justice, but could we not pay Thomas's fine for him? It is surely a pittance for you, Father, but to him it is the difference between life and death."

"I am to pay commoners' fines for them now!" his father exclaimed while Robert and Hugh burst out laughing. "Let me inform you of your family's current economic situation, Simon. Since King Richard set sail on his wars of conquest, we have struggled to make ends meet. The Saladin Tithe all but stripped England's noble families bare to finance the great crusade. Pay a miller's fine? Hah! My coffers are empty! Why do you think I am going to such lengths to see that Robert marries the Lovetot heiress? And you seem to make it your business to thwart us at every turn!"

"Me?" said Simon, wondering how the conversation had turned suddenly against him. "What have I done?"

"I just thank God that you are my third son and not my firstborn," said his father. "The way you carried on with that servant slut at Rotherwood when we were there last! Don't think we didn't see you. Your behaviour in the house of my friend was shameful! And then your conduct when the steward was here last night! It's a wonder he agrees to be our guest at all, the way he is spoken to by my own son!"

"That bloody steward!" said Simon. "The way you kiss that bastard's arse makes me sick! I have heard you curse him often enough when he is not our guest! Isn't his hall at Hallam Head the very hall of our ancestor, Earl Waltheof? Why are you so keen to reclaim all our family has lost yet at the same time you play host to your own usurper and tolerate his insults?"

"Because I'm not Cedric of Rotherwood, that's why! I don't barricade myself in my hall and pretend the last hundred years didn't happen. We need to move up in the world but we can only do that by playing the game by their rules. That's what Cedric doesn't understand."

"So you are content to be the friend of a man who not only despises us but tyrannises the inhabitants of Locksley Chase with his extortion and his corruption!"

His father sighed. "I don't like the man, it is true. But one day we will sit in our ancestral hall at Hallam Head and I shall be steward, if not lord of the manor while your brother rules from Sheffield. I only pray that when that day comes, you will understand all I have done and know that I did it for you and your brothers."

Simon slammed his fist down on the table and rose from his seat. "Politics and currying favour! Small wonder it has taken this family an age to reclaim a fragment of what we lost."

He left the hall and made for his chamber. John appeared from the doorway to the kitchens, chewing on a chicken leg. "Any joy with your father?"

"None," Simon replied, grumpily. "As far as he is concerned, the poor can go burn so long as he marries Robert to that wretched Lovetot girl and reclaims his precious pride."

"Such is the way of it with lordly folk," John replied. "Present company excepted of course," he added with a wink. "Although I must confess I am surprised that you have taken this business so hard."

"You are surprised that I care for the fate of a man I consider a friend?" Simon said sharply, not liking John's assessment of him.

"I spoke out of turn, master, and I apologise. It's just that you've never been one to care much about anyone's future, not even your own."

"Because I can *afford* not to care about my own, I suppose. But you're right about one thing, John. This has hit me hard. How can I sit by and do nothing while Thomas and his family face starvation?"

"I don't rightly know what you can do, master."

They had reached Simon's chamber now and he closed the door behind them before sitting down on the edge of his bed. "Gilbert said that he and his bailiff were staying at Endcliffe tonight before arriving at Sheffield Castle tomorrow, didn't he?"

"That's what I heard," said John.

"Then he will be taking the road south through Crookesmoor tomorrow morning," Simon pondered. "And he only has that oafish bailiff for protection."

"What are you thinking?" said John with a frown.

"I'm thinking that we should rise early tomorrow, ride out and meet our dear steward on the road to Sheffield."

"And do what, precisely?"

"Persuade him to exercise his Christian charity. He has a fat purse and some of it will relieve at least a little of the pain he has caused."

"Rob him?" said John. "The steward of Hallam. At sword point presumably?"

"Or arrow point," said Simon. "I'll do the robbing but I'll need you to keep an arrow trained on that bailiff to stop him interfering."

"And suppose I feel that hedge robbing is beyond my duties as your servant?" said John, folding his arms.

Simon's heart sank. "I'm sorry, John. You are right of course. I cannot press you into committing a crime for the penalty for you would be worse than it would for me."

"Rubbish. If we're caught then we'll both swing from the gallows tree, side by side. The rope makes equals of us all."

Simon saw a glint of grim humour in John's eye. "Then you'll help me? I can't ask it of you, John …"

"No, you can't. But I'm not about to let you risk your neck by robbing that bastard steward all on your own. Besides, Thomas is my friend too and I have as much of a score to settle with Gilbert of Tankersley as you do."

Simon grinned. He knew the soberness of dawn would rob him of some of the courage he felt now but he couldn't help but feel elated. It was a mad scheme but he was confident they could pull it off; saving Thomas's family from ruin and giving Gilbert a taste of his own medicine into the bargain. "We'll have to disguise our faces," he said.

"Leave that to me," said John. "I know where I can get some black cloth to use as masks."

"Very well," said Simon, rising. "We'd best get some sleep then. Wake me early, John. It will be a hard ride to Crookesmoor to beat Gilbert to the Chase, late riser though he is. We need plenty of time to prepare and I don't want to take any chances. We'll only get one shot at this."

The morning was cold but thankfully dry as Simon and John took their horses from the stables and rode out of Stannington Hall dressed as simple yeomen. Simon wore a brown cloak fastened with a dull bronze brooch and the hood pulled up while John was dressed in the garments of his former employment; a hunter's green tunic and hooded mantle. As soon as they were in open country and the houses of Stannington were in the hazy distance behind them, they bound masks of black cloth around the lower part of their faces, obscuring their identities. Then, as the rising sun melted away the morning mist, they broke into a gallop and headed east.

As the road from Endcliffe dipped into the wooded valley that cut through Crookesmoor, it was overshadowed by the thick branches of the trees. Despite being largely leafless at this time of year, the tangled tops of the woods all but screened the iron-grey sky above.

Simon and John hobbled their horses behind a dense thicket atop the valley some distance from the road and began making their preparations for the ambush. Between them they dragged a thick, rotten log across the road to form a crude barricade. Simon took up position on it and sat in full view of anybody who might be approaching from the north.

John scrambled up a tree that had an ample branch overhanging the road. From his position, Simon could only just make out his companion's figure squatting in the tree, arrow nocked to his bowstring. He only hoped John would be just as invisible from the road ahead.

The longer they sat there the more nervous Simon grew. It had seemed like a great plan last night when his head was buzzing with anger and wine but now, as he had predicted, the cold, harsh light of day had banished the courage from his veins. He was still sincere in his mission to aid Thomas the miller but sitting on the road, waiting to rob a man as powerful as Hallam's steward was a nerve-racking way to spend the morning.

Just as Simon was starting to consider abandoning the whole plan as a foolish idea John gave a low whistle from his perch. Simon squinted and could make out his companion waving a warning to him. Somebody was coming.

Simon's mouth was dry as the two horsemen approached. They could see him now and advanced cautiously. It was the steward and the bailiff and

Simon could see the smugness on their faces. They clearly did not feel threatened by a single man blocking the road.

"Move that log, ruffian," Gilbert called out. "I am Malvoisin's steward on important business."

Simon rose and drew an arrow from his quiver, nocking it to his bowstring slowly and deliberately.

"Do you run mad?" Gilbert said. "Think you to rob us? I'll have you dangling from the gallows oak!"

The bailiff drew his sword and urged his horse on a few paces, testing the lone bandit to see if he really meant to shoot.

The arrow streaked out of the branches above, snatched the felt hat from the steward's head and nailed it to a tree trunk on the other side of the road. The bailiff whirled around to try and see the second bandit while the steward clutched his naked head and tried to retract it down into his shoulders as if he were a frightened tortoise.

"Hand over your sword, good bailiff," Simon said. "Or the next arrow will be aimed at you and find its mark somewhat lower."

The bailiff turned pale but did as he was told, holding his sword by the blade, pommel offered to Simon. Simon replaced the arrow in his quiver and shouldered his bow, confident that it was no longer required. The steward and the bailiff had no idea how many bandits were lurking in the trees, arrows trained on them.

He took the offered sword and thrust it into his belt. Then, drawing his hunting knife, he stepped up to the steward and severed the cord that held his purse to his belt.

"I'll find out who you are," the steward seethed. "I'll find out and I'll see you hanged myself!"

Simon said nothing, not wanting to take any further chance that the steward might recognise his voice. Purse in hand, he stepped away from the horses and, cutting a short bow to the men he had just robbed, turned and headed up the wooded bank.

John dropped down from the trees behind the steward and the bailiff and hurried after Simon. Before the steward and the bailiff realised that they had just been robbed by only two men, John and Simon were retrieving their horses from behind the thicket and galloping back down the bank.

They re-joined the road several yards ahead and rode hard south. When they were confident that they were not being followed, they left the road and cut south east across country, heading deep into the woods of Locksley Chase.

CHAPTER V

Ascalon, April 1192

The blazing heat of the sun made the blood dry to a sticky consistency on Wilfred's face and arms. It clung to him like syrup, making his hair matted and his skin itchy. He sat astride Jago who plodded through the field of the slain, trying to navigate a course through the corpses without disturbing them.

He gazed down upon the carpet of unarmed Saracen bodies. Their faces gazed back at him with glazed eyes and slack jaws. They had started to rot and their bellies were distended with gas. The stink was unbearable in the heat of midday and Wilfred felt his stomach rise with nausea.

Jago's right hoof caught against one of the bloated carcasses and the flesh split. A cloud of flies rose from the opened cavity and engulfed Wilfred, crawling all over his face, feeding on the sticky blood. He choked and coughed as they entered his mouth and nose, tickling him with their foul little legs, suffocating him.

He woke with a start, his heart pounding in his chest. He was soaking wet and could still feel the flies crawling all over him. He realized with relief that it was only sweat that drenched him, not blood. *But the flies.* There were one or two buzzing around the room (there always were), but hardly enough to cause the awful crawling sensation that made his skin shiver with revulsion.

It was not the first time he had dreamt of the flies. The massacre at Tell al-Ayyadiyya stayed with him like an open, festering wound in his mind. It had changed things irrevocably, and he knew he was not the same man that had sailed from England two years ago.

He got up and drank deeply from the clay water jug by his pallet, washing the dryness from his mouth. He left the room and stared out over the ongoing building works of Ascalon. Nearly a year had passed since they had set out from Acre and, although it had been an eventful year, they had come full circle and returned to the coast achieving virtually nothing for their efforts.

Not long after the massacre, the army had marched south with the intent of taking the coastal city of Jaffa before attempting an assault on Jerusalem. It had been a struggle to drag the troops from the brothels and taverns for they had grown accustomed to such comforts and were reluctant to tread the path of war once more, despite their vows.

The king shamed and threatened them and eventually got most of the soldiers moving. They followed the coast with the fleet keeping pace with them and supplying them when needed. The heat of summer was relentless and men fell from their saddles, stricken by exhaustion and sunstroke, some even dropping dead in their tracks.

Every step of the way they were harried by Saladin's raiding parties that swept down from the mountains to their left, keen for any vengeance they could claim for their butchered brothers. They shot arrows from horseback and, if they could get close enough, struck out with their vicious clubs embedded with sharp teeth. King Richard kept the formations tight, with the footmen guarding the flanks of the riders and crossbowmen forming the outermost ranks. It was little more than nuisance attacks and it was clear that Saladin did not dare risk a pitched battle by blocking their path.

They marched in the mornings and rested in the blazing afternoon heat. At night they were plagued by gigantic spiders called *tarentes* that crept into camp like imps sent by the infidels. Their bites caused agonising swellings and poor Leonard received one the size of a pomegranate on his wrist which Wilfred treated with poultices of vervain and stonecrop according to local medicine. The creatures seemed to be scared of noise and the Christians took to clashing shields and pots and pans to frighten them off.

It was with some relief that they reached the city of Haifa where they stopped for two days and recuperated before moving on to the town of Merle which lay deserted in the face of their advance. They finally reached Caesarea at the end of August and found it largely ruined by Saladin's forces. It was situated on the banks of a river known for its terrifying scaled beasts that could rip a man limb from limb and Wilfred began to despair that the Holy Land offered nothing but death by heat, disease, infidel attacks, or vicious creatures.

As they journeyed south, the terrain changed and the old Roman road they were following became overgrown with thorny scrub and thick bush which forced them inland, away from the coast. Twelve miles of oak forest lay north of the city of Arsuf and, even as they entered the cooling shade of the trees, the Christians were unable to relax for they knew that these woods were the perfect place for Saladin to conceal his army.

Saladin, who had contented himself with hit-and-run attacks so far, surely knew that to prevent the Christians from reaching Jaffa, he would have to confront them head on and he chose his spot well. As the trees petered out and they began to cross the plain north of Arsuf, there arose a great cacophony from the woods to their left as Saracens beat on cymbals and drums, and blew pipes and horns in a dreadful din designed to frighten the Christians. Then, they rushed down from the trees and began assaulting the crusader lines in their usual hit-and-run tactics but with increased intensity, focusing particularly on their rear guard which was held by the Knights Hospitaller.

The king demanded that the line hold firm and that they stay their course, defending themselves against the enemy as best they could without actively engaging them. Any break in formation could result in disaster and was exactly what Saladin was hoping for. The horses fared the worst of it and many knights had to continue on foot after their unprotected mounts dropped dead, riddled with arrows. Still they marched on, sometimes walking backwards so that they might protect the rear of the column with their shields.

The desperation of the Saracens could be smelt and it was clear that Saladin was throwing everything he had at them in an effort to draw them into a fight. Wilfred marvelled at the mix of nations the great sultan had marshalled under the banner of Islam. Black-skinned Nubians charged forward on foot, launching javelins at them before retreating. The desert-dwelling Bedouins, who were known for being the fleetest of foot, followed up with volleys of arrows while the cavalry, made up of Kurds and Mamluks – military slaves whose ancestors came from the steppes north of Persia – charged at regular intervals, churning up great clouds of dust that blotted out the sun.

They had just reached the outskirts of Arsuf when the pressure grew too much to bear and the Hospitallers broke rank and charged. It was only one or two knights who led the attack, cries to Saint George on their lips, but the rest of the Hospitaller corps followed suit. As soon as the king saw what had happened he uttered a foul oath and immediately ordered a general charge.

As horses and men wheeled about in the dust to face their enemy, Wilfred was astonished at the king's quickness to abandon his plan and ride out to support his insubordinate followers. Not for the first time did he appreciate why men had started to call King Richard the 'Lionheart'.

The battle was a hot, mad press of chaos and slaughter. The enemy ranks were tightly packed as they slammed into them in a flurry of flashing blades and spurting blood and the dust made it impossible to tell friend from foe.

The enemy's right wing soon crumbled under the charge and bolted. Wheeling his mount around and bellowing like a pagan thunder god, King Richard led a second charge, this time on Saladin's centre and drove them further back. They rode back to the column and escorted it to the shattered city walls. But by the time the first ranks had reached the ruins of Arsuf, the Saracens had regrouped and tried to assault their rear once more.

King Richard called a third charge and they pursued the Saracens all the way back to the woods, halting before they reached the treeline. Pursuing the enemy into the cover of the forest would be madness.

Thousands of dead Saracens littered the plain between the city and the forest and, with the Christian dead numbering around seven hundred, the battle was considered a victory. It was a costly one, though, and nobody felt the sting of its price more than Wilfred for, in that first mad charge against the enemy, Harry of Leicester had fallen.

They found him the following morning while recovering the dead to be given Christian funerals. His body was a broken, ruined thing hacked and slashed about like a side of pork in a butcher's shop. Wilfred found himself grieving more than he might have expected at the death of one when so many others had fallen. But Harry had been the one to take Wilfred under his wing, even before they had landed in Outremer. With Roger of Hambleton's execution in the aftermath of the massacre and now Harry's death, Wilfred felt as if he had been stripped of all his mentors and, although he had made other friends, he had never felt quite so alone as he did when they marched south to Jaffa the following morning.

They spent seven weeks at Jaffa and busied themselves repairing the city's defences while Saladin licked his wounds at Ramleh, some fifteen miles to the east. It became known that he had razed the city of Ascalon which lay further along the coast in an attempt to deprive the Christians of its strategic importance. Ascalon was the link between the Holy Land and Saladin's core kingdom of Egypt and the sultan clearly preferred to have it in ruins rather than in the hands of his enemies.

At the end of October, Richard's army marched out and camped on the road to Jerusalem between two ruined Templar fortresses that once protected the passage of pilgrims to the holy city. The king set his men to work refortifying Casal Maen while the Templars rebuilt Casal des Plains. It was during these efforts that a group of Templars strayed too far from the safety of the fortress and had to be rescued.

A rider galloped into Casal Maen crying that Saracen cavalry had attacked the Templars who were guarding the gathering of grass and horse fodder. They were vastly outnumbered and the king, ignoring the advice of several of his followers, rode out himself, every mounted knight that was available struggling to keep up.

They were able to drive the Saracens back and rescue the Templars and it was with some amusement that Wilfred noticed Brian de Bois-Guilbert in their number, looking appropriately sour-faced at being rescued by the king he despised while his French allies remained at Jaffa.

It was during their time at Casal Maen that negotiations with Saladin's brother, al-Adil, took place. This aroused suspicions among Richard's critics that he was altogether too keen to compromise with infidels but it mattered little as the talks came to naught and the army soon marched on Ramleh.

Saladin fell back to Jerusalem but by then it was December and torrential rain and hail assailed the crusaders. Camps flooded, food stores rotted and their very armour rusted on their bodies. It was a miserable time where nothing seemed to be gained and skirmishes with the enemy were constant.

They spent Christmas at a ruined Templar castle called Toron des Chevaliers, halfway between Ramleh and Jerusalem. It was a sombre place to celebrate the birth of Christ but they made the best of it. A highlight was the entertainment provided by a young, fair-haired troubadour who went by the name of Blondel and whose strumming lute and lilting voice kindled a warm glow in the candle-lit hall of that rain-lashed fortress.

After Christmas, they advanced to the village of Beit Nuba which was a mere twelve miles from Jerusalem but, with the weather only getting worse and the army ravaged by disease, Richard was forced to concede that Jerusalem could not, at present, be taken. Saladin had fortified it and stockpiled food while the Christians were stranded in the middle of nowhere, their supply lines to the coast vulnerable to attack. They were too few and the walls of Jerusalem too wide. With heavy hearts, they turned around and headed back to Ramleh.

It was there that Richard expressed his controversial plan to capture Ascalon and refortify it. This caused outrage, particularly from Hugh of Burgundy and the rest of the French. They accused him of abandoning his oath to reclaim Jerusalem in favour of building his own kingdom in Outremer for Ascalon was an advantageous staging point for an invasion of Egypt.

Richard grew more and more exasperated as he explained over and over that his interest in Ascalon was in building a stronger foothold in Outremer so that they might take Jerusalem all the more efficiently later in the year. With Ascalon under their control they could cut Saladin off from Egypt and utilise its supply lines themselves. But the French and those Templars who supported Conrad de Montferrat wouldn't listen. They did not like the possibility of King Richard, ruler of the mighty Angevin Empire, adding Egypt to his domain as well.

Hugh of Burgundy and many of the French refused to follow him any further and departed for Tyre, leaving Richard and his remaining followers to march on to Ascalon alone. They arrived in late January, starving and exhausted.

As the weather improved, supply ships were able to dock in Ascalon's harbour and Richard began rebuilding the city walls. He was keen to renew his assault on Saladin as soon as possible and wished to let bygones be bygones with Conrad of Montferrat and his French supporters, provided they agreed to join him at Ascalon. A meeting was arranged but bad news came down from the north which spelled doom for any reconciliation.

Acre was in turmoil. The Pisans and the Genoese, bitter rivals at the best of times, had declared war on each other over some slight and the city was now in the hands of the Pisans. The Genoese had appealed to Conrad of Montferrat and Hugh of Burgundy for aid. They laid siege to the city and, as soon as he got word of what was going on, Richard marched north. Not wishing to go to war over Acre with the Lionheart, Conrad and Hugh abandoned their siege and retreated to Tyre.

While Richard was able to calm the quarrel between the Pisans and the Genoese, his negotiations with Conrad fared less well. Conrad refused to reconcile and the rest of the French knights who had marched with Richard deserted him to be with Hugh at Tyre. The only Frenchman of any note who remained with the English was Henry of Champagne, and that was mostly due to him being Richard's nephew.

It was a bad blow. Even with Ascalon under his control, Richard could hardly mount another attempt on Jerusalem with the Christian force split in two. All they could do was refortify Ascalon and hope that some opportunity to heal the rift between the two parties would present itself.

Wilfred breathed the morning air deeply, hot and dry though it was, and tried to calm his thumping head. He had drunk too much wine last night. That had become a habit of late. Easter had been a debauched affair and hardly a fitting way to mark the crucifixion but, with Lent over, everybody was keen to wash away the bitter disappointment of the previous months with as much food and wine as they could consume. Wilfred had never really stopped celebrating and spent most of his evenings in the wine shops, retiring to his bed as dawn was breaking over the partially rebuilt walls of the city.

He climbed down the ladder that led from his rooftop sleeping quarters and made his way to the nearby stables to check in on his horses. Leonard, like many of the squires, slept in the stables with the horses and Wilfred found him brushing Jago's glossy coat. Both Jago and his courser were eating hay.

"Why aren't they eating fodder?" Wilfred asked. "I specifically asked for fodder, not hay."

"I tried telling the stable owner that, master," said Leonard. "But he says there isn't any. Hay is all he's got."

Wilfred felt anger rise in his gut and he stormed off to find the stable owner. "You!" he bellowed upon seeing him. "I specifically told you that my horses were to be fed on alfalfa or millet, not hay. My destrier, Jago, especially requires a very strict diet."

"Apologies, sire," the Egyptian stable owner said. "But there have not been any fresh deliveries of fodder for several days."

"You lie!" said Wilfred, seizing the man by his tunic. "I saw sacks of millet in here only yesterday! Where is it?"

"All gone, sire!"

"You mean you gave it to the horses of other knights. Fodder that I already paid you for!" He raised his fist to strike the stable owner who desperately tried to wriggle out of his grasp.

"Please, sire! It is business! They pay me more so naturally I prioritise their horses over yours! I cannot help it if the stock runs out!"

"You mean to say you'll gladly sell fodder I already paid for to those who offer more coin?" He lifted the poor man up by his tunic and hurled him headfirst into the wattle partition of a stall. The partition splintered under the impact and the man was thrust halfway through it. Wilfred drew his dagger, keen to teach the dishonourable wretch a lesson.

"Master, no!" Leonard cried, running forward to grab Wilfred's arm.

"This bastard has been cheating us, Leonard!" he said.

"But killing him would be a great sin!"

Wilfred blinked. He looked from Leonard's pleading face to the terrified man lying at his feet and then to the knife in his hand. *Killing him?* Was that what he had been about to do? Christ, Jesus, he didn't even know what he had been thinking when he had drawn his knife. His mind had been so clouded with rage that it had just sort of *appeared* in his hand.

"I swear, sire," said the stable owner, one hand raised to ward of the anticipated attack, "from now on, your horse gets fed first! Only the finest fodder!"

Wilfred sheathed his dagger and found that his hand was shaking. "Very well," he said. He turned and left the stables, his head swimming as he stepped out into the sunlit street.

Had he really been about to kill that unarmed man? He could barely believe himself capable but then, he knew that he was fooling himself. He had already killed unarmed men and had been complicit in the butchering of thousands more. He found it increasingly hard to reconcile the naïve youth that had boarded a ship in Dartmouth two years ago with the man he now found himself; the man so quick to anger over the smallest slight.

He felt utterly wretched. It was this city, this damned sense of being stranded. They should be marching on Jerusalem, not toiling away on the coast while Saladin's forces undoubtedly grew in the east. He was stagnating here, drinking too much, sleeping too little and constantly plagued by nightmares which were surely a punishment from God for tarrying when they should be trying to reclaim the holy city.

Fulk d'Oilly rode down the street, calling for all knights to marshal at the royal pavilion for the king had some important news to share. Wilfred briefly contemplated that his prayers had been answered and that some sort of resolution had been reached with the French meaning that they were moving out soon. But Fulk's words soon dashed that hope. "A letter from England, by all accounts. News from home!"

Wilfred strangely felt little disappointment at this. The simple word 'England' was all it took to raise his spirits for the word was entwined with another that occupied pride of place in his heart. *Rowena.* The letter to the king would of course, make no mention her but

Wilfred felt his mood lift anyway as he followed Fulk to the royal pavilion, eager to be distracted by whatever the king's letter contained.

As soon as King Richard stepped out of his tent to speak with the arranged knights, barons and bishops, all could see that the news from England was bad and had struck him like a malady.

"William de Longchamp, it seems," the king said, "my trusted justiciar, has not only been deposed, but has been forced to flee England. The efforts of Walter de Coutances, whom I dispatched from Sicily to quell the disputes between Longchamp and my brother John, appear to have come to naught. As it stands, Longchamp is in exile and my brother is now in control of England."

There were groans at this for most of Richard's followers had about as much faith in his younger brother's leadership skills as he did.

"There is worse," the king went on. "It also seems that my brother has become rather cosy with King Philip who, as we can well imagine, is safely back in France by now, free to pour honey into John's ear and turn him against me. John has even agreed to pick up where I left off and marry Philip's sister, Alys. It appears that he is being groomed for my throne."

There were cries of outrage at this and stifled curses directed at the king's traitorous brother. While they were struggling here in Outremer, their very homeland was being stolen. Richard made it clear that he had no alternative but to set sail for England and abandon his efforts to capture Jerusalem.

This caused a degree of panic for it seemed as if the entire crusade was falling apart around them and, if Richard should leave, there was a very real threat that Christian rule in Outremer was doomed. Guy de Lusignan was an ineffectual king and was largely seen as Richard's puppet. Without Richard there to support him, there could very well be revolt against Guy's rule and Saladin would like nothing more than the further fragmentation of his enemies.

A council was hastily arranged and riders were dispatched to gather the lords of the Christian territories in Outremer to discuss the future of the crusade and the very lands they called home.

Wilfred found himself alone with the king atop the city wall after the messengers had been dispatched and they watched the dust churned up by their passing settle on the road north.

"I should never have backed Guy," the king said. His eyes were fixed on the horizon as if it might offer some answers to the predicament they all found themselves in.

"Sire?" Wilfred asked, not sure if the king was addressing him.

"I felt that I had to, for Guy is my Poitevin vassal, but Conrad is by far the better king."

"I agree that Guy is the less charismatic of the two …" Wilfred hazarded.

"That's putting it mildly. Guy has all the charisma of a dead mackerel. And when I return to Europe, he will never maintain control of these lands we have managed to win him. I was a fool to back the man who lost Jerusalem for that is a man who will never be loved." He hammered his fist down on the stone wall with resounding force, giving vent to his pent-up frustrations. "I've made a bloody hash of this, haven't I? The whole crusade is coming apart at the seams and here we are, no closer to Jerusalem than we were a year ago."

"It's not all bad, sire," said Wilfred. "When we landed, all that could be called Christian in these lands were Tyre and a siege camp around Acre. Now we control the coast, not to mention Sicily and Cyprus."

"Cyprus!" the king scoffed. "Cyprus is all but lost after the locals revolted. Lucas de Beaumanoir, it seems, is a tad heavy-handed in his rule and I believe the Templars are starting to regret purchasing the island from me for they can't control it."

They retired to the royal pavilion and the king called for wine and song to cheer his mood but neither drink nor the gentle strumming of Blondel could do much to clear the thundercloud that hung about his head.

"Tell me of your home, Ivanhoe," the king asked. "What have you to look forward to on your return?"

Wilfred was a little taken aback for these were things he spoke of to no man and not in little part due to a sense of shame at how he had left things in England.

"I have a great deal to look forward to, sire," he said. "not least of all my estate which you so kindly granted me."

"Yes, yes, but what else? Who were you before you took the cross? What drives you here, at the ends of the earth?"

Wilfred knew that he should say that it was the chance to do God's work that drove him but, as it was the king who asked, he felt compelled to be as honest as he could. "I am afraid to disappoint you, sire, in admitting that there is a woman involved."

"Not at all!" the king replied, almost smiling. "I love a good romance, as Blondel here can attest." He winked at his troubadour who smiled and nodded in response. "A woman for Ivanhoe, by God! Who is she?"

"Her name is Rowena, sire, and she is the ward of my father, Cedric of Rotherwood."

"Indeed? I am sure Cedric of Rotherwood will be keen to see his son and his ward married upon your return."

Wilfred grimaced, and only in part due to the king's French pronunciation of his father's Saxon name. "No, he opposes our union."

"What on earth for?"

"He has a mind to marry her to his friend." And then, for Wilfred was not about to discuss his father's plans for a renewed Saxon royal line with King Richard, he quickly said; "It was the source of a quarrel and I did not leave on the best terms. He disinherited me as a matter of fact. I had hoped that my taking the cross would prove my worth to him and that upon my return he might let me marry Rowena. But every day I spend here is a day he might decide to marry her to somebody else."

"Hmm," the king said. "I am no stranger to the quarrels between a father and his son. In fact, my brothers and I could surely teach you a thing or two about family strife."

Wilfred smiled but said nothing, not knowing how he could possibly comment on the bitter conflict between King Henry and his sons that dominated the end of the old king's rule.

The king sighed. "What am I to do, Ivanhoe?" he asked. "While I struggle to keep this crusade on track here in Outremer, my Norman territories face conquest and England descends into chaos. Thank God my mother is there to keep John from running completely amuck. It was her who stopped him jumping on a boat to France to marry Philip's sister at the drop of a hat. Without her, England would no doubt already be under French rule but she cannot keep Philip and John from each other indefinitely. I need to be there. What are we to do? If we remain here, I risk losing my kingdom and you your Rowena. But if we return before achieving our goal, then all we have gone through was for naught, all the lives lost in vain, not to mention our oaths desecrated. What in God's name do we do?"

Wilfred was momentarily flummoxed. It was probably all rhetorical but it felt as if the king was asking him for advice. He had to admit that the thought of deserting this detestable land with its incessant quarrels and returning to England was a greatly pleasing prospect. With any luck, Rowena would yet be unmarried.

But deep in his heart, he knew that would be a hollow victory and a shameful return. He would have to face his father's smug victory at being right about the crusade, about the king, about everything. Worse, he would have to face Rowena, knowing that he had failed in his vow to her and his oath to God. He thought of how she had once compared him to Perceval and could have cried at the memory. Whatever path he was walking, it was very far from that of King Arthur's perfect knight.

And yet, even the worst sinner was not beyond redemption. That was the very basis of the scriptures. He had to believe that his soul could be saved along with the souls of every man here in Outremer. And there was only one way to do that. There was only one way to wash the shame of the massacre of the Acre garrison from his soul. The recapture of Jerusalem.

"In truth, sire," Wilfred said with a sigh. "I felt a sense of relief when you said that you may have to return to England for there is nothing I want more than to go back to my Rowena. I dread to think that my father has forced her into a marriage in my absence, but …"

"But?"

"But I promised her that I would return having trod the streets of Jerusalem as one of its liberators. That may even be enough to persuade my father to change his opinion of me enough to give us his blessing."

"And if, by remaining here to see your oath through, you lose Rowena forever?"

"If that happens," Wilfred replied, swallowing heavily, "then I must content myself with the knowledge that I have earned God's favour at least, if no one else's. Better to return home too late and live with my loss than return too soon and live the rest of my life knowing that I betrayed my oath to God."

The king smiled as he considered Wilfred's words. "You are a brave man, Ivanhoe. Perhaps braver than myself, even."

The outcome of the council was that Conrad of Montferrat would finally be recognised as King of Jerusalem, and Guy de Lusignan was effectively usurped. Predictably, Guy was outraged and King Richard had to explain patiently to him the precariousness of his situation. If he returned to Europe, Guy would be on his own in a land filled with lords who despised him. It would never have worked. In the end, Richard was finally able to placate his vassal by selling him Cyprus for a meagre forty-thousand bezants. The Templars, deciding that the island was more trouble than it was worth had already sold it back to Richard. Thus, Guy gained a kingdom and the Templars were rid of the troublesome island Lucas de Beaumanoir had made such a hash of ruling.

While the coronation of Conrad and his wife, Isabella, was hastily arranged at Tyre, Richard busied himself chasing Saracens across the plains of Ramleh. The castle of Darum, some twenty miles south of Ascalon was an important Saracen stronghold and the king entertained designs of capturing it to really put a chokehold on Saladin's supply line out of Egypt.

The Christians had made camp for the night and Wilfred was just getting his supper from the cookfires when a group of knights were spotted approaching from the north. One of them was Count Henry of Champagne whom the council had dispatched to inform Conrad that he was to be king.

"What news from Tyre?" King Richard asked, calling for wine and food to be brought. "How did Conrad take the news that he is to wear a crown at last?"

"Conrad of Montferrat is dead, Uncle," said Henry.

"What?" the king cried. "How can this be? Tell me everything."

"He was dining with the Bishop of Beauvais and, on his return home, two of the men in his employ turned on him, one jumping up onto his horse and stabbing him in the back."

"His own men?" Richard asked, incredulously.

"One was slain on the spot and the other fled into a nearby church," said Henry. "He was dragged out and interrogated. It appears that Conrad had two members of the Assassins in his service."

There were gasps at this for the Assassins were a group that conjured a cold feeling of dread throughout Outremer. It was a derogatory term for members of the Nizari Isma'ili state; a Shia sect based in the mountains of Persia and Syria who were often at odds with the Sunni dynasty of Saladin. The leader of the Syrian branch of the Assassins, Rashid al-Din Sinan, was known as 'the Old Man of the Mountain' and ruled from his stronghold at Masyaf, dispatching his agents to infiltrate the companies of notable Muslims and Christians alike. They had murdered scores of emirs and sultans, always finishing their targets with a knife. It was said that even Saladin feared the Assassins.

"Tyre must be in an uproar," said Richard.

"It is. Hugh of Burgundy tried to claim the city on King Philip's behalf but Conrad's widow, Isabella, barred the gates against him."

This caused some mirth in the camp but Richard was clearly unamused.

"I admire her courage but she can't hold Tyre against the French," he said. "And the French won't hold it against me once they take it. To think that our crusade should descend into bloodshed between Christians! Saladin must be laughing at us from his perch in the holy city!"

"There will be no need for bloodshed," said Henry, "for a solution has presented itself. The barons of Outremer have elected a new king."

"Who do they have in mind?"

"Me, Uncle."

The camp was silent, hanging on every word the young count was saying. They remained quiet as this last bit of news was imparted, none knowing exactly how the king would react.

"Well, I feel right in saying that you are a perfect choice," said Richard. "And a far better one than either Conrad or Guy. As the nephew of both myself and King Philip, you are acceptable to both the English and the French."

"That is the feeling in Tyre. They have also offered me Conrad's widow to legitimise my rule."

Richard raised his eyebrows. "They marry her off while her husband's body is not yet in the ground? What does the Lady Isabella have to say about that?"

"I am told that she is amicable to the idea. Her marriage to Conrad was a forced one, after all and she seems to know that it is the only way to prevent Outremer from being watered with yet more Christian blood. She is, however, pregnant."

"Pregnant!" Richard exclaimed. "You can back out of this you know, Henry? No one can force you to raise a child that is not your own, and heir to the crown of Jerusalem at that."

"I know," said Henry. "But to refuse the bride would be to refuse the crown. I can't have one without the other."

"True. Well, if it is what you want, Nephew, then you have my backing."

"Thank you, Uncle."

The camp erupted into cheers. Few of King Richard's followers liked Conrad of Montferrat and, although Henry of Champagne was a Frenchman, it was like seeing one of their own ascend to the throne. Most of all, it was a turn for the better in relations between the various Christian parties. Perhaps now they could all put their differences behind them and focus on what they were here for.

The coronation and wedding plans for Isabella and the late Conrad did not go to waste and were hastily reshuffled to allow for Henry's insertion as the groom. A mere week after Conrad's assassination, Henry and Isabella were married and crowned King and Queen of Jerusalem. Now all they needed was a kingdom.

Richard was still determined to take Darum Castle and there were worries that he intended this to be his parting gift to Henry; his way of contributing one last boon to the crusade before heading back to England to put his own kingdom to rights.

Richard didn't even wait for Henry and his men to march down from Tyre and set out along the coast with three disassembled trebuchets transported by ship. They approached Darum and, apart from an initial half-hearted skirmish, the Saracens retreated to the castle and hunkered down for a siege.

Richard ordered the siege engines be carried from the beach and the men struggled and sweated under the hot sun, carrying the pieces for almost a mile before constructing them within range of Darum's towers. King Richard and the English operated one, the Normans another and the Poitavians the third. All day and all night, they pounded the walls and towers of Darum and succeeded in smashing the Saracen mangonel atop the castle keep which had been a bother to them as soon as they had come within range.

A delegation from the castle came out offering to surrender Darum if they would be allowed to depart in peace with their families. The king was in no mood to negotiate and sent them back, telling them to defend themselves as best they could.

"We're not going to accept their surrender?" Wilfred asked Fulk d'Oilly.

"The king is in a victorious mood," Fulk replied. "He wants nothing less than an unconditional surrender."

One might call our king 'the ruthless' in addition to 'the lionheart', Wilfred thought nervously, though he kept that thought to himself, instead saying; "And he will spare the families inside once the castle falls?"

Fulk glanced at him. "Of course. King Richard isn't a butcherer, despite what the Saracens say."

Wilfred prayed for that to be true.

Richard had a group of Saracen sappers who had defected from Aleppo after some dispute with their sultan. He put them to work and they were able to bring down one of the towers and a section of the wall. The command was given to storm the breach and, swords drawn, Wilfred and Leonard joined the mad charge into the castle precinct.

Darum did not hold out long. First they cleared the walls of remaining Saracens and then focused on the keep which was barred against them. It took a day for the Saracens to surrender but they did eventually after losing all hope that a relieving force would arrive. They were not well met by their besiegers, mostly due to an act of particular barbarity before the castle had fallen. It was discovered that they had hamstrung all the horses in the stables rather than let them fall into Christian hands.

"Damned savages," said Fulk d'Oilly, as they put the horses out of their misery. "I'd rather cut off my own hand than use it to maim a defenceless horse."

It was a sentiment shared by all for a knight valued the life of a horse far higher than the life of a man and to see those poor beasts so brutally treated, made the blood boil in the veins of every man there.

There was some consolation to be found when the cells beneath the keep were opened and around forty Christian prisoners were freed from their shackles. They came blinking into the sunlight, praising the Lionheart for rescuing them. The dungeons were then given over to the holding of the Saracen garrison and their families.

It had taken four days to take Darum and, on the fifth, Henry of Champagne and the French arrived from Tyre, too late to be of any help. Wilfred and the other knights had plenty to occupy themselves with. Repairs had to be overseen, horses fed, prisoners organised and regular patrols sent out to guard against Saracen reprisals.

It was on returning from one of these patrols that Wilfred stopped by the armoury to have a dent knocked out of his helm. Normally he would give such an errand to Leonard, but the lad was nowhere to be found and Wilfred wanted the helm fixed as soon as possible. He had received the blow from a Saracen club when they had stormed Darum's breached wall and had thought it was only a minor thing but, while out riding on patrol, he had noticed the discomfort of the dent through his coif and decided that it couldn't wait.

"Lost your squire, Ivanhoe?" said a voice from the shade of a nearby canvas awning.

Wilfred turned around and saw Brian de Bois-Guilbert lounging on a bench, a cup of ale in his hand. The Templar had been part of the assault on Darum and had distinguished himself in slaying a large number of infidels. Two of his servants loitered in the shadows behind him. They were Saracens, part of the group that defected from Aleppo to join the Christian effort, and Bois-Guilbert had purchased their services from King Richard. Wilfred wondered what Lucas de Beumanoir's thoughts on infidel servants were and realised that it was irrelevant. By all accounts, Beaumanoir had returned to England after his disastrous reign over Cyprus had been cut short, leaving his followers in Outremer to conduct themselves how they pleased.

"I suppose it was only a matter of time before your squire left you in search of a knight who could actually pay him," Bois-Guilbert went on. "This crusade has not yielded much in the way of profit and it is always the pockets of the poorest knights that suffer first."

"You misjudge me," Wilfred said, feeling his face colouring. "And my squire. He is loyal to a fault and not just because I am able to pay his wages."

That was only half true. Leonard had shown nothing but loyalty in the year they had been together, despite Wilfred being unable to pay him anything in the last three months. The money he had won in the tournament had dwindled recently and, with no great conquests to its name, Bois-Guilbert had a point about the crusade being unprofitable.

"Perhaps I do you both a disservice," said the Templar with a smile that was almost apologetic. "Still, soon you will be back in England, no doubt, free to collect the rents of your tenants. I understand the fief of Ivanhoe has a yearly yield almost equal to that of Ecclesfield Priory."

Wilfred knew the Templar was goading him but it was the casual inference that King Richard would soon abandon the crusade that made his blood boil. "I do indeed look forward to acquainting myself with my fief," he replied. "And I pray that it will be soon. As soon as Jerusalem is a Christian city once more."

"God willing," said Bois-Guilbert. "And I pray too that those who have sworn to recover the holy city do not turn their backs on their oaths. Treachery is all around us these days, but betrayal of the holy crusade is surely the gravest of all."

"Treachery is indeed all around us," said Wilfred. He looked from Bois-Guilbert to his Saracen servants. "I would take care who I let get close to me in these times, Bois-Guilbert. Considering what happened to Conrad of Montferrat."

"Hamed and Abdallah here are beyond reproach," said Bois-Guilbert coldly. "I even forgive them their paganism for their loyalty to me outweighs it. And besides, I do not fear the Assassins, for all know who was really behind Conrad's death."

Wilfred gritted his teeth. It had been the French who had spread the rumour that King Richard had played a hand in the murder of Conrad, claiming that the Assassin they had interrogated had confirmed this before he was dragged to death through the streets of Tyre.

The English refused to believe it. It was well known that the Old Man of the Mountain had his own axe to grind with Conrad after he had captured a ship belonging to the Assassins that had docked at Tyre, confiscating their goods, and drowning its crew. It was not hard to imagine the Assassins exacting their revenge.

And yet, even Richard's staunchest supporters could not deny that Conrad's death had cleared up a number of issues and breathed new life into the crusade when it had been on the verge of collapse. Richard's frustrations at the refusal of the French to follow him had been well known and the ascension of his nephew to the throne of Jerusalem had offered a solution overnight.

Wilfred had no desire to entertain these suspicions, yet he found it hard to come up with a response to Bois-Guilbert's barb. Instead, he turned his back on the Templar and led Jago to the stables.

They celebrated Pentecost at Darum before making their way back to Ascalon. Trepidation hung over the English as they marched north. They had given Jerusalem's new king the foothold he needed to march on the holy city. Was this it? Had they won their last victory in Outremer? Would the king announce his plans to return to Europe once they had reached Ascalon?

On the way it became known that the king had received further letters from England. Unlike before, he did not address the army but details of their contents began to circulate and told of the worsening situation in Europe. King Philip had attempted to invade Normandy but fortunately had not been able to convince enough of his barons to attack the lands of a crusader. In England, John's powerbase was growing and he had even begun to circulate rumours that King Richard was dead. The queen mother was doing her best to keep her youngest son under control but she desperately requested that Richard return home.

It seemed like the crusade was over at last. The refusal of the king to talk to his men only confirmed their suspicions that he was intending to do precisely what his mother asked of him. He remained in his tent for over a day, seeing no one but his Poitavian chaplain. Whatever was going through his head, he clearly needed spiritual guidance.

It was as they camped in the orchards surrounding Ascalon that the king finally spoke to his men. They assembled in silence, shaded by the fruit trees, eagerly awaiting the king's words.

"My loyal followers," he said, the sun burnishing his mail and making his tawny curls seem golden. "I owe you all an apology. Since I received word from my lands back in Europe, I have not given our efforts here my fullest attention. The treachery of King Philip and my brother John have tugged me away from my oath, away from our mission and away from you, and for that I am truly sorry.

"My selfishness has been reproached by men closest to me who pointed out that it would be to my eternal shame to dim the splendour of our bright beginning in Outremer by too hasty a return. Why consign the lands we have saved to their doom by deserting them now?"

Wilfred felt his spirits and the spirits of all the men who stood with him rise with the king's words. Could it be true? Did the king mean to stay?

"But we cannot remain here in Outremer forever," the king went on. "Every day I am absent from my kingdom is a day my enemies conspire against me. Therefore, I have decided upon an ultimatum. I will remain here until next Easter and shall do what I can to ensure that King Henry of Jerusalem has a kingdom to rule long after I have departed. I hereby give my word that until Easter, nothing, not even the threat of losing my kingdom, shall draw me from my task here in Outremer."

There was a great cheer at this for although many, like Wilfred, had found the idea of returning home tantalising, the sense of shame at deserting their task and their comrades had weighed heavily on their shoulders in the past few weeks. Easter it was. They had an ultimatum and they would throw all their strength behind their mission to take Jerusalem and if they couldn't take it before Easter, then they could depart knowing that they had served God to the best of their abilities.

"Now, my brave followers," the king continued. "Prepare yourselves for battle for tomorrow, we march on Jerusalem!"

CHAPTER VI

Sheffield Castle, June 1192

Eight months had passed since Rowena had come to Sheffield Castle and, on the whole, she had settled in rather well. The castle was a modest motte and bailey fortification at the confluence of the rivers Sheaf and Don with the town to the west of it, clustered around the main street that led from the castle to the parish church.

Lord and Lady Malvoisin had formidable reputations but, thankfully, Rowena saw little of them. Lord Philip de Malvoisin was often away, visiting various allies. In his absence, Lady Honora Malvoisin ruled the castle with an iron fist and put the fear of God into the servants. Then there was the object of Rowena's employment. Contrary to her expectations of a snooty, spoiled little madam, Maud de Lovetot was a delightful girl, full of life and mischief and she seemed to take to Rowena from the start. She was short, with dark hair and a face that seemed younger than her fifteen years. Her immediate affection for Rowena made her realise how lonely the poor girl must be in such a joyless castle. In no time at all, it seemed, they were talking and laughing as if they were indeed actual friends instead of mistress and servant.

To her surprise, Rowena began to feel happy at Sheffield Castle. She still thought of Wilfred and kept him in her prayers every day and night. But when she thought of how lonely and bored she would have been back at Rotherwood, she could not deny that her employment had been most beneficial to her and had in fact saved her from months of misery.

There was only one fly in the ointment: Constance de Folvais.

Constance was Maud's other lady-in-waiting; a thin-lipped, sharp-tongued woman of about twenty-five whose only qualification for being Maud's companion that Rowena could see was that she was the niece of Lady Honora. Rowena soon realised that she was not the only one who had been placed in Sheffield Castle with an ulterior motive and she had to feel a little sorry for Maud who hadn't a true friend in the world, only companions surreptitiously paired with her for the benefit of her elders.

Constance had immediately taken a dislike to Rowena and Rowena could only assume that this was largely due to some sense of rivalry. She had no idea what Constance's relationship with her predecessor had been like but there was a clear feeling of jealousy, as if Rowena had somehow usurped Constance's position as Maud's closest companion.

But for heaven's sake, it was only natural that the girl would take more easily to someone closer in age. Besides, Constance was such a domineering figure that she came across as more of a nursemaid than a friend and Rowena was sure that everything Maud said or did was reported to Lady Honora. How could the young heiress trust a companion like that?

Nothing Rowena did met with Constance's approval. As soon as the elder woman set eyes on her, Rowena could see that she was inwardly mocking her clothes and the way her hair was plaited; indicators of her Saxon heritage. Constance came from a wealthy Norman family and certainly dressed the part with her brightly coloured robes that fitted tightly around the waist, their edges tapering into tongues. Not to be outdone, Rowena quickly purchased fine damasks and velvets in Sheffield's marketplace and had them cut in to garments in the Norman style. She dreaded to think what Cedric would have thought of her betrayal of Saxon fashion but she'd be damned if she'd play the part of the unsophisticated bumpkin in this most Norman of castles and company. Pride of her heritage was one thing, but there were other forms of pride that she could not suffer to have damaged.

One afternoon they were sitting in Maud's bower in the Great Tower reading a copy of Chrétien de Troyes's *Lancelot, the Knight of the Cart* which told of the brave knight Lancelot's rescue of Queen Guinevere from the wicked Meleagant. Composed for the king's older sister, Countess Marie of Champagne, it had become one of the most popular romances in high-born households in both France and England. Lady Honora had lent Maud her copy which must have cost her a pretty penny.

Rowena did the reading while Maud and Constance listened. It was a chance for Rowena to practice her French although she winced every time she stumbled over a particularly difficult pronunciation and could see the corners of Constance's mouth turn up in a smirk when Maud had to help her out.

"Isn't it wicked to love another man's wife?" Maud asked once Rowena had finished the tale.

"Yes, but Lancelot's love for Guinevere is the love of a knight for his lady," Rowena explained. "It has nothing to do with marriage or the, ahem … *corporeal* love Meleagant accuses Lancelot and Guinevere of indulging in."

"So there are different forms of love?"

"Certainly. Even though Lancelot knows that Guinevere belongs to his king, he still loves her and strives to make himself worthy of her by acting bravely and nobly. It is love for love's sake, not with any other aim in mind."

"But is it possible for a man to love his wife in the way a knight might love his lady?"

"Through years of intimacy, I am sure it happens," said Rowena. She knew that Maud was thinking of her own future, her own marriage to a man she didn't love, and shared some of her fear as she thought of Athelstan of Coningsburgh. "The sacrament of marriage is a partnership between man and woman who may certainly learn to love each other."

"And what of corporeal love?" Maud asked. "What sort of love is that?"

Rowena coloured as an image of Simon of Stannington's white buttocks thrusting back and forth while Gunhild gasped with pleasure flashed through her mind. "That's a very different sort of love," she explained. She hoped Maud wouldn't press her further on that particular type of love for she wasn't sure she understood it herself. "I would say that is more lust than love."

"Have you ever been in love?"

Rowena blinked, surprised at the question. She did not want to bring up Wilfred's name, not in front of Constance. "Yes, I have," she replied.

"Who was he?" Maud's eyes were alight with excitement and not for the first time Rowena realised how little contact the girl had with boys, men and the outside world in general.

"The son of my guardian. His name is Wilfred."

"Will you marry him?"

Rowena sighed. "I don't know. His father does not wish it and in any case, he is fighting in the Holy Land with the king. I don't know when he will return."

"War changes a man," said Constance. "I expect he will have forgotten all about you by now. Don't take it hard, it was only a childish love, after all."

Rowena ignored her. "I know that he still loves me. I just know it deep inside."

"And you still love him?" asked Maud.

"Yes. Very much so." To her surprise, a tear had welled up in her eye. She quickly wiped it away with her wrist before Constance could see but Maud had noticed. The girl said nothing and Rowena was deeply grateful for her discretion.

"Oh, look at the sky!" Constance said, gazing out of the window. "There isn't a cloud in sight. Why are we sitting indoors when we could be out riding in the sunshine?"

And so it was decided. They put aside the book and donned their riding cloaks before heading down to the stables to fetch their horses.

They rode out and followed the old Roman road that led south-west through the Crookes Valley. It was deeply wooded and the dappled sunlight and birdsong made for a very pleasant afternoon ride.

They cut a wide circle and, by way of return, made for the town's southern gate. The road cut across rugged moors and common land where the hay harvest was in full swing and the villeins were out in force, scythes swinging. It was sheep shearing season too and bales of wool were being piled up ready for transport to market.

They came within sight of a hamlet although it was such a sorry and run-down heap that they would be forgiven for thinking it was abandoned. Thatch was black with mould and there were no milk cows or pigs about the place that usually gave such clusters of dwellings a semblance of life. There weren't even any chickens scratching about in the dirt. As they drew closer, they heard a baby wailing and an old man shambled into view, an axe in his hand and a couple of logs under a very thin arm. His back was stooped and his appearance so haggard that he looked more like a beggar than a woodsman.

"What hamlet is this?" Rowena asked.

"Sharrow, I believe," said Constance. "Although it was in better shape the last time I came this way."

"Where have all the people gone?" Maud asked the old man, riding closer so that he might hear her.

"Gathering the harvest, what's left of them, my lady," said the old man.

"And the rest?"

"It's been a hard year, my lady. We lost two to sickness, including my grandson. He was weak with so little food to be had."

A woman emerged from the hovel at his back carrying a squalling baby on her hip.

"This is my daughter," the old man said. "It was her eldest son we lost."

"Let us ride on, my lady," said Constance, holding a handkerchief to her nose. "These wretches are probably riddled with disease."

"Is food really so scarce that the people starve?" Maud asked.

"We turned to grinding acorns for flour last autumn," said the woman. "But even they are hard to get what with the Chase being off limits to foragers."

"What of the alms for the poor?"

"Few have anything to spare these days," said the old man. "These high taxes have been hard on everyone."

"The Saladin Tithe," Maud murmured. "Preparations for the holy crusade …"

"Aye, my lady. And since our king has been gone, God give him victory, we've seen no relief."

"But why?" Rowena asked. "Why are the taxes still so high when the king isn't even here?"

"His brother, John the Count of Mortain, is now regent, or so it is said. He keeps the taxes high to pay for England's defences against the French."

"Or to pay his own way to the throne," the man's daughter said bitterly.

The man quickly hushed her, panic written on his face. "My daughter is grieving," he pleaded to them. "She cares for nothing these days, not even for her tongue in front of her betters."

"Do not fret," said Rowena. "We are but ladies, not lords and certainly not friends of the king's brother."

"We really must press on," said Constance.

The man bowed as they rode off but the woman stared after them and Rowena could feel her resentful eyes boring into their backs.

Two days later, there was a feast at Sheffield Castle to honour Gerard de Furnival and his family who had come to visit. Gerard had news from his father who was fighting alongside the king and they listened eagerly as he read the letter but there was little of interest. Jerusalem still had not been taken and the king was at a place called Ascalon which, as far as Rowena could make out, was on the coast.

Rowena hadn't forgotten her purpose of influencing both Maud and Philip de Malvoisin's opinions in favour of Robert of Stannington but it was a seemingly impossible task. She had mentioned him several times in conversation with Maud, exaggerating his qualities, few as they were, but there was a limit to how many times she could drop his name without it coming off as unnatural. And unnatural it certainly was, for she had no liking of the man and how many reasons could there be for bringing him up in polite conversation with a fifteen-year-old-girl?

Besides, even if by some miracle, she made young Maud think favourably of this boorish stranger ten years her senior, it would never be Maud's decision to make. It was up to the king to decide who she would marry, perhaps on Malvoisin's recommendation, and as for persuading him, a chance would be a fine thing! He was rarely at the castle and even when he was, what business would a mere lady-in-waiting have for speaking with him? It all seemed so hopeless that Rowena despaired of her task.

As she watched the endless parade of dishes being brought out from the kitchens, she felt her stomach turn. There was enough food being prepared for this one meal to feed the wretched hamlet of Sharrow for a month. The memory of those bones showing through the skin and the grief of a mother for her dead child were still so fresh in her memory. How could one section of society gorge themselves on pies, pasties and roasted meat while another section not two miles away literally starved to death? Is this what God had intended for His children in the world He had created? A barbarous free for all?

And everyone was at it, not just the allies of Count John. Oh, Geoffrey of Stannington Hall claimed to be trying to oust Malvoisin by marrying his son to Maud but nobody would ever be fooled into thinking that he was doing it for the good of the shire. All Geoffrey wanted was one of his own installed in

Sheffield Castle and his family in control of its surrounding manors as they had been of old.

For the first time in her life, Rowena saw the greed all around her and it made her sick. And she was no better. When she thought of what she had spent on fancy clothes just to compete with the likes of Constance de Folvais, it made her cringe with shame. What silly, girlish nonsense! Well, there had to be something she could do. She would gladly go hungry herself if it meant giving her portions to the people of Sharrow. In fact, she would even go so far as to redistribute some of the castle's ample stores to people in more desperate need of it. Not enough that would be missed, of course. *But how to do it?*

As the feast rolled on into the evening and yet more dishes appeared from the kitchens, Rowena lost herself in her plans. *There has to be a way*, she determined. *I'll do something for the poor. Even if no one else will.*

Over the following days, Rowena began to steal small amounts from the cellars, only a little at a time and things that would not perish: salted pork, fruit preserves, smoked fish and a sack of dried oats. She hid this little stockpile in the stables. Maud occasionally sent Rowena or Constance to the market on errands and the next time she sent Rowena, she decided it was time to distribute the items to the people of Sharrow.

When the stable boy's attention was occupied by some other task, Rowena quickly uncovered her secret hoard and loaded up the mare's saddlebags. When she was done, the saddlebags were bulging with stolen food and she began to regret her plan. How on earth would she explain all this if somebody inquired as to why a lady-in-waiting was leading such a laden horse out of the castle?

But there was no turning back now. The weather was warm and she took off her riding cloak and draped it over the mare's hindquarters, covering the saddle bags. Then, swinging up into the saddle, she rode as casually as she could out of the stables and down the hill to the gate.

When she arrived at Sharrow and handed the food over to the old man and his daughter, they were entirely overwhelmed and Rowena thought it sad that kindness was so rare in this world that a little of it could bring tears to an old man's eyes.

"God bless you, my lady," he said.

"It's only a little," said Rowena. "I dare not take more for fear that it would be noticed. Will you see that some of it goes to others in need? I know there are several families here and I wish that I could bring more."

"This here is a banquet for all Sharrow," said the old man. "I'll see to it that everyone gets a share."

She rode back to Sheffield with all haste, knowing that she had already used up too much time on her detour. As soon as she got back from her errand, she began stockpiling food once more, elated by her achievement and determined to continue her good work.

She managed one other visit before the thing she dreaded came to pass.

Discovery.

It was Constance who informed them of the events unfolding in the Great Hall. She had been down to get a pitcher of water and had overheard the outrage. "There's a thief in the castle," she informed Maud and Rowena, closing the door behind her, her face filled with excitement. "Lady Malvoisin is in a dreadful flap."

"A thief?" Maud exclaimed, echoing Constance's excitement. Gossip was rare in the castle and every scrap was to be seized upon ravenously.

"What have they stolen?" Rowena asked, doing her best to appear innocently curious.

"Food from the stores," said Constance. "Cook suspected something was amiss last week but couldn't be sure. Now he's convinced. He's been keeping a closer eye on his stocks and there is no doubt about it. Someone's been filching meats and cheeses."

"Is Lady Malvoisisn awfully cross?" Maud asked, biting her lip in sympathy for the thief should they be caught.

"She's threatening to have the hide whipped off them in the courtyard if only she can find out who it is."

"Has she any idea?" Rowena asked.

Constance shook her head. "My guess is it's that new vintner. He's a shifty looking fellow and he's always hanging around the stairs to the cellars. I saw him there twice last week and I'm sure he was trying to get a look up my skirts."

When Rowena was brushing Maud's hair that evening, Maud turned to her and said; "I know it was you."

Rowena's heart froze. She glanced at the door to the bower which was ajar. Constance was fetching fresh candles and they were alone.

"I saw you one night," Maud continued. "Stealing food from the cellars."

"Even if that were true," said Rowena, trying to keep her hands from shaking as she continued to brush Maud's hair. "What were *you* doing in the cellars?"

"Also stealing."

The answer was so frank that Rowena was momentarily taken aback and she stopped brushing. "Stealing?"

"Yes. I sometimes like to sneak some of those almond cakes late at night."

Rowena considered this. She and Constance slept in Maud's bower with her. Surely one of them would have noticed if she left the room in the middle of the night? But then, Constance was a heavy sleeper (she certainly snored loudly enough) and Maud was something of a little night owl, always fidgeting and whispering to Rowena when she was trying to get to sleep. Perhaps their little lady did indeed go wandering the castle at night.

"It's not what you think," Rowena found herself saying. "I wasn't stealing for myself. I took it to that hamlet we passed through a few weeks ago."

"Sharrow?" Maud asked. "Those poor, starving villeins?"

"Yes. I just wanted to help them. There is so much food in the castle that I didn't think any would be missed if I … oh, dear. What a mess!"

"I won't tell," said Maud, conspiratorially. "*If* …"

"If?"

"If you let me help you next time."

"You want to help?"

"Yes! I think it's wonderful, you being such a good Christian. Those poor, starving wretches living on my land while the likes of Philip de Malvoisin get fat on the stores of my castle. I can't do anything about it, not yet. Things will be different when I'm married and a lady and in charge of the whole place. But until then, I want to do my bit too."

"But Constance …"

"We'll leave her out of it. She'd never understand anyway. It'll be our little secret!"

She winked at Rowena and turned around just as Constance returned with the candles. Rowena picked up the brush and continued brushing Maud's hair, wondering how she had strayed so far from her mission at Sheffield Castle.

CHAPTER VII

Stannington Hall, July 1192

"Why does Malvoisin have the right to try a criminal case?" Simon demanded. "This is surely a thing for the county court or the hundred court at least."

"Let me guess," said Hugh, with a sneer. "This poacher is one of your drinking companions."

"Why else would he take such an interest in the law and order of the shire?" Robert agreed.

"I know his father, it is true," said Simon. "But that is by the by."

It was hard not to feel emotionally involved. Young William of Studley had been caught red-handed poaching deer in Locksley Chase and had spent the past week in the cells of Sheffield Castle. His father was frantic and Simon felt awful for him. Food prices had risen of late and even a respectable hooper like Harold of Studley could not afford much in the way of fresh meat. Young William had only been trying to feed his family.

But it was a serious crime. The Chase was leased to the Lovetot estate by the king and, as its administrator, Philip de Malvoisin saw the poaching of deer in the Chase as the serious theft of property he was the custodian of. But such things came under common law and were not matters for a manorial court.

"Malvoisin has obtained a court leet from the sheriff," Simon's father explained. When he saw Simon's blank expression he sighed and went on; "Occasionally the king, and by extension, his sheriffs, can grant a lord the legal authority of the hundred court. This privilege includes the old Saxon right of *infangthef*; the right for a lord to dispense justice on a thief caught on his own lands."

"The sheriff," said Simon. "Hugh de Bardulf? He is John's sheriff, not the king's. The king appointed Oswald de Longchamp Sheriff of Yorkshire."

"As far as the likes of Malvoisin are concerned, John is as good as king. We don't even know if the king yet lives."

"Whether he does or not, his brother is edging his backside closer and closer towards his throne," said Simon, bitterly. "And his supporters are already enjoying the benefits of backing him."

It was a frightening thing to think that Malvoisin now wielded such power. There would be no waiting around for the hundred or county courts to make up their minds on criminal cases now. And, if Simon knew Malvoisin, there would be no waiting around for coroners or Justices of the Peace to arrive before a man might be set swinging from the gallows.

The Great Hall in the tower of Sheffield Castle seethed with people on the day of William's trial. Simon accompanied his father and brothers and, after leaving their weapons in the ante chamber, they forced their way into the Great Hall, realising immediately that they were going to have to stand. A few benches had been placed opposite the dais upon which was a long trestle table.

Simon's father spotted Maud de Lovetot and her ladies-in-waiting, including Rowena of Rotherwood.

"My lady," said Simon's father, addressing Maud. "And fair Rowena. I hope you are both well."

"Oh, do you know my newest lady-in-waiting?" Maud asked.

"Her father is a good friend of mine," said Geoffrey. "I trust you are settling in well, Rowena?"

"Very well, I thank you, my lord," said Rowena.

Simon saw his father hold Rowena's eye a little longer than necessary as if to try and extract some information on his little spy's progress. Rowena looked flushed, as if she would rather be far away from the Stanningtons. Simon didn't blame her.

The steward called the court into session and the jurors took their seats. The first matter of business was to oversee of the oaths of peacekeeping of all the freemen in the manor. Then a few mundane matters concerning the upkeep of roads and ditches were attended to following the fining of an alewife who had sold her ale after its best. Finally came the trial of William of Studley.

The lad was brought up from the cells, his hands manacled before him. His nervous eyes sought out his mother and father who sat on the benches before the dais and he looked as if he might weep at any moment.

Malvoisin's keeper of the Chase, a man called Hubert, was brought forward as the first and only witness. He was asked to describe how he had come across the accused skinning a deer in the northern part of Locksley Chase and burying the offal, his hands red with blood.

The jury discussed the evidence given. Some comments were passed on the reputation of the Studley family but there was little to be done in the way of defence. The lad had been caught red-handed in the most literal sense and all that remained was for the jury to decide on his punishment.

"William of Studley," said the steward after some moments of deliberation with the jury. "It is the decision of this court that, two days hence, you shall be taken from here to the oak tree on the border between the manors of Sheffield and Hallam. There, that tree will put to the use it has served before and you shall be hanged by the neck until you are dead."

William's mother broke out into loud sobs at this and was comforted by Harold whose face was stone-grey and emotionless. William looked about in desperation, his eyes pleading. But there was no one to plead to. His trial was over. The reality of his sentence suddenly sank in and tears began to stream down his cheeks as the bailiff and the constable of the court seized him by the arms and took him back to his cell.

The court dispersed and, as the people filed out, there was much gloomy murmuring sympathetic to young William's fate. Simon overheard some trying to look on the bright side.

"Hanging is a better fate than what some get," said one. "Blinding and castrating is the way of it in some courts."

"Aye, the lad is lucky he wasn't caught on Front-de-Boeuf's lands," said another. "I heard he once sewed a poacher up inside the skin of the deer he killed and then set his mastiffs on him."

"That was no court's sentence," said the first. "That was Front-de-Boeuf acting on his own. He never was one to mind the law. Nor was his father."

"He'll be much worse now the king is gone, I'll wager."

Talk quickly turned to politics and poor William was forgotten as easily as any afternoon's entertainment. Simon felt resentful that everybody could be so callous when a young lad had just been condemned to the gallows. He made his feelings known on the ride back to Stannington Hall.

"I dare say Malvoisin wants to set an example," said his father. "Locksley Chase has seen a rise in lawlessness in past months. You remember that Hallam's steward was robbed on his way to Sheffield by two ruffians last October?"

"Yes, I remember …" said Simon.

"It has to stop. I don't like Malvoisin any more than the next fellow, but the law must be upheld and criminals brought to heel."

Simon felt a crawling sensation of guilt creep over his body. He and John had been jubilant after their robbery of the odious Gilbert of Tankersley last year. They had struck a blow for the common man and had never considered any consequences outside the risk to themselves. To think that their contribution to the rise in lawlessness may have led to the need to make an example of young William of Studley made Simon sick to his gut.

"Can't something be done?" he asked in desperation.

"The boy has been tried and found guilty, Simon!" said his father.

"And sentenced to death for trying to feed his family!" Simon retorted. "How is that justice?"

"You might not like it, but it *is* justice."

"You had best control yourself, master," said John once they were back at Stannington Hall. "It does not become you to care so deeply about the struggles of commoners."

"I'm surprised at you, John," said Simon, angry at his servant's attitude. "You know that I care more for them than I do for my family's opinion of me. And are you not just as outraged as I am about the trial today?"

"Indeed I am, master," said John. "And I did not mean to suggest that you did not care. I just wished to point out to you that if you intend to do something about young William, then you had best play the part of a disinterested nobleman. In the interest of appearances."

"Do something? What makes you think I can do anything about William?"

John shrugged. "You were keen to help Thomas the miller when he was in need. I assume it's no different with young William."

Simon wasn't sure if John was playing some sort of game with him. "Stealing some money to pay a man's fine is one thing. How are we to stop a boy from being hanged?"

"As you said, master. There has to be something somebody can do."

That night Simon and John rode to the Cross and Cup and sent somebody to fetch Harold of Studley. The man was in no mood for drinking, not even for the drowning of his sorrows, but Simon took him to a dark corner of the inn where the three of them would not be overheard.

"I appreciate the thought, Simon," said Harold after Simon had expressed his intention of rescuing William. "But we all know it's hopeless. My son sits in a cell beneath Sheffield Castle guarded by scores of men. He will only leave that cell when they take him out to execute him." This last bit made him choke on his words and tears welled in his eyes. "I beg your pardon, sirs. I have made my peace with God and accepted William's fate, but it's my wife I fear for. She's inconsolable."

"You are right that we cannot aid your son while he sits in his cell," said Simon, pouring Harold some more ale from the jug that stood on the table. "It's when they take him to the gallows oak that we will have our one and only opportunity."

"He'll be closely guarded then too," said John. "The sheriff himself will oversee the execution."

"That is why we must be quick and use every advantage surprise gives us. We will need fast horses and a spot in mind to take young William. Once we snatch him from the gallows, he will need to live a new life. He will not be able to appear in public again, I fear."

"Harthill Walk is a good spot," said John. "It's densely forested and has plenty of game to sustain him."

"Harthill Walk is in Front-de-Boeuf's lands isn't it?" said Simon.

"Aye, far enough from Malvoisin's lands and Front-de-Boeuf has fewer men than he used to. His debts with the Jews have made him a poor man and Torquilstone Castle is a shell of what it once was. William will be safe enough."

Harold looked from Simon to John. "You're seriously considering this, aren't you?"

"Yes," said Simon. "But the reason I called you here tonight is not to involve you in the rescue – you must show your face at your son's execution so that no doubt falls on your own shoulders. But once William is sprung, he will need your help to survive in the greenwood. Will you be able to bring supplies to Harthill Walk? Food, tools, that sort of thing. We can look in on him from time to time but it will be a lonely life for him. He will be an outlaw for the rest of his days, you do understand that?"

"Better an outlaw than dead," said Harold. "Bless you, Simon, I mistook you in the past. I don't know where you get the courage for this mad scheme but I'm with you all the way. How else can I help?"

"By playing the part of a bereaved father. There must be no suspicion that you knew. Perhaps it would be best not to tell your wife."

"Aye, that would be for the best but it'll break my heart not to ease her suffering."

"Two days, Harold," said Simon. "Just two days."

"I agree that Harold shouldn't be involved," said John, "but there'll be plenty of armed resistance. Two don't stand a great chance against them."

"True but two might manage to cause a distraction while a third makes off with William."

"A third?"

"Aye. Drink up, John. I thought we might pay a visit to our friend the miller tonight."

The old gallows oak on the border of Sheffield and Hallam was well-chosen for its vicinity to the scene of William's crime. South of it stretched a thickly wooded portion of Locksley Chase which was perfect for what Simon had in mind. He sent John ahead on foot to spy on the proceedings while he and Thomas the miller waited with the horses, screened by the trees.

The miller had been gobsmacked to learn that it had been Simon of Stannington Hall and his servant John who had tossed a full purse of coin through the wooden bars of his window late at night last winter. There had been enough money to pay his fine and a little left over besides which had been the saving of Thomas's family that winter.

After revealing that it had been he and John who had robbed the steward of Hallam, Simon informed the miller of their plan to rescue William of Studley from the gallows. Simon wanted his help. Thomas, like most millers, was a strong man with powerful arms and not yet too along in his years that he wouldn't make a formidable opponent if it came to a fight.

At first, Thomas was reluctant to get involved but his conscience quickly reminded him that Simon and John had risked their necks to help him out. How could he turn his back on another in more dire straits? Besides, Harold of Studley was a friend down at the Cross and Cup. Friends had to stick together in these times, whatever the risks.

The noonday sun was just beginning to make the air beneath the leaf canopy stiflingly hot when John came hurrying back, moving as quietly as he could through the undergrowth, the sweat beading on his bald pate.

"They're approaching the oak now," he said in a low voice. "The sheriff is there along with a few soldiers from the castle. No more than five. Two of them have crossbows."

Simon swore. He had been afraid of that. Rescuing William would do no good if one of them took an arrow in the back as they made their escape. "Is there much of a local presence?"

"Some," John nodded. Harold and his wife are there, along with the local priest. A few other hangers on. Less than I would have thought. I think most can't stomach the hanging of a young lad, especially with Malvoisin as hated as he is."

"Very well," said Simon. "I had hoped for a high turnout. The more confusion the better."

"The fewer there are, the less chance there is of us being recognised," said John.

"True enough. Come on, let's make our move. We don't want to be late, for God's sake."

John mounted his horse and each of them donned their disguise; a hooded mantle and a black mask that hid the lower portion of their faces. Long cloaks hid any recognisable clothing and the three of them looked like spectres moving through the greenery.

John and Thomas rode around to the east. Armed with quarterstaffs, their job was to ride straight at the gathering and make them scatter like hens. Then, with the crowd held at a distance, Simon would ride straight for the gallows oak, seize William and then the three of them would bolt for the trees.

Through the foliage, Simon could see the gathering assembled around the oak. William stood beneath its thickest branch which jutted out at an opportune angle while a soldier wearing the green and yellow colours of Malvoisin tossed the rope over it. The priest stood by, reading the last rites, and beyond stood William's parents, the mother needing to be supported by the father in her grief.

The noose was looped over William's head and fastened. One of the soldiers gripped the other end of the rope in his hands, ready to haul the boy up and set him dancing. Simon glanced desperately at the thicket to the east. Now was the time and not a moment later!

John and Thomas burst from the thicket at a gallop, quarterstaffs raised. There was a cry of alarm from the crowd. The soldier holding the rope dropped it and drew his sword. One of the men with a crossbow fitted a bolt and raised the weapon.

"Watch it lads!" Simon muttered. But by then, his comrades were upon the soldiers.

John had spotted the one with the crossbow and nearly rode him down, lashing out with his staff. The blow rang against the side of the man's helm, knocking him silly. The bolt from the crossbow went wide.

Thomas had gone for the man who had held the hanging rope and was unleashing a barrage of blows which the soldier desperately tried to deflect with his sword. Thomas had the advantage of range and height and soon enough the man was sent sprawling by a nasty blow to his head.

Now it was Simon's turn to pitch in. As John and Thomas drove the terrified crowd back and engaged the rest of the soldiers who rushed forward to battle the masked attackers, Simon spurred his horse into a gallop.

Few saw him as he rode up to the gallows and William nearly leapt out of his skin when he felt the noose around his neck go taut as Simon grabbed it and began cutting through the rope. He turned to gaze up at Simon with wide eyes.

"Come on, lad," said Simon through his mask. "The hangman will have to look elsewhere for his prey today. Up on my horse."

"My hands!" said William.

Simon cursed and slid down from his horse to cut the rope that bound William's hands behind his back. He glanced up and could see that John and Thomas were having a tough time of it against the soldiers, two of which had mounted horses and were using spears to jab at them.

Once William was free of his bonds, Simon boosted him up into the saddle. John and Thomas had done all they could and were now riding back towards the oak tree. Simon scrambled up into the saddle behind William just as they passed on their way to the treeline.

Before Simon could kick his mount into a gallop, a hand seized his mantle and tried to wrench him from the saddle. One of the mounted soldiers had caught up to them and was insistent on preventing the prisoner's escape.

Frantic that his opponent's tugging might pull down his hood and expose his face to the awestruck crowd, Simon turned in his saddle, grabbed the soldier's arm and slashed at the wrist with his dagger.

The man roared and released him, briefly clasping his wounded hand before using it to reach the hilt of his sword. Simon thanked God the man had lost his spear in the fray with John and Thomas or he would have been done for. Just as the soldier's blade rose into the air, Simon galloped off, narrowly missing having his skull split by the downwards chop.

He rode hard and fast towards the treeline which had already swallowed John and Thomas. Just as he reached it, a crossbow bolt whickered through the air a few paces to his right and vanished into the foliage.

Simon didn't look back. He skirted the dense underbrush and kept to the more open parts of the woodland. Up ahead he could see John and Thomas, keeping their heads low as they rode beneath the lower branches of the trees. It was a path they had planned beforehand but, after risking a glance over his shoulder, Simon could see the soldier he had wounded and one of his companions following them into the woods. If they weren't careful, the pair would follow them all the way to Harthill Walk.

John led the way, being far more knowledgeable of the Chase's hidden paths than Simon. He kept a hard pace and, with the extra weight of William, Simon's horse struggled to keep up. Eventually they lost their pursuers as the woods grew deeper and deeper. When they judged it was safe, they reined in their horses and had a quick rest.

"By Christ," said Thomas, removing his black mask so he could breathe the air more freely. "I thought that was the end of us when they gave chase. Where the hell are we?"

"A little north of Dronfield," said John. "We're about halfway to Harthill Walk."

"Thomas?" asked William, gazing at the miller's unmasked face. "What's going on?"

"Haven't you got it figured out yet, lad?" Simon asked, pulling down his own mask. "We've just rescued you."

John removed his mask too and William looked from one face to another, his eyes goggling. They all laughed. It had been a close call but they had managed it and the combination of adrenaline pumping through their veins and the relief that they were all still in one piece was exhilarating.

"I don't know how to thank you," said William. "I had given up all hope. I thought they'd hang me for sure."

"There's a lot of things Malvoisin and Count John's new sheriff will be unsure about now," said Simon. "Now that there are a few in Locksley Chase who are prepared to fight back. Your father was in on it too, but he had to play dumb for the sake of appearances. He will be coming to visit you in a few days. I hope you realise that you can't go back, lad. The greenwood is your home now."

The smile faded from William's face as this realisation sank in. He nodded. "Still, I'm alive, eh? Thanks to you three."

"We've prepared a few things to get you started," said Simon. "John?"

"Right here," said John, reaching for a long, thin bundle strapped to the side of his saddle. He passed it to William.

"A few scraps of food, a good cloak and hood and a bow with a quiver of arrows. You'll need to shoot your own food, but I hear you're no poor shot when it comes to fallow deer." He winked at William.

They all laughed again and continued onwards to Harthill Walk.

CHAPTER VIII

Jaffa, August 1192

As soon as they saw the saffron flags fluttering from the walls of Jaffa, all hope was sucked out of them. They were too late. Jaffa was lost.

"God's legs, I thought Saladin would need at least two months to take Jaffa," said King Richard as they gazed across the stretch of water at the fallen city. "And he has taken it in three days!"

They had been in Acre when word reached them that Saladin had launched a lightning strike against the port city. King Richard had quickly thrown together a relief force made up primarily of infantry and Genoese crossbowmen, loaded them onto thirty ships and set off against the wind in a desperate attempt to save the city. King Henry and the rest of the Christian army marched along the coast but it would be several days before they reached the besieged city and Richard couldn't wait that long. Now that they were here, they realised they hadn't a chance of retaking it.

Wilfred leant against the gunwale of the king's crimson flagship and peered across the water at the fallen city. The Saracens were coming down to the beach north of the harbour and were jeering at the approaching Christian fleet. Some shot arrows but they were too far away to reach their marks. Smoke hung in a fug above the shattered walls and several houses in the city were burning. Wilfred glanced from the walls to the Great Tower of the citadel, proud and stern above the chaos below.

"Sire," said Wilfred, glancing at the king who was also looking forlornly at the scene. "There are no banners flying from the citadel. Only from the city walls."

"By God, he's right!" said the Earl of Leicester.

"There are no banners flying from the citadel, it is true," said the king, gloomily. "But there are no signs of life either."

"No, look!" cried another knight. "On the wall of the citadel!"

They all squinted, shielding their eyes from the glare of the noonday sun off the water. High up on the western wall, a figure wearing nothing but his undershirt was scrambling over the battlements.

"Does he run mad?" the Earl of Leicester exclaimed. "He'll break his neck!"

They watched as the figure plummeted to the wet sand below. He survived the fall, got up and ran towards the surf before plunging in and taking long strokes towards the fleet.

The nearest galley picked him up and conveyed him to the king's ship. The man, dripping wet and heaving with exertion, appeared to be a priest and the news he brought from the citadel was good.

"We held out for as long as we could," said the priest. "When the curtain wall fell we retreated into the citadel."

"Are there any left alive?" the king asked, kneeling down in the puddle forming on the deck from the priest's dripping garment.

"For now," the priest replied. "But they await the butcher's knife like lambs for the slaughter. They will all perish if you do not act now!"

"Head into the shallows!" the king said, rising quickly. "Every man of us prepares for battle!"

"We're storming the beach?" asked the Earl of Leicester, glancing nervously at the assembled war host on the shoreline.

"God sent us here to die if need be!" the king snapped. "Shame on any who tarry now!"

As the king's flagship was rowed into the shallows, the rest of the fleet followed it and there was a great flurry of activity on board as soldiers seized their weapons and girded themselves for battle. Then, without warning, the king leapt overboard to land up to his waist in the foaming surf, a sword in one hand and a crossbow in the other.

"Christ Jesus!" said the Earl of Leicester. "Protect the king!"

As one, they leapt over the side to join their king as he waded ashore, seemingly intent on storming the beach single-handedly.

Crossbows thudded as they launched their bolts into the charging Saracens. Wilfred saw the king swing his sword at the first to get near him and shear the infidel through the collarbone. The Christians roared oaths and pushed forward, surrounding their king and driving the Saracens back.

They met with surprisingly little resistance which Wilfred put down to the sudden and unexpected nature of their attack. Minutes ago the Saracens were jeering the Christians for refusing to make landfall.

Now they were fleeing up the beach; those who tarried were being cut down by Christian swords.

Having established a beachhead, King Richard gave orders for trenches to be dug and barricades constructed. The city was still in Saracen hands and had barred its gates against them but they had at least made landfall. As for entering the city, it was the king who remembered a small postern gate accessible only by a small, very narrow stairway.

Wilfred found himself one of a small band of knights handpicked by the king to accompany him on a scouting expedition. They followed the city walls to the stairway cut into the rock. Hurrying up it single file and keeping an eye out for any Saracens on the battlements above, they reached a small oak door.

"This leads into the Templar quarter," said the king. "If we can get in undetected, we could sneak into the citadel and rally the survivors for a rush on the gates. Furnival, have that door down, please."

The elderly knight had brought an axe with him and made to swing it at the door.

"Shouldn't we have brought more men?" the Earl of Leicester cautioned.

"If we did then we'd draw attention to ourselves," said the king. "And I want the eyes of every Saracen in the city fixed on our beachhead. They'll never see us coming! Furnival, the door!"

It took several blows of the axe to break in the postern door and as each one landed, Wilfred felt sure the Saracens would come running to investigate the noise. But none did and they quickly filed in through the splintered remains of the door to find themselves in the back room of a wealthy townhouse.

None speaking, they crept to the front of the house and looked down into the street below. There wasn't a soul about although there were plenty of corpses, mostly Christians. Swords drawn, they climbed down the wooden stairs to street level and, King Richard leading the way, made their way through the deserted streets towards the citadel.

There was a fug of smoke that hung over everything and the stench was acrid. As they rounded a corner, they found themselves in the town square where the remains of a large bonfire still smouldered. White ash drifted on the breeze and the shape of the charred remains did not suggest that the Saracens had been burning wood.

"What in God's name …" said Gerard de Furnival, as they approached the smoking pile of blackened debris. "There are bones in those ashes!"

"They haven't!" the Earl of Leicester exclaimed. "Have they?"

"And over here, look!" said Gerard, pointing to a corner of the square that was slick with blood. A large knife, red with gore, lay upon a chopping block.

The thought that their Christian comrades had met such a grisly end made the stomachs of every man there recoil with disgust and a red rage settled over them at the barbarity of their enemies.

"Wait!" said Wilfred, kneeling down by the burned-out fire and inspecting it closely. He picked through the charred bones with the tip of his sword. "Pigs!" he exclaimed. "It's not people, it's pigs!"

"Can you be sure?" asked the Earl of Leicester.

"Aye, my father's people live off pork. I used to help old Gurth the swineherd with the slaughtering every winter. I'd know pigs' bones anywhere."

"Of course!" said the king. "The infidels can't abide swine. It goes against the teachings of their prophet. They must have butchered and burned every hog in Jaffa!"

Despite the grisly surroundings, the crusaders broke into laugher born of the relief that their comrades had not been butchered.

They continued towards the citadel but before the gates of the inner wall could be seen, they found their way blocked by a group of Saracens who were busy stockpiling weapons and armour looted from the dead. Swords were drawn and, with cries to God on their lips, both sides charged at each other.

The sound of blows rang out in the street as the Christians desperately tried to fight their way through to the gates of the citadel. Wilfred hacked through a Saracen's neck, nearly severing his head, and booted him to one side just in time to catch the blow of his companion's sword on his own.

The Saracens were outnumbered and, after several of them had been felled, the rest cut a retreat towards the citadel. The Christians pursued but stopped short as a group of Saracen archers came running to reinforce their comrades.

"Take cover!" the king yelled and Wilfred hurled himself into a doorway as a volley of arrows whistled down the street, thudding into wooden doorframes and bouncing off stone walls.

Peeping out, Wilfred could see a dozen or so archers fanning out, taking up positions where they could pick off any Christian that broke from cover. The Saracens they had chased had now turned around, their courage rekindled, and were shouting taunts and curses at the Christians.

"We're pinned down!" Wilfred called to the king. He could see Richard loading his crossbow and aiming it down the street. The Earl of Leicester dragged him out of danger as an arrow narrowly missed him.

"Look, the gates are opening!" said Gerard de Furnival.

Wilfred risked another peep around the doorway. Sure enough, behind the enemy, the gates to the citadel were swinging wide. Armed men could be seen hurrying through the gap and charging the enemy from behind.

"The survivors from the citadel!" Richard cried.

The Saracens were taken by surprise and whirled to face their attackers, their attention drawn away from the Christians further down the street.

"Now's our chance!" shouted Richard. "Charge them!"

As one, they emerged from cover and ran up the street, blades keen. The Saracens were caught between two forces and quickly surrendered.

The survivors from the citadel were a rag-tag band wearing dulled and bloodied armour. Many had wounds bound with dressings. Richard approached the one who seemed to be the leader. "We thought to rescue you but, by God, it was you who rescued us!"

"This time yesterday, there was talk of surrender," said the soldier. "But as soon as we saw your fleet arrive we knew it was only a matter of time before the Lionheart would put the infidels to the flight! When we heard fighting in the street beyond the gates, we decided it was now or never."

"A good thing too, they had us by the balls!"

Once King Richard's standard was flying from the walls of the citadel, the Saracens that remained in the city deserted it and re-joined the bulk of Saladin's army to the north. Despite having retaken Jaffa, the Christians could not feel altogether victorious for the presence of the massive Saracen force now stood between them and Caesarea where King Henry and the rest of the Christian army were now stuck. They did their best to refortify the ruined walls and patch up the breaches but there was more demoralisation when it was learnt that the Saracens had not only slaughtered every pig in the town but they had also broken open very barrel of wine and emptied them into the gutters.

Oaths singed the air as Wilfred looked out over the shattered battlements at the scorching land to the east where their goal lay, so close yet so far.

Earlier that year, their second attempt to reach Jerusalem had been rebuffed once again after they had come so tantalisingly close that they had actually seen the walls of the holy city from a distance. As before, they had made their camp at Bait Nuba but, if they had been beaten back by rain and hail during their winter campaign, it was the scorching heat and desperate thirst that plagued them on their summer one. Aware of their advance, Saladin had poisoned every well for miles around Jerusalem and the crusaders had to send out dangerous scouting missions in search of natural springs.

It was on one of these expeditions that Wilfred and a company of knights were ambushed by a party of Saracens. After a brief skirmish, they put the Saracens to the flight and, as they rounded a hilly pass, they drew up short, their quarry forgotten as they gazed at the sight ahead. Wide, limestone walls encircled a mound of dwellings and domed buildings that shimmered in the heat as if they were only a mirage that might vanish at any moment.

"God in Heaven," said one of Wilfred's companions. "Is that it?"

"Yes," said Wilfred, unable to tear his eyes away. "That's Jerusalem."

They rode back to tell the king that the holy city was within sight, thinking that he would be keen to lay eyes on it but he surprised them by refusing. "I will not lay my eyes on the holy city until I am confident that we can take it," he explained.

And clearly, their king was not confident.

Yet more negotiations ensued and Saladin was willing to allow Christian pilgrims to visit the Holy Sepulchre and for them to keep the coastal territories Richard had won for them. All except Ascalon. This was the keystone upon which the campaigns of both sides rested. Without Ascalon, Saladin's supply lines were ever under threat, not to mention the safety of Egypt. But if the Christians did not keep the city for themselves, then their small, fledgling kingdom would be like a green sapling in a storm.

Richard refused to give up Ascalon and, as a result, the negotiations fell through. They retreated back to the coast and once again, the crusade seemed on the verge of being over; a situation not improved by the news that Saladin had suddenly taken Jaffa.

But these days it seemed to be negotiations that were interrupted by war and not the other way around. By the time King Henry and a small force had circumvented the Saracens via a sea voyage to Jaffa, he found King Richard camped outside the city and engaged in yet more discussions with the sultan's delegates. Still the matter of Ascalon stood in the way of peace. Richard would not budge and Saladin was prepared to wait. With the bulk of the Christian army still at Caesarea and King Richard and his small force camped at Jaffa, Saladin saw a rare opportunity to defeat the crusaders and took it.

Wilfred awoke to the sound of panicked shouting. Men were hurrying through the camp raising the alarm.

"Master, wake up!" Leonard said, as he gathered together Wilfred's helm and sword belt. "The enemy is upon us!"

"They attack?" Wilfred exclaimed, snatching the sword belt from his squire and buckling it on. "And we are camped out here like sitting ducks!"

"It was one of the Genoese crossbowmen who spotted their advance when he was emptying his bowels a few miles from camp," said Leonard.

"I bet that made him empty them a bit quicker."

They hurried off to find the king and were relieved to see that he was already ordering men into defensive formations. He had every man-at-arms kneel in a line with the butts of their spears jammed into the dirt, their iron heads angled at the height of a horse's chest. Between each of them, protected by their shields, he had the crossbowmen in teams of two for the purpose of faster reloading.

"We'll keep up a constant barrage while the men-at-arms hold the enemy cavalry at arm's length," said the king.

"What about the knights?" asked the Earl of Leicester, as he strapped on his helm.

"We brought few horses with us for we had planned on a siege not open battle," said the king. "Every man with a mount will remain with me. Those who have none shall take their places alongside the men-at-arms."

Thankfully, due to his rare horsemanship, Wilfred had been one of the knights whom Richard had instructed to bring his horse in the ships from Acre. He bade Leonard farewell and sent him off to join the spear lines. The mounted group that stood with the king was a pitiful band. They had nine horses between them. If it came to a cavalry charge, they would be slaughtered and Wilfred began to wish that he had left Jago in Acre. That way he would be in the front ranks of spearmen. It sat ill with him for his squire and so many others to face the enemy while he hung back in relative safety.

They could see the enemy now; a massive force of riders and flapping pennons. Dust rose in the air, obscuring them, and the hot noon sun made them appear as approaching shadows.

As they came within range, the crossbowmen took aim and shot, the strings of their weapons thudding in unison as hundreds of bolts flew at the enemy. At the same time, the enemy bowmen sent a volley of arrows in their direction which mostly bounced of the shields of the men-at-arms.

The cavalry charged but drew up within spitting distance of the spearmen, their horses unwilling to get too close to the bristling wall of spear heads. Arabic curses were hurled at them and some even tried to hack through the shafts of their spears with their swords which only resulted in them and their horses being impaled by the screaming Christians. And all the while the crossbowmen kept shooting, bolt after bolt into the mass of enemy cavalry.

Infuriated at being held off by such a small band of Christians, the Saracens wheeled their mounts around and retreated. A second charge was attempted but it was repelled. Again and again they tried, with increasing desperation, only to be held back by the Christians who found their morale gradually increasing with their continued success.

A man from the city garrison came running towards the assembled Christian host crying urgently that the city was under attack.

"Keep that man quiet or I'll have his head!" Richard ordered the knights nearest to him.

The man paled at the threat and shut his mouth like a clam. Richard rode over to him. "Now, what's this nonsense you're spouting?" he demanded.

"Sire, the Saracens have crept past our lines and snuck into the city. The inhabitants are fleeing for the ships!"

"Impossible!" King Richard growled, turning in his saddle to gaze at the city behind them. "Speak of this to no one," he told the men around him. "You, Ivanhoe, and you, Furnival, come with me. We must investigate. Bring some of those Genoese crossbowmen."

Wilfred and Gerard de Furnival shared a nervous glance. It was sensible of the king to stifle any potential panic but did he really have to tackle everything himself? They rounded up a score of crossbowmen and, as inconspicuously as possible, rode away from the front lines and made for the city gates.

Jaffa was in a state of panic. People ran through the streets carrying belongings under their arms and dragging children along with them as they moved in the general direction of the harbour. Richard shook his head in exasperation and led the small troop up the main street towards the citadel which had once again barred its gates.

Three mounted mamluks rode down the street towards them, swinging their swords at the fleeing townsfolk. Richard charged them head on and slew one of them before Wilfred and Gerard managed to catch up to him. The remaining two assailed the king on both sides and, while Wilfred engaged one of them, Richard was able to slay the other.

Realising he was outnumbered, Wilfred's opponent turned tail and attempted to flee but the king, now in a murderous rage, hacked him down from his saddle before he could gallop away.

"You're making a red name for yourself, sire," said Wilfred. "Three mamluks to your name before Furnival and I could wet our blades!"

"I'm sick of the lot of them!" the king replied. "Would that they could all offer their necks to my blade as easily as these three and I could rid the Holy Land of them once and for all!"

There were several Saracens on foot further up the street but, after one look at the dripping blade of the feared King of England, decided that perhaps it would be better to re-join their comrades on the other side of Jaffa's walls.

They rode on to the harbour and Richard did his best to rally what was left of the garrison and persuade the terrified civilians that the danger was over. The battle in the plains beyond the city was still raging but for now, the city itself was resecured.

Upon their return to the front lines, they found that the Saracens had grown reluctant to attack the ranks of footmen and were marshalled across the plain, licking their wounds.

"Now is the time to take the fight to them," said the king. "Every mounted man, prepare to follow me!"

"Sire, we were too few!" the Earl of Leicester protested.

"Nonsense!" the king replied. "Those men over there are exhausted and demoralised. Besides, it's the last thing they will expect. I just slew three mamluks because I charged them head on before they had a chance to realise what was happening. It's now or never, lads! Onwards!"

Wilfred swallowed and grimaced at the dryness of his throat which was parched by dust and fear. Leicester was right; they were hopelessly outnumbered. But the king's courage was boundless and they were doomed to follow his lead or else face eternal shame. With a blast of a trumpet, the king set off, the hooves of his horse churning up dust which Wilfred and the paltry force of knights could only chase.

The Saracens were in no mood for further fighting. Most retreated from the oncoming Christian knights and those who remained to face them found themselves up against the mad bloodlust of men who were giving their very last effort.

The king distinguished himself yet again, slaying men right and left, even riding to rescue the Earl of Leicester whose horse was knocked from under him by a Saracen javelin. Outnumbered they may have been but the Christians showed the fighting spirit and eagerness of ten-thousand men with which the worn-out Saracens could not hope to compete. Before they knew it, it was over and they found themselves surrounded by corpses while the surviving Saracen ranks held fast, refusing to engage.

King Richard, in another astonishing display of foolhardy courage, galloped along the enemy lines inviting any of them to fight him. None did.

"His own courage will be his downfall, I have no doubt of it," said the Earl of Leicester. "How long can a man stretch his luck?"

Wilfred nodded agreement with this sentiment but this day, at least, Richard the Lionheart's luck held out and the Saracens retreated.

The repulse from Jaffa marked the end of hostilities. Both sides were exhausted, severely weakened and utterly fed up with war. As Richard fell seriously ill with another bout of quartan fever, delegates were sent to Saladin to reopen negotiations. A three-year truce was negotiated, on the condition that Ascalon would be razed to the ground so that it could offer no strategic importance either to Christian or Muslim. The Christians would be allowed to retain the coastal strip from Tyre to Jaffa while Saladin retained Jerusalem but would allow Christian pilgrims to visit the city. It was the best they could hope for.

Wilfred, for his part, was thrilled with the result. Not only was this damnable war over at last, but he could now fulfil his promise to Rowena and visit the holy city before returning home. He joined the second of three parties that headed to Jerusalem and found that it was everything he had hoped it would be.

First they visited the Church of the Holy Sepulchre which had been built around the site of Christ's execution and resting place. Atop the small hill of Calvary they gazed upon the stone into which Christ's cross had been fitted. True to his word, Wilfred plucked a stone from the ground and kept it for Rowena. At the entrance to the tomb it had always been the custom for each pilgrim to leave a small gift such as a ring or some coin but it was learned by the first party of pilgrims that the Saracens had taken to stealing the small offerings so Wilfred, along with many others, decided to give their tokens to the poor Christian wretches who had been taken captive and were now toiling away in chains within the city.

They saw other sites that had borne witness to Christ's life; they kissed the table of the last supper, paid homage to the tomb of the Holy Virgin and entered the cell that was the chamber that held Christ on the eve of his execution. Although it distressed them all to see how these holy sites had been neglected by the occupying Saracens who had even given some of them over to the stabling of their horses.

Once the pilgrimages had been completed, the army left Jaffa and returned to Acre where King Richard began making his plans to depart the Holy Land at last. Queen Berengaria and his sister Joan left first, on the 29th of September, boarding a ship that would take them to Sicily where they would continue over land. Such a route was not desirable to Richard who feared that the many enemies he had made such as the Holy Roman Emperor and Duke Leopold of Austria, might make his passage difficult. The exact route he would take and the date of his departure were kept a closely guarded secret.

He called Wilfred to his side one evening and, as Wilfred entered the lamp-lit tent, he had trouble recognising the courageous Lionheart who had been so victorious at Jaffa in the man who lay before him now. The king was horribly pale and the sweat stood out on his brow. Despite his illness, the king still managed a smile as Wilfred knelt at his side.

"How was Jerusalem, Ivanhoe?"

Wilfred was surprised by the king's question. He remembered Richard's words on the day they had set eyes on the holy city from afar and understood why he had not wanted to visit. He may have ensured three years of peace and the safety of Christian pilgrims, but his vow to retake Jerusalem had not been fulfilled.

Wilfred gave the king a full report of his pilgrimage, detailing every sight they had seen. The king closed his eyes as he listened so as to better imagine the places Wilfred described. When he was done, the king sighed.

"Such is my punishment for failing in my vow," he said. "That I must forever imagine walking the streets of Jerusalem while the brave knights under my banner tread those cobbles in my stead. I am glad for you, Ivanhoe. Cherish those memories."

"You may walk those streets yet, sire," Wilfred said. "Jerusalem will be a Christian city once more, I am certain of it."

The king smiled. "As am I. But I may not live to see it."

"Your illness, sire? But the physicians …"

"My illness comes and goes. No, it is not fever I fear, but my journey home. I have made many enemies here, Ivanhoe. King Philip, whom I once called friend, despises me with a hot vengeance. Emperor Heinrich is determined to act on his wife's claim to Sicily and will never forgive me for handing it to Tancred. I have enemies in Spain, Germany, France and Italy. My journey home will be fraught with danger."

"Surely you do not suspect these men of trying to hinder the passage of a returning crusader?" Wilfred asked.

"You do not know these men as I do, Ivanhoe. Their jealousy, their pettiness and their vindictiveness know no bounds. I wish to give you something, Ivanhoe, for safekeeping." He reached over to the small table beside his bed and picked up a small reliquary by its silver chain and handed it to Wilfred. "This reliquary contains a splinter of the true cross, one of several relics I have collected here in Outremer. I want you to keep it for me."

"Sire, I don't know what to say," said Wilfred.

"I am dividing all my holy relics between my most trusted men. That way, if I am captured or killed on my way home, they will not fall into the hands of my enemies. Guard it well, Ivanhoe. Guard it as loyally as you have served me."

"I will, sire," said Wilfred, slipping the silver chain over his head and tucking the reliquary beneath his tunic. "I will guard it with my life."

Wilfred spent his last days in Acre running errands for King Richard who had many debts to settle and supplies to purchase before he set out. It was while returning from one of these errands that Wilfred realised he was being followed. His route took him through a part of Acre that still had not been wholly repopulated. Footsteps echoed and the fading light of the late afternoon sun deepened the shadows in the ruined buildings on either side of him.

He quickened his pace and was alarmed to hear the two sets of feet following him quicken also. Before he could reach the sunlit square at the end of the passage, hands grabbed him roughly.

He tried to twist out of their grip, his hand reaching for the hilt of his sword, but they were ready for that, one hand grasping his wrist like a vice while another seized his sword.

They were Saracens, he could see that, but he also found that he recognised them. These were the two turncoats who served Brian de Bois-Guilbert: Hamed and Abdallah.

A fist landed in his gut, making him double over in pain, the wind knocked from him. Then they were hustling him over to an open doorway of a ruined building.

It was pitch black inside. His captors forced him down onto a chair that seemed to have been placed in the room especially for him and rope was produced to bind him. As his eyes grew accustomed to the dimness, he became aware of a fourth person in the room; one who had been waiting for him.

"Bois-Guilbert?" Wilfred hazarded.

The figure stepped closer, the light from the doorway glinting off his polished mail and illuminating a handsome face framed by black locks and a thick beard.

"Ivanhoe," said the Templar.

"What's the meaning of this? Do you run mad to set your heathen dogs on a fellow Christian?"

Bois-Guilbert smiled. "Christian you may be, but you and your false-lipped king are no fellows of mine nor any true brother of my order."

"What do you want?"

"Your king is due to leave Acre any day now. As someone who has wormed his way into his close circle, you naturally know the date of his departure and the route he will be taking. Tell me both."

"You overestimate King Richard's opinion of me," said Wilfred. "Only a few men close to the king know those things and I am not one of them."

"I don't believe you."

At a nod from Bois-Guilbert to one of his servants, a Saracen fist slammed into Wilfred's gut again, making him gasp in agony. His involuntary reaction was to double over as he did before but the bonds that held him to the chair prevented him so he was forced to sit in an upright position as the pain radiated throughout his belly.

"You had best give up the pretence of ignorance," said the Templar. "Hamed and Abdallah are most efficient at inflicting pain."

"I don't know anything!" Wilfred said weakly.

Another blow to the abdomen brought tears to his eyes. Then, one of the Saracens tipped his chair over so he landed heavily on his side. What followed was a brutal barrage of kicks and blows that succeeded in shattering the chair Wilfred was tied to, not to mention cracking some of his ribs. Although free of his bonds, he was in no position to fight back and the savage beating continued until a word from Bois-Guilbert stopped the exertions of his servants.

Wilfred lay in a ball, blood seeping from his mouth and his body screaming in protest. He was sure they would kill him once they were convinced he knew nothing. He prayed to God to give him the strength to hold out that long. Of course he knew when King Richard would leave Acre as well as his planned route. But he would never tell Brian de Bois-Guilbert. The Templar's savage determination to extract the truth from Wilfred told him that there had to be some plot against the King of England, some treachery on the part of the Templars who had supported Lucas de Beaumanoir. He must not betray his king!

"You are really willing to die rather than tell me what I want to know?" Bois-Guilbert said, as if reading his mind. "I'll find out anyway, you know? You can't save Richard. He'll never make it through Europe, whichever route he takes, not without being captured or killed."

Wilfred tried to mouth an insult but his jaws would not work. He was glad of that and instead spat out a glob of blood that nearly reached the Templar's feet. Bois-Guilbert sneered and said something to his servants. Wilfred only remembered them moving towards him to continue their beating and then knew no more.

Wilfred never found out how he left the ruined building the Saracens had dragged him into. All he knew was that he must have regained consciousness after being left for dead and stumbled his way into the market square only to collapse into a heap. It was Leonard who told him he had been found bleeding and broken and carried to the Hospitaller quarter to be treated for his wounds.

He was a mess. Several ribs were broken, his nose was smashed and his entire body was one blue-black bruise. He had difficulty speaking for his jaw was swollen and his mouth full of loose teeth but as soon as he was able, he told Leonard that he must speak with the king as soon as possible.

"The king has departed, master," said Leonard. "He left two nights ago."

"Two nights ago?" Wilfred said. "How long have I been unconscious?"

"Almost a week, master. You ran a high fever and the Hospitallers thought you might not make it."

"Who went with the king?"

"Around twenty men. William de l'Etang, Warin Fitzgerald, Baldwin de Bethune. Some of the Templars."

"Templars?" Wilfred croaked.

"Yes, master."

"Where is Bois-Guilbert?"

"Left also, master. Most are making their way home now, before winter."

Wilfred ignored the pain as his crushed lips curled into a frantic grimace. He tried to rise but the pain in his body was too great and he fell back, cursing his wounds. He had to get out of here and catch up with the king somehow. He had to warn him of the Templar plot before it was too late.

CHAPTER IX

Locksley Chase, October 1192

The cold autumn wind rattled the bare branches hanging above the road that led from Sheffield to Copmanhurst. The last of the fiery leaves drifted on the breeze and the road beneath the hooves of Rowena's mare was carpeted with reds and golds.

She often rode out alone these days, sent off on some excuse of an errand by Maud while in reality she would ride to nearby settlements and distribute small packets of food, medicine and even coin and other items of value that could be exchanged for food. Sometimes her and Maud told half-truths and explained that Maud wished to make a donation to a nearby church but felt too ill to ride out herself and so Rowena would be sent in her stead. The money would go directly into the hands of the needy, bypassing any risk that it might fall into a corrupt churchman's coffer.

Constance suspected something of course. She'd be mad not to with Rowena off on some obscure errand every other week or so. But exactly what her and Maud were up to was beyond Constance's powers to comprehend. And they hoped to keep it that way. Not that what they were doing was bad – quite the contrary – but Lord and Lady Malvoisin might take exception to any suggestion that they were not running their ward's estates to her satisfaction and that she had taken to distributing alms to the poor from the castle stores.

In truth, Rowena felt that Maud enjoyed having a secret and somebody to share it with. The girl did not like her guardians much and she was desperately bored. Relieving the tedium of castle life as well as the suffering of the poor was like killing two birds with one stone.

Copmanhurst was a small settlement south of the River Don and, like many such settlements in the West Riding, it had more than its share of needy folk. Rowena had visited it twice before and had become known to the elders of the settlement who blessed her and her mistress for their charity.

It was as the road veered away from the riverbank and passed through a densely wooded portion of the upper part of the Chase that Rowena realised she was not alone. Several figures had emerged from the trees to her right to block the road ahead. Her heart caught in her mouth as she took in their appearances. Each of them wore the rough spun, undyed cloth of woodsmen and their faces were obscured by hooded mantles of green and black masks that covered their noses and mouths. Each of them had a bow with an arrow nocked to its string.

It had always been a danger that she would be accosted by robbers on her travels but it was only now that it was happening to her that she suddenly took the threat seriously and realised how foolish she had been. There had been an increase in banditry in the Chase of late. A single lady-in-waiting travelling those wooded roads alone was madness but it was too late now.

"Where does a fair maiden go on her own in Locksley Chase?" asked the lead robber. "Does she not know that these are dangerous times?"

"I go to Copmanhurst," said Rowena, trying to keep her voice steady. "And my business is important enough that gives me the courage to risk encounters with hobhoods."

"Hobhoods?" said the lead robber, his voice laced with laughter. "Is that what we are? Trust old Cedric of Rotherwood to fill his ward's head with tales of hobhoods and hodekins."

Rowena felt a chill creep over her. It was true, 'hobhood' was an old Saxon word for a magical forest creature who robbed and beat unwary travellers, sometimes driving them mad so they lost their way in the woods and were never seen again. But how did this hedge robber know she was the ward of Cedric?

"Do I know you, sir?" she asked the robber. "How are you so acquainted with my guardian that you recognise his ward on sight?"

The robber seemed taken aback by this, as if he'd let his mouth run away with him. *Who is this man?* Rowena thought.

"Aye, I know Cedric," said the lead robber. "But what business would draw the Lady Rowena from Sheffield Castle to a poor little place like Copmanhurst?"

"Delivering Christian charity to those in need," said Rowena. "You'd not rob a woman for trying to help the poor, now would you?"

A snort of mirth told Rowena that there might be a grin behind that black mask and the robber stepped forward to examine her saddle bags. When he was finished, he glanced up at her, surprise in his eyes.

"You steal food from the castle kitchens and give it to the poor?"

"When I can," Rowena replied.

"Sounds like a dangerous pastime for a lady-in-waiting. Your days at the castle would be numbered if you were caught."

"Why is that a concern of yours?"

"It isn't. Just a passing interest."

"Well then, hobhood. Will you let me pass or will you and your band fill your bellies tonight on food meant for hungrier mouths?"

"I am honour bound to take something from you by way of a tax."

"Tax?"

"On principle. All who pass through Locksley Chase must pay a tax. Your charitable business is most commendable but what of the poor outlaws who have no beds but the leafy loam and no roofs but the branches of the trees?"

"I dare say such outlaws should have thought of that before they broke the law."

"Then I dare say that Rowena of Rotherwood has led a sheltered life. The law of this land does not favour the poor who are not free to hunt or forage in the chase or mill their own grain. When the law seeks to hang men for trying to feed their families then men must live without the law and seek aid from those who pass through their realm."

Rowena felt herself flush at the implication that she was blind to the plight of the commoners. "I am but a lady-in-waiting," she said. "I do what I can for the poor. You are welcome to take the food in my saddlebags if you feel that you are more deserving of it than the folk of Copmanhurst."

"Food is something we do not lack," said the robber. "But that gold ring on your finger may buy us many things that do not grow so freely in the Chase. Give us the ring and you can go about your business."

Rowena instinctively withdrew her hand from the reins and cupped the finger that wore the ring protectively. "This was given to me by my guardian, Cedric," she said.

The robber shrugged. "The ring or the food, it is your choice."

She dared not push her luck with this robber further. It had been friendly banter so far but it was clear that he would not let her pass without robbing her of something. The ring or the food. It was absurd to compare a small trinket to a bundle of food that could feed several families for a week and yet … Cedric had given her this gold ring with its inlaid sapphire on her twelfth birthday. It was very dear to her and she hated to lose it to some common outlaw who would probably barter it for a jug of wine. Oh, blast it! She slipped it off her finger and held it out for the robber to take. She just couldn't let these rogues steal the food she and Maud had prepared for the poor. Those families had to eat, even if it meant losing her ring.

The outlaw snatched it from her fingers and slipped it into his purse. Then, without another word, he and his band vanished back into the woods from whence they had come.

Her thumping heart still had not returned to normal once she entered the outskirts of Copmanhurst. She had tried to put a brave face on things but there was no getting past the awful sense of violation. She had been robbed. She had been lucky, it was true, but she had been robbed nonetheless and of her favourite ring too! She was just glad they had not spotted the reliquary Wilfred had given her that she wore around her neck beneath her chemise. If they had taken that from her she may have just died.

There was another visitor to the settlement of Copmanhurst and a rather unusual one at that. Building what looked to be a simple shelter was a Cistercian lay brother. He wore the brown tunic and black scapula of his order, both of which were tucked up into his belt of rushes to keep them from being soiled by his labour. He was a stout and hale man with a barrel chest and a ruddy face that sweated from his exertions despite the chill of the season. He was pounding thick wooden stakes into the ground which would presumably support a roof.

"Lady Rowena, you return to us!" said an elderly man of the village.

"Hello, Godfrey," said Rowena, accepting his hand as he helped her down from her horse. "I haven't brought as much as last time, I'm afraid."

"Now, don't you worry about that, my lady. You've been more than kind to us. There are many here who remember you in their prayers. Your hand, my lady. It's shaking."

"Yes," said Rowena, clearing her throat. "I am a little shaky. I was robbed on my way here and my nerves haven't quite settled."

"Robbed!" Godfrey cried. His alarm drew other members of the settlement to them, their faces greatly concerned. "My lady, you must sit down and rest yourself!" He turned to one of the others. "Fetch some ale!"

"I'll be quite all right, I assure you," said Rowena. "Fortunately they did not take the food intended for you. Their minds were set on gold apparently and only made off with my ring."

"Curse the buggers!" said Godfrey. "Well, that settles it. The Chase has become too dangerous for a maiden to be travelling alone. We can no longer accept your kind charity, not when you risk your very life in bringing it to us. Besides, God has blessed us with another kind stranger. Come, let me introduce you."

He waved at the monk who had taken a rest from his labour and was leaning against one of the stakes he had implanted and was gratefully accepting a cup of ale from one of the villagers. He spotted Godfrey and, after draining his cup, made his way over to them.

"So this is the heavenly creature God has allied with the efforts of my own order to relieve the suffering of the poor!" said the lay brother. "Brother Broch, is my name, a monk of Fountains Abbey."

"This is the lady Rowena of Rotherwood," said Godfrey. "Didn't I say she was the very picture of an angel? Her beauty matches her courage for she has come again today bearing parcels of food despite being assailed by robbers on the road."

"Robbers! By Saint Dunstan!" Brother Broch cried, his face appalled. "They did not mistreat you, I trust?"

"No, I am quite unscathed," said Rowena.

"Although they did take a ring," said Godfrey.

"Stole a ring from the hand of so charitable and good a lady?" Brother Broch said in outrage. "These woodland fiends should be beaten from the brush like plump partridges ready for the hunter's arrow!"

"The arrow seems to be their own choice of weapon," said Rowena, "for they all bore bows."

"Poachers turned outlaw no doubt," said the monk, tutting. "The oppression of hunger drives weak men down such sinful paths. That is partly the reason of my mission here. My abbot, the blessed Ralph Hagget of Fountains Abbey, is keen to do what he can to relieve the suffering of the poor. He has dispatched brothers such as me to build shelters for the homeless."

"I took you for a lay brother but you are a full monk? Should you not be making your way back to your abbey? Fountains Abbey is a long ride north."

"Abbot Ralph is a little unconventional in his way of doing things. He has granted me permission to dwell outside the abbey's walls and conduct myself as if I were indeed a lay brother, free to mingle with the secular world. Such is his dedication to the welfare of the poor and his trust in me. Copmanhurst is my home for the foreseeable future. These good folk have accepted me into their fold in return for my efforts. I am building a shelter for those poor wretches who have found themselves without homes. Winter will soon be here."

"As will dusk," said Godfrey. "I wonder, Brother Broch, would you be able to spare yourself a few hours to escort the good lady Rowena back to Sheffield? I fear for her safety, especially as night draws in."

"Not only would it be a pleasure," said the monk, "but a sure duty. Besides, I have the perfect antidote to woodland robbers." He walked over to where he had been working and picked up a large club. "Crab tree wood does for most rogues," he said with a wink.

Rowena was pleased to have some company on the ride back and not just because it made her feel safer. She found the jolly monk fascinating and wanted to know more about his business.

"Why Copmanhurst?" she asked, as they rode towards Sheffield, her on her mare and him on his mule. "There are many there in need it is true, but the same can surely be said of settlements closer to your abbey."

"Alas, that is true, my lady. Famine and high taxation have devastated all England but we must choose our battles. There is another reason for my choosing Copmanhurst. In the vicinity of the settlement is a ruined chapel to Saint Dunstan, long neglected and overgrown. I have a mind to repair it and return it to its former use for the people of Copmanhurst require spiritual guidance as well as charity."

"And you intend to be their priest?"

"If Abbot Ralph gives me permission."

They arrived at Sheffield just as the sun was setting over the wooden palisades of the castle. After stabling their horses, Rowena led Brother Broch into the kitchens and went to find Maud. When they came back down, Constance hurrying behind, wearing her usual expression of concern-bordering-on-outrage, they found Brother Broch sitting at a table with a chunk of bread and lump of boiled beef in front of him lifting a foaming cup of ale to his lips.

"I thought monks didn't eat meat," said Constance, looking him up and down with distaste.

Brother Broch, startled, set down his cup and wiped the foam from his lips with the hem of his sleeve. "Only on special occasions, my lady, or if we are ill. And your cook here was good enough to notice that I was feeling faint after a lengthy journey and bade me sit and eat."

"I thought you only came from Copmanhurst," Constance said, turning to Rowena.

"Oh, never mind that!" said Maud. "Eat your fill, good monk, and then you can tell us all about your mission from Fountains Abbey."

The monk did so and they joined him at the table for their own supper of pottage. The monk devoured the boiled beef and gladly accepted two more cups of ale as he settled in to answer all of Maud's questions of which there were a good many.

"Well, the monks of Fountains Abbey seem perfectly wonderful," she said at length. "It's good to know that somebody cares about the poor. We are so surrounded by greed and political wrangling that I had all but given up hope that anybody did."

"We do our best," said Brother Broch. "But even the sincerest efforts of a handful of monks do little in the larger scheme of things. Take Copmanhurst, for instance. I will have built a shelter for a score or so homeless wretches before winter. But that will do them little good when there is nothing to eat."

"No, I suppose not," said Maud, sharing a glance with Rowena. "Could food not be grown for them?"

"Indeed it could, come spring. We Cistercians pride ourselves on our affinity with the plough and field, for their bounty is the true wealth of the world, not rare metals pressed into coins."

"Are the Cistercians not known for building granges?"

"We are and a grange is by far the most efficient way to turn waste into arable land. But before we can begin the rooting and planting and making habitable of the waste, the waste must first be granted to the abbey."

"I'll give it to you!" Maud said. "Copmanhurst lies within my lands. I can give you all the land you require for your grange!"

"That is very generous, my lady. But there would be much to organise. Food and materials from the abbey, plus half a dozen or so lay brothers to build a monastic community."

"This is nonsense, my lady," said Constance. "You are getting carried away. Your lands, like you, are the ward of Lord Malvoisin. You will not be free to do as you please with them until you are married."

Maud looked down at the table, her spirits dashed. "And even then my husband will have charge of my property," she said bitterly. "Whoever he turns out to be."

"It was a nice thought, my child," said the monk. "You have a good, Christian heart and I am sure you will come to rule your lands as a just and charitable lady."

They bade the monk goodnight and retired to Maud's bower. Rowena could see that Maud was not utterly defeated and over the next few days, she could see that a plan of some sort was forming in her mind.

Later that month they were visited by Prior Aymer of Jorvaulx Abbey; another Cistercian community a few miles north of Fountains. Prior Aymer was a friend of Philip de Malvoisin's and Rowena knew that Maud did not like the man. He was a plump figure with a pointed beard who dressed in cloth and finery unbecoming to a monk of his order. Although they were both Cistercians, there couldn't have been a starker contrast between the Prior of Jorvaulx Abbey and Brother Broch of Copmanhurst. The Cistercians were known to pride themselves on their anti-materialism to the point of calling themselves the 'poor of Christ' but the vast wealth the order had amassed in recent years through land grants and its involvement in the wool trade presented them with something of a conundrum. For all their talk of poverty, the Cistercians were beginning to look more and more like the Cluniac and Benedictine orders they had broken away from and Prior Aymer represented the worst of their hypocrisies.

The feast went on late and the ladies excused themselves, leaving Lord Malvoisin and Prior Aymer alone in the Great Hall to discuss important matters. It was when Rowena went down to fetch some clean linen from the laundress that she overheard their conversation. They were speaking in low tones, clearly not wishing to be overheard but their voices carried well enough through the empty, vaulted hall so that Rowena could hear them from the stairwell. Their words froze her in her tracks.

"The count is desperately trying to raise an army," Malvoisin said. "After his mother stuck her oar in and ruined his negotiations with King Philip, he feels increasingly vulnerable. He fears his brother could return any day."

"Surely we would have had word of his return from Outremer if that were true," said the prior. "The last we heard of the king, he was at Jaffa fending off Saladin, no closer to his goal than he was a year ago. His expedition to reclaim Jerusalem has been a shambles from the start. He may even be dead by now."

"He lives, I am sure of it," said Malvoisin. "And as long as he does, John will need men, men his loyal supporters had best provide."

"I see. You fear that you do not have enough, Philip? The Lovetot estate the king entrusted to is considerable …"

"It is large certainly, but there are few nobles with any retinues to speak of. Not with so many good fighting men with the king in Outremer …"

"You think to hire mercenaries."

"Yes. And I need the silver to do so."

"I understand. Well, the sheep pastures between Anesacre and Bradfield have long seemed attractive to the abbey. I could make you a very good offer, considering our friendship and our mutual support of the king's brother."

"As always, Your Reverence, your generosity is to be commended."

"I will have the charters drawn up as soon as I return to the abbey."

Rowena dared not loiter any longer for fear of discovery and hurried down to the laundress. By the time she climbed the stairs again, the Great Hall was empty but for the servants who were clearing up.

"My lady, I must speak with you!" Rowena said, as she entered Maud's bower. Constance was brushing Maud's hair and they both looked at her expectantly. Rowena set the fresh linen down on the bed. "I just overheard Lord Malvoisin and Prior Aymer discussing the sale of some of your land to Jorvaulx Abbey."

"Well that's hardly surprising," said Constance, as she continued brushing. "As Lady Maud's guardian, Lord Malvoisin is custodian of her lands and can do with them as he sees fit. It's not the first time he's sold some of it off."

"No, it isn't," said Maud in a sad voice. "He gets to enrich himself at my expense while I can't even grant Brother Broch a few acres of land to build a grange for the welfare of the poor."

"Lord Malvoisin is hardly enriching himself by selling off parcels of your estate," said Constance.

"These business transactions are to preserve your inheritance. He knows what he is doing."

"I wouldn't be so sure," said Rowena. "He intends to use the money to buy mercenaries to support Count John."

Constance stopped brushing as Maud swivelled in her seat to look at Rowena. "Are you sure?" she asked.

"I heard them say it. John fears the king's return and is building an army, perhaps to fight him when he does return."

Constance and Maud did not remark on the certainty in her voice that the king would indeed return. They knew whose return she was really thinking of.

"Well, it's not for us to disagree with what Lord Malvoisin thinks is best," said Constance. "Perhaps supporting Count John is the best way forward. He may well be our king before Christmas."

"The king *will* return," said Rowena defiantly.

Maud said nothing but Rowena could see that she was deep in thought once more.

The following morning, Maud confronted Philip de Malvoisin as he was breaking his fast in the Great Hall and put to him her desire of gifting a parcel of land near Copmanhurst for the monks of Fountains Abbey to build a grange upon.

"My dear child," said Lord Malvoisin. "Your inheritance is not to be frittered away on trivial matters. This monk of yours, Brother Broch, sounds like a hopeless bumpkin little better than the people he has taken it upon himself to benefit."

"Brother Broch is a selfless man of God!" Maud protested. "He loves the poor and will do anything to help them."

"Then maybe it is the people of Copmanhurst who seek to take advantage of him. I won't allow them to take advantage of you too. Your inheritance has been entrusted to me for this very reason."

"But the people of Copmanhurst are starving! There are many who have lost their livelihoods and their homes due to the recent high taxes and England's unjust laws."

"Unjust laws?" Malvoisin said, his eyebrows raised. "You really have been taken in by them, haven't you? There are only two types of men who call the laws of England unjust: criminals and idlers. Perhaps I should pay more attention to whom you spend your time with."

"My lord," said Maud, stifling an exasperated sigh. "I only ask that you give a small parcel of my inheritance to Fountains Abbey. If you won't do it for the poor, then do it for me. It *is* my land, after all."

"Not yet it isn't, my dear," piped up Lady Malvoisin, as she popped a slice of pear into her mouth. "Until you are married, Philip is your guardian and can do what he wants with your land."

"Including selling it off to men like Prior Aymer?" Maud countered.

Lord and Lady Malvoisin froze. Rowena and Constance, who had remained silent at Maud's side, looked to the ground nervously.

"How did you …" Lord Malvoisin began.

"Yes, I know you intend to sell a chunk of my inheritance to Jorvaulx Abbey," Maud continued, a defiant fire in her voice. "And I know what you intend to do with the proceeds too. You deny me a small request to gift some land for the good of the poor while at the same time you seek to use my inheritance to bolster support for Count John's rebellion!"

"Oh, this is childish stubbornness!" snapped Lord Malvoisin, although his face had gone quite pale. "These matters are beyond your comprehension. I have been chosen by the king to manage your estate precisely because you have no understanding of such things. You might consider showing more gratitude."

"And you might consider showing more caution. I am sure the king's mother would be very interested to hear who is funding rebels intended to fight the very king who entrusted my estate to you."

"You think to blackmail me!" Malvoisin seethed, his jaw clenching dangerously. "You don't know what you're getting yourself into, little lady!"

"Perhaps not," said Maud. "But I'm sure a lot of bother could be saved all round if you would just let me use a little of my inheritance. Then Queen Eleanor need not know of your hiring mercenaries to overthrow her favourite son."

She did not give her guardian a chance to answer and he seemed to be struggling for one anyway. Rowena and Constance hurried after her as she spun on her heel and headed for the stairs.

Rowena had begun to regret telling Maud what she had overheard for it had set the young heiress against her own guardian and for what? She didn't know what Maud could do about it all but felt that blackmailing Philip de Malvoisin may not be the wisest course of action.

Apparently her fears were for naught and Maud's gambit had worked. Within a few days, Philip de Malvoisin journeyed to Fountains Abbey, where, in the abbey's chapterhouse, he signed over to them a parcel of land near Copmanhurst.

CHAPTER X

Locksley Chase, October 1192

It was to be their last robbery of the year. One big score before settling in for the winter and winter in Locksley Chase promised to be long and cold. Already the mornings were chill and frosty. *But at least William would not be alone*, Simon thought.

It had not been long before William of Studley was joined by two more outlaws who had fallen afoul of Malvoisin and Front-de-Boeuf for poaching on their lands. Rather than take their chances by standing trial in increasingly corrupt courts, Ralph and Ulric, two villeins from the Chase, had fled deep into the greenwood. There, after crossing William's path, they took the young lad under their wing.

Simon and John visited their small camp in Harthill Walk as often as they could, bringing them food and supplies but they quickly found that the trio of outlaws were more than equipped for life in the forest, all three being fine shots and used to stalking prey.

It was those inhabitants of the Chase who still lived within the law that suffered most during winter. Food was scarce and few dared poach game now that Malvoisin and Front-de-Boeuf were free to exercise their own cruel forms of justice in the king's absence. Simon had grown more and more aware of the suffering of the common folk who were starved into submission and crippled by extortionate fines and taxes. He remained determined to do something to help them and so he began organising the trio of outlaws into a band of robbers, joining them along with John and occasionally Thomas the miller, making them a band of six.

They would lie in wait by the side of the road that led south from Sheffield through the Chase towards Sherwood Forest and plunder the traffic that made its way to and from Nottingham, robbing merchants, clerics and knights. They even headed east and preyed upon England's other great artery; the Great North Road which led from London to York and offered even greater prizes. Few dared offer any opposition to six hooded thieves armed with bows and the wealth they gathered was more than any of them had ever dreamt of seeing in their lifetimes.

But coin and jewellery were of little use to men who had made their homes in the greenwood and Simon had other plans for it besides. They began distributing the wealth among the poor denizens of the Chase, still dressed in their hooded disguises and, although the people began to fear the reports of increased banditry on the nearby roads, they also began to speak of hooded angels who rode from hamlet to village distributing alms for the poor. They had to be careful about what they distributed of course; it wouldn't do for the poor to draw attention to themselves by suddenly coming into possession of silver and finery so Simon had taken to selling the more valuable pieces and buying up sack loads of food, grain, clothes, blankets and other household items and distributed those instead.

He found it exhilarating. All his life he had been bored, lazy and sheltered. Now he felt as if he had a purpose. The danger and the thrill of the hunt played its part too and all too often he retired to his bed late, exhausted and more often than not sporting bruises, black eyes and other injuries from rough encounters on the road. His family despaired of their wayward member who, they assumed, did nothing but drink, whore and fight his nights away over at the Cross and Cup. Little did they know the real reason, and Simon was keen to keep it that way.

It was John who learnt of the visit of Prior Aymer to Sheffield Castle. He heard it from one of the castle laundresses whom he was still on speaking terms with, and she told him when the prior was expected to return to Jorvaulx Abbey. Now the outlaws waited a little distance from the road, screened by the foliage before it petered out into the fields south of Barnsley.

Their horses nickered impatiently and the cold was sinking into their very bones for they had been there a good hour already. Simon had provided the gang with horses and they had built a small stable at Harthill Walk to house and feed them. Mounts ensured a much faster getaway as well as giving them an edge if it came to combat. Most of their marks were mounted so it made sense to face them on an equal footing.

William came running towards them from the direction of the road where Simon had told him to keep a lookout.

"The prior is on his way!" he gasped, as he scrambled up into his saddle.

"Good," said Simon. "How many does he have?"

"Two lay brothers and six men in mail with shields on their backs. I couldn't see the sigil."

"Malvoisin's men, no doubt," said Simon. "On loan to see the fat prior safely home. Six, you say? This will be a tough one, lads. We can't afford to make any mistakes. William, I want you and John covering us from the treeline but make sure you're visible. We need to show this lot we're not messing around. The rest of you, stick close to me and have your blades ready. They'll fight back, you can be sure of that."

He could not see the nervous expressions of his men beneath their black masks but he knew they were there. They didn't often attack armed posses of men. Of the six of them, Simon was the only one with any training in sword work. He had given them some pointers but they were still simple commoners, not soldiers.

"Don't worry about the armed escort," he told them in an effort to raise their spirits. "I know a man who'll pay well for six blades and coats of mail. Now, come on, let's give that prior a warm welcome and pray that his purse is as fat as he is."

They emerged from the woods a few yards ahead of the prior and his retinue who reined in their mounts in surprise. The men-at-arms immediately knew something was up and drew their swords, pushing the holy men on their mules aside as they forced their way to the front. Simon and his men broke into a gallop and charged the small group with their swords raised high.

Two arrows sailed out of the trees to the side of the road. One struck the foremost man-at-arms in the side and the other embedded itself in the shield of another. Malvoisin's men spotted the mounted bowmen and their attention was drawn from Simon's party just for a split second.

It was all the time Simon needed to turn the battle to his favour. As they slammed into the distracted soldiers, their leader was still reeling in his saddle, clutching the feathered shaft that protruded from his side.

Simon grunted as his blade clanged against the helm of one of the soldiers and quickly brought it down to parry the man's own thrust. As the blade slithered against his own, the man slammed the boss of his shield into Simon's chest, pushing him backwards. Caught off guard, Simon gasped in pain as the man's blade raked against his shoulder, cutting deep and he instantly felt a warm gush of blood.

Ignoring the urge to clutch his wounded shoulder, Simon raised his blade to counter his opponent's inevitable follow up. It never came for, suddenly, the man-at-arms was leaning back in his saddle, his face a grimace of pain, an arrow jammed into his throat.

"You're finished!" Thomas the miller cried. "Throw down your weapons!"

Simon turned and could see that it was true. The day was theirs. Two of Malvoisin's men were pierced by arrows and a third had been knocked from his saddle and was lying in the mud cradling an arm that looked to be broken. The remaining three looked around nervously, seeing that they were outnumbered and fearful at being struck down by one of the bowmen. The three holy men cowered to the side of the road, their faces pale.

"Alright, hand over your blades," said Simon, sheathing his own and clamping his hand over the gash in his shoulder. "And start stripping those hauberks off."

He rode over to the prior and his attendants. "Morning, Prior. Hand over your purse."

"Is there no decency left in England?" said Prior Aymer. "That a holy servant of God is robbed by brutes on his way to his abbey?"

"Apparently not, else I'd have no need to rob you," said Simon. "But a little of your vast wealth will go some way in helping those you and your brother leeches have sucked dry."

"I and my brothers?" the prior asked in astonishment. "What blame do we have that warrants your thievery?"

"Come now, Prior. You know as well as I do that the Cistercians are as bad as the Jews when it comes to squeezing coin out of folk."

"You blaspheme when you compare my order to those dogs of unbelievers!"

"I'm not going to discuss theology with you all morning, Prior. Hand over your purse and we'll be on our way."

With a snarl, Prior Aymer untied his bulging purse and handed it over.

"And those rings on your fingers while you're about it."

"The habit off my back too, no doubt! By the rood but you are a godless rogue!"

"But a charitable one. I'll not leave you to freeze on the road. Your habit you can keep, though it is of finer stuff than the clothes of those who till your lands. I'll see to it that your donation keeps them warm this winter."

"Ha! You pretend that you rob me in the name of charity? You must think I'm a fool if you expect me to believe that the coin in my purse will find its way into the hands of the poor instead of being squandered on sinful pleasures at the nearest tavern."

"Shows how little you know," said Simon. "And I don't much care what you believe anyway."

"Who are you?" the prior demanded, grinding his teeth in frustration as he plucked the rings off his fingers and handed them over. "By your speech you are a high-born man."

Simon winked at the prior and then gave him the name he had given others who had questioned his identity in the past. "I am Hob of Locksley."

By the time they left the party on the road, the soldier with the arrow in his throat had died. That pained Simon for he did not take pleasure in the deaths of those who stood against them, especially when they were employed men just doing their job. Malvoisin may be kin of the devil himself but his soldiers were probably just local lads from Sheffield and he hated to think that some poor widow and her babes would now mourn a man slain by their hands.

"Who was it who skewered that fellow in the throat?" he asked his band, as they rode back to Harthill Walk.

"Who was it who saved your life, you mean?" asked John. "That would be me."

"Thank you," said Simon. "It's true, you did save my life. And I'm sorry it was you. That fellow could have been one of your old comrades from Sheffield's garrison."

John shrugged. "It was him or you. How would I explain your death to your father? Besides, few of my old comrades stayed on at Sheffield after Malvoisin took over. He mostly filled the garrison with men from his other estates."

As soon as they got back to camp John took a look at Simon's shoulder. It was a deep cut but a clean one and Simon sat and patiently winced as John sewed it up with catgut. Once they had shared out the loot and eaten a meal, it was nearly time for Simon, John and Thomas to ride back to Stannington. Simon always hated to leave Will and the other lads. It was ironic that he was the one with a life of luxury to return to while they had nothing but the forest and yet he was the one who would have swapped his life with any of them in a heartbeat. It was in the greenwood that he felt free; properly free for perhaps the first time in his life. Here he wasn't a nobleman's son. Here he was an equal among thieves and outlaws and he relished it.

On the ride back, John gave Simon a hard time for his recklessness. It had become a common theme between the two of them. John valued his master so highly (or feared his father's wrath should anything happen to his youngest son) that he had taken on something of a mother figure in Simon's mind. He regularly joked that John's true calling was that of a wetnurse but today John was in no mood for joking.

"I could see right from the start that you were going to get too close," John said. "The way you charged them was like a knight charging into battle."

"Well? It was a battle, wasn't it?"

"It needn't have been. We have bows. We could have made them throw down their weapons at a distance."

"Aye, and lose the element of surprise. It's surely best to rush them head on before they have a chance to think."

"Best for the robbery or best for you?"

"What do you mean?"

"I mean, you seem to enjoy the violence a tad too much. The rest of the lads just want to make off with the loot as quickly and as quietly as possible whereas you always turn the thing into a pitched battle."

"Come on, John! Surely you're not turning craven?"

"I'm no craven, but I'm no fool either."

"And I am?"

They had stopped riding now and faced each other. Thomas hung back, looking uncertain at this sudden tension between his two comrades.

"I don't think you're a fool, master," said John, remembering his place now that they were closer to Stannington than to Harthill Walk. "I just think you're in this for the fun of it while William, Ralph and Ulrich have little choice but to rob folk."

"How dare you?" Simon snapped. "It was I who organised this band into a gang of thieves and I did it for the benefit of those in the Chase, those like Thomas here or the scores of others we have helped who have no employment and empty bellies."

"Noble intentions, I'm sure," said John. "I just wonder how much of it is an excuse for a nobleman to play the hedge robber, knowing full well that as soon as he rides back into Stannington, he can take off his green mantle and put on his fine robes."

"Still you doubt me, John," said Simon, gritting his teeth. "You of all people. I thought I could count on your faith but you're just like my family. And just like them, you sorely underestimate me!"

He kicked his horse into a gallop and rode back to Stannington alone, his rage burning.

Simon had still not cooled down three days later when he and his family rode to Sheffield to dine with Philip de Malvoisin and the occasion did little to improve his mood. His father was still trying to curry favour with Malvoisin in the hopes of marrying Robert to the Lovetot heiress but, with the king still gone, it was a long and slow business. Word had it that Malvoisin was entertaining a similar proposal from the

Furnival family whose patriarch was currently with the king in Outremer, and Simon's father was desperate to put on a good show.

Simon loathed to be part of this charade, made to dress in his finest clothes and be on his best behaviour like a performing dog. But he found there was a single bright spark to be had in an evening at Sheffield Castle. If there was one thing that had occupied his mind in the past few weeks other than the robbery of Prior Aymer, then it was Rowena of Rotherwood. Ever since they had unexpectedly encountered her on her way to Copmanhurst that misty autumn afternoon, he had been captivated by the thought of her. Previously he had considered her nothing more than another spoiled nobleman's daughter, albeit an orphaned one. She was very beautiful of course, even though he tended to prefer coarser fare that didn't put on quite so many airs, but when he had opened those saddlebags and saw that her claim to be feeding the poor was no lie, he saw her in a whole new light.

He was not the only one, it seemed, who was doing good deeds in Locksley Chase, nor indeed, was he the only thief. The dangers she had to be risking were immense! How did a mere lady-in-waiting go about pilfering stores from Sheffield Castle and distributing them among the poor without detection? Did she have help or was she acting alone? And what of her mistress, the young Maud de Lovetot? Did she know? Whatever Rowena of Rotherwood was getting up to at Sheffield Castle, Simon decided, it was something very different to what she had been sent to do and he was keen to find out more.

He only caught a glimpse of Rowena as she accompanied Maud down to dinner before retreating into the shadows. Not for the first time he was struck by how beautiful she was. For a moment, Simon amused himself with an attractive fantasy in which he revealed his secret to Rowena and they joined forces in the pursuit of a common goal. Many powerful and wealthy people passed through Sheffield Castle and Rowena would know about all of them in advance. If she could pass knowledge to him and his gang, then they could rob every prior, knight and bishop who visited Sheffield. It was a pleasant thought, but an idle one and Simon pushed it from his mind as Maud was seated and the dining commenced. Rowena and the other lady-in-waiting, the older one with the sour face, stood by, ready to attend to their lady should they be required.

The meal was a tiresome affair in which Simon's father grovelled and flattered his way through the various courses while Robert did his best to appear dignified, suave and every bit the desirable suitor. Lady Malvoisin and Simon's mother made polite conversation while Malvoisin himself looked as bored by the proceedings as Simon was.

At last, when the eating was done and the tables were cleared and pushed up against the walls, there was dancing and Maud coyly accepted Robert's hand as the feasters formed up to begin the first carole. Simon, pleased to see that Maud's ladies-in-waiting were to join in too, made a beeline for Rowena but found himself thwarted by his father who got to her first. Instead, he was forced to take the hand of the colder, sterner one and, before he could object, the musicians struck up the tune and the carole was off.

The wound in Simon's shoulder, despite John's attention, was still fragile and the tugging and jerking of the dance pulled at the stitches and made Simon grimace in pain. The lady-in-waiting – whose name he learned was Constance – began to give him funny looks and he did his best to hide his agony. Before long, he felt a damp patch growing on his shoulder and knew that the wound had opened and had begun to bleed.

He excused himself from the next dance and rearranged his cloak to cover the patch of blood on his tunic, willing his wound to stop bleeding. He retrieved his wine cup and drained it, holding it out to be refilled by one of the serving lads. He was drunk, bored and fed up with the whole evening but, as his eyes scanned the hall, he spotted Rowena back in her spot by the candelabra. She had apparently made her own excuses not to partake and was watching the dance.

He sidled up to her, amused by the whole situation. She had no idea that he was the one who had robbed her earlier that month. She glanced at him as he approached and her face curled into one of distaste.

"How goes castle life?" he asked her. "Somewhat different to Rotherwood Hall, I'd imagine."

"Bigger," she said. "And they speak French here. But apart from that, a Norman castle isn't so different to a Saxon hall."

"Still, you must miss Rotherwood. It's been, what, a year?"

"To the month," Rowena replied.

"Any idea how long you'll be here?"

"Until my lady Maud is married, at least. And that won't happen until the king returns."

"Ah, yes. The ever hoped for return of the king. It has become such a prophesised event that I'm beginning to wonder if we ever had a king at all."

"We do and he will return," said Rowena, a hint of determination in her voice. "And when he does, many things will be put to rights in England."

Simon glanced at her. "Yes, the blame for a lot of England's woes is placed on King Richard's absence. Famine, oppression, corruption of the courts. It's almost as if people think such things did not exist before he left for Outremer."

"You seem to feel that the blame for such things should be placed elsewhere."

"Perhaps. Whose fault do you think it is?"

Rowena thought for a moment. "It is true that people have suffered before, but surely you can see that things have worsened in the king's absence? Certain lords have taken advantage and are fighting to increase their power in case Richard doesn't return and we find ourselves with his brother as our king."

Simon glanced around the hall, impressed by Rowena's audacity. They were speaking English but it was still possible that one of Malvoisin's lackeys would overhear them and notice the implied criticism of her employer.

"All things wait upon the king's return," he said slowly. "Maud's marriage. Your employment here at the castle. And the welfare of the poor. If only people were willing to step in to help them until his return."

"People do, but the poor are many and Christian charity is in short supply these days."

"Nevertheless, there are some kind souls who redistribute the wealth of the rich for the good of the poor. Or so I have heard."

Her eyes widened as she turned to look at him and he knew he had made her nervous. *She suspects that I know.* But there was little she could do about it without incriminating herself further. Simon decided to push a little bit more.

"It's dangerous for such people to work alone, especially when they live under the very noses of those who are the cause of the poor's oppression. Better to work in tandem with someone of a like mind. Favours for favours, that sort of thing."

He winked at her, drained his cup of wine and placed it on a nearby table. "Do you know, I feel like dancing?" He held out his hand. "Come, let us join the fun."

She glared at him, her face suddenly thunderous. "I don't know what you think you know about me but I will not be threatened or bullied. Tell what you want about me to whom you like but if it's a dance you want and a chance to put your lecherous paws on my body then you can whistle that tune at somebody else."

Simon was taken aback by the venom in her words. He had only been having a bit of fun with her but she seemed to possess a thorough dislike of him that he couldn't account for.

"Lecherous paws?" he said, affecting a hurt expression. "You do me a disservice, my lady. I am no letch."

"No? Well let me inform you that you are not the only one who knows a few secrets. Do you remember Gunhild?"

Simon blinked as he tried to recall the name.

"No, I suppose you don't. She was just another pretty face out of many I am sure. Well, let me remind you. She was the serving girl at Rotherwood Hall whom you pawed and leered at all evening the last time you and your family visited us."

Simon cast his mind back. *Gunhild? Ah yes, that Gunhild …*

"Would it interest you to know that Cedric had her thrown out of Rotherwood Hall for an unvirtuous harlot? And he did not know the worst of it for I kept that from him. I saw you that night, having your way with her, your breeches around your ankles."

Simon felt himself flush. This conversation was not going at all to plan. Was the girl lying about having seen them? But no, it had happened exactly as she said.

"Well, what of it?" he snapped, feeling defensive. "I'd say your guardian's estimate of Gunhild was accurate for she hardly beat off my advances."

"What serving girl would when a nobleman's son takes a fancy to her?" Rowena countered. "She'd be damned for her haughtiness if she spurned your advances, no doubt, and damned for a slut if she didn't. And now you seek to make me one of your whores by threatening me. Well, this maiden *will* stand up to you."

"You mistake me, Rowena," Simon said, aware that the girl's outburst had caught the attention of his father who was moving hastily towards them, his face crimson. "My aim was not to threaten you and my request of a dance was just that; a request to dance. My real reason in talking with you was to offer an alliance."

"An alliance? What are you babbling about?"

He reached into his tunic and seized the ring that hung around his neck by a cord. He had kept it since that day on the road to Copmanhurst as a keepsake, hoping for some chance to return it to her somehow. He tugged on it and the cord snapped. He handed the ring to her.

She gazed at the ring, her eyes wide as sudden understanding dawned. "My ring!" she gasped.

"It was only taken as a test," he said.

"A test?"

"Aye, a test of your sincerity. And you passed."

"My son is not bothering you, I hope, Rowena?" Geoffrey of Stannington said, planting a hearty, but heavy, hand on Simon's wounded shoulder which nearly made him buckle in agony.

"Not at all," Rowena said but her face was pale and she did a poor job at not appearing flustered.

"Well, we should say our farewells to our host," Simon's father said, pulling him away. "We must prepare to ride back to Stannington. Good evening, Lady Rowena."

As Simon's father led him over to where his mother and brothers were waiting, he hissed into Simon's ear. "Just as I feel we are making progress with Malvoisin, you start upsetting things."

"Upsetting things? Father, I …"

"I won't have you ruin Robert's chances with your lecherous carryings on. And with Rowena of Rotherwood too! You know she's the ward of my friend Cedric. He'd have both our hides for hearth rugs if he found out she'd been seduced by you!"

"I don't think it at all likely that Rowena of Rotherwood would be seduced by me …"

"Well, I'm glad she has some sense at least. Although not for want of trying on your part, I'm sure. You are to stay away from her, and any other female in Sheffield Castle, do you hear!"

Simon said nothing. The evening hadn't been a total loss after all and, despite his father's wishes, he was pretty sure he'd be having further dealings with Rowena of Rotherwood.

CHAPTER XI

Gorizia, December 1192

The heat. The stench of blood and opened bowels. The buzzing of the flies. Wilfred knew he was back on the plains of Tell al-Ayyadiyya.

The nightmares didn't get any better. They didn't get any worse, but they weren't going away either. He relived his participation in the slaughter over and over, night after night. Time slowed to a trickle as he raised his sword and brought it down on the skull of the man he had slain that day. The face of the man always eluded him and he wasn't sure he ever saw it before the edge of his blade had crunched into bone and drenched its features with blood.

He didn't want to see it and always tried to avert his eyes but, every time, he found himself trying to catch a glimpse of the face of the man he was butchering.

Except this time, he did see the face.

It was not a man's face, but a woman's and a beautiful one at that. Her mouth gaped open in horror and agony as his sword bit deep. Her eyes were wide and livid in the mask of gore as the blood ran down her forehead and he cried out her name in anguish at what he had done.

"Rowena!"

He awoke in a sweat and knew that he was wrong. The nightmares *did* get worse. The dead were finding new ways to taunt him and now they had found his Achilles heel. Wilfred felt that every day that passed carried him farther and farther from Rowena and his salvation as if he were flotsam on the tide.

All around him was blackness and, as the sweat rapidly cooled on his skin, he remembered that he was no longer in Outremer.

The mountains that surrounded Gorizia were capped with snow and the wind that whistled between the cob-plastered buildings was bitterly chill. It was hard to believe that less than a month ago, Wilfred had been in Acre which, although considerably cooler in winter than the baking heat of high summer, was an oven compared to this north-eastern Italian town at the foot of the Alps.

It was only when Wilfred heard the bells chiming for the third mass of the day as he had entered Gorizia that he realised he had arrived on Christmas Day. It had been a gruelling journey and, after a month of travelling, he was half-starved, his face thickly bearded and his skin wind-chapped and raw.

It had taken him almost two weeks to recover from the savage beating Brian de Bois-Guilbert's Saracens had inflicted upon him and a further two to procure passage for himself and Jago on a ship heading west. Men were departing Outremer in droves and the price of passage was high, exacerbated by the lateness of the season. Few captains wanted to brave the coastal routes when the going promised to be so rough.

Wilfred had to let Leonard go and that had been hard. During their months together, the Pisan squire had become more than a servant. Wilfred counted him as a friend and he paid him handsomely upon their parting. His supply of coin was short but such was his gratitude that he wanted to make sure Leonard would be all right in the days to come.

"Are you sure you won't come with me?" Wilfred had asked him. "I'll pay for your passage. You can continue to serve me until we reach Pisa and then we can part ways there. You must miss your homeland."

"I do, master, and I thank you for your kindness. But we Pisans, great seafarers though we are, are not so foolhardy as to voyage in winter. I will remain here in Outremer and return home in the spring. There are still a few knights who need a squire. I will be all right."

"You are perhaps a wiser man than I, Leonard," said Wilfred. "But I must brave the storms, you see. It is urgent that I find the king and warn him of the Templar plot against him."

Wilfred had to sell his helm and armour in order to pay for the trip, although he had kept the fine sword King Richard had given him. He could not bring himself to part with that, even if it meant going hungry on the long voyage.

He *had* to catch up with the king and warn him that he was headed into danger. Richard would still not have reached England but he would probably have landed in Marseille by now and who knew what had been waiting for him there? Perhaps he had fallen into the hands of King Philip who, it was now well-known, was plotting with the king's brother to steal his territories in England and Normandy. Wilfred was determined to find the king and stand by his side, even if it meant wandering into the same trap. Besides, the king had entrusted him with his piece of the true cross. He knew now that the king had been right to worry for the fate of the holy relic and Wilfred was duty-bound to return it to him once the king was out of danger.

It was late November by the time he found a buss heading to Sicily. It was when they had put in at Corfu for water and supplies that Wilfred learned that the king's journey had gone badly wrong. The king had apparently got as far as Sicily where he was warned by King Tancred that King Philip's agents were waiting to capture him as soon as he came ashore at the port of Marseille. It was just as Wilfred had feared. There were few other safe havens in the Mediterranean open to the king. Barcelona was out of the question as it was part of the combined kingdom of Aragon and Catalonia and therefore the enemy of Queen Berengaria's homeland of Navarre. The island of Majorca was in Saracen hands and home to fleets of corsairs who would like nothing better than to capture the famed Lionheart. Genoa was against Richard too, having allied themselves with King Philip. Even Pisa was dangerous despite the Pisans having previously supported Richard, for they had recently thrown in their lot with the Holy Roman Emperor. The entire Mediterranean, it seemed, was against him. There had been no other option open to the king but to return to Corfu and that is exactly what he had done.

One possible route home had presented itself; north to Hungary which was ruled by King Bela who was a friend to Richard's family. From there he could cross into Saxony which was ruled by Richard's brother-in-law, Henry the Lion. Crossing the belly of Europe with no maps and not speaking the local languages was incredibly ambitious and the people of Corfu thought the King of England a fool for sailing up the Adriatic in December but they did not know Richard the way Wilfred did. It may have bordered on suicidal but it was the only way home.

Finding another captain foolhardy enough to take Wilfred up the Adriatic in King Richard's wake was not easy and he was frustrated to lose several days in Corfu bargaining with captains. He eventually found one who would take him as far as Ragusa and no further. The *Bora*, the captain explained, using the local term for the fierce Adriatic wind, was too strong this time of year and even navigating the islands off the Dalmatian coast was a risky business.

Nevertheless, they made it safely and at Ragusa, Wilfred heard a tale of a group of pilgrims who had been shipwrecked on the island of Lokrum that lay at the entrance to Ragusa's harbour. There, they had been taken in by the small Benedictine priory and one of the pilgrims had sworn to spend 100,000 ducats to build a new church on the island as thanks.

Such a lavish offer had become legend in the short time since it had occurred and all Ragusa was talking of it. Wilfred took heart in the tale for in it he recognised the reckless spending and quick oaths of his king and knew he was on the right track.

Wilfred knew he would find no captain to take him further up the Adriatic so he saddled up Jago and followed the coastal road north. He guessed the king would have landed at Zadar, a Hungarian port from which he could travel through King Bela's lands to Saxony. As he had done at Ragusa, Wilfred found evidence of the king's passage and again, he had met with misfortune.

The fearsome Bora had swept the king's ship out into the middle of the sea and, from what the locals had heard, he had again been shipwrecked somewhere in the marshy, bandit-infested region of Aquileia. He had overshot the borders of Hungary and was now dangerously in lands that owed allegiance to the Holy Roman Emperor. The only reason the locals knew this was because word had reached them of the King of England's presence at the town of Gorizia to the north-east. Richard, it seemed, was still pushing on for Hungary and Wilfred was alarmed that everybody else seemed to know it.

He pushed Jago as hard as he dared, lamenting the brutality such a fine warhorse had been put through the past few weeks. He reached Gorizia to find the ghost of his quarry who, evidently, had moved on yet again.

Language was a constant problem for Wilfred. Although his French was more than good enough, there were few along the Adriatic coast who spoke it. Latin was a possibility for there was no shortage of churchmen, but his was poor. It was Leonard who came to his rescue, despite being hundreds of miles away, for during their time together in Outremer Wilfred had picked up a smattering of his squire's tongue.

Gorizia was a meeting point between Italian, German and Slovenian cultures and the languages that rang in its cobbled streets reflected this. Wilfred was able to pick out the Venetian traders and had struck up conversation with one the previous night. Everybody knew the King of England had been here, the Venetian explained, for he had made his presence known to Count Engelbert up at the castle.

Wilfred couldn't believe Richard had been so foolish as to reveal his identity to a minion of Emperor Heinrich when the safety of Hungary lay many miles to the east. He had to find out what had happened. The Venetian knew a guard from the castle and promised Wilfred that he would bring him to the local tavern that morning and act as translator.

Wilfred used some of his dwindling supply of coins to purchase a meagre breakfast of dark bread, boiled beans and weak ale while he waited for the Venetian and the guard. They arrived as he was sopping up the last of the beans with his crust. To show his gratitude, he ordered ale for the pair of them and eagerly listened while the Venetian translated the guard's story.

A merchant by the name of Hugo and his servants had arrived in Gorizia in early December. They were foreign to these parts and had sent one of their number up to the castle to ask Count Englebert if they could purchase a guide from him that would take them through the mountains to the north-east and into Hungary. Payment was offered in the form of a large ruby ring.

Wilfred clutched his forehead with his hand. Richard's generosity would be his downfall one day, he was sure of it. Whoever heard of a simple merchant with such wealth?

Count Englebert certainly hadn't and made his suspicions known; this 'Hugo' could be none other than the King of England whom, it was said, was travelling through these parts, and he had been ordered to seize by Emperor Heinrich.

"And was he seized?" Wilfred asked the Venetian, dreading the guard's answer.

"No," replied the Venetian, once the guard had spoken. "Count Engelbert is a pious fellow and feared God's wrath should he arrest a returning crusader. But neither could he accept the ring, for it would be seen as a bribe. He sent the servant with the ring back to Hugo – or King Richard, rather."

"Then what?"

The Venetian shrugged. "Your king and his friends left Gorizia."

"In which direction? Surely they would not attempt to cross the mountains at this time of year without a guide?"

"It is not known. They left quickly and quietly."

Wilfred thanked the Venetian and the guard and left the inn to consider his next move. The Holy Roman Emperor had issued orders for King Richard's arrest. That boded ill. As Wilfred gazed north-eastwards he realised, as the king and his party had surely done, that Hungary would now be too dangerous to attempt. The only other route to Saxony was through Bohemia whose ruler, Duke Ottakar, was currently at odds with the emperor.

Crossing the central Alps in December with its avalanches and deep snow drifts would have been madness even for a hopeless optimist like Richard. They would have tried to skirt its eastern range and pass through the basin that separated the Alps and the Carpathians. But this would bring them perilously close to Vienna whose ruler, Duke Leopold, was a vassal of Emperor Heinrich and had surely not forgotten the incident in Acre where Richard's men had torn down his banner and cast it into the moat.

Wilfred made some further enquires and learnt of a long valley that led eastwards through the Alps and emerged in Austria. It was accessible north of the village of Udine which he had passed on his way to Gorizia. He made his way back west and spent the evening asking around. While the residents of Gorizia had merely suspected that the King of England had been in their midst, the locals of Udine were well aware that he had passed through their town as he had narrowly avoided arrest. There had been a street battle it seemed, in which eight of King Richard's knights had been captured. Wilfred was alarmed to hear this and struggled along in broken Latin until he was satisfied that the king had once again escaped.

There were a myriad mountain passes north of Udine known only to locals but the surest road north was the old Via Julia Augusta; a Roman highway of cracked stone. Wilfred spent the night in the stables of one of Udine's inns and set out the following morning.

As he followed the road north, he passed the town of Venzone and made his usual discreet enquiries, though they knew nothing but what they had heard from Udine; that the King of England had escaped by the skin of his teeth and vanished into the mountains.

The road led to the Pontebba Pass which crossed the deep valley that led eastwards through the Alps. As Wilfred descended, he entered a country of glacier-gouged gorges and dense pine forests that grew thick and dark on all sides. At night, the thunder rolled through the blackness like the anger of forgotten gods.

He encountered few people as he followed the frozen river east but there was a night's lodging to be had at a monastery. There, the good monks confirmed that a party of Templar knights had passed by earlier that month. Wilfred didn't know how to feel about this news. Templars could mean one of two things. From what he had heard in Gorizia, Richard was attempting to travel in disguise. Perhaps he had traded Hugo the merchant for a Templar knight? On the other hand, Wilfred knew he was not the only one seeking Richard out. He had heard nothing of Brian de Bois-Guilbert since leaving Acre but he did not doubt for one second that the Templar was not still involved in some plot to find King Richard and bring him to calamity.

At last, the walls of the valley sank down into the Vienna Basin and the town of Villach could be seen up ahead. Wilfred followed the northern shore of the Ossiacher Sea and imposed himself on the hospitality of the Benedictine brothers at the Gerlitzen monastery before continuing on to Feldkirchen and St Veit. Nobody could tell him anything that matched the story of a foreign king and his retinue passing through and Wilfred began to worry that he had lost his quarry in these wooded valleys. But then, the king had probably skirted these towns in the interest of keeping a low profile. Wilfred set his jaw as he rode on, the hopelessness of the situation gradually dawning on him. If King Richard had been successful in keeping his passage through these lands a secret, then what chance did he have of finding him?

The town of Friesach was a cultural melting pot, a boom town founded on a silver mine and the babble of different languages was a welcome change to the quiet, monolingual villages and hamlets Wilfred had recently passed through. Here somebody had to know something, surely?

He used up yet more of his precious coins on food and lodging for himself and Jago for one night. His rumbling belly wouldn't let him keep his purse closed. While drinking ale in the low-ceilinged common room, warming his aching bones by the hearth, he was able to strike up conversation with an elderly local who spoke good French.

"King Richard whom they call the Lionheart?" the old man said when Wilfred commented on the possibility that the king had recently passed through this country.

"Yes."

"Why, he has been captured."

Wilfred seized the man by the hem of his sleeve. "Captured? By whom? Duke Leopold?"

"Where have you been? All Europe surely knows this by now."

Wilfred ground his teeth. Perhaps all Europe did by now, except the monasteries and small towns in those deep valleys he had passed through. "Where is King Richard now?"

"Nobody knows. He'll be spending Christmas as a guest of the duke in some castle I should think. Or perhaps he has been handed over to the Holy Roman Emperor already."

"How was he captured? Was there much bloodshed?"

"The duke was waiting for Richard to turn up in his territory and had sent one of his barons here to Friesach to seize him upon arrival. But your king is a canny one. He snuck out of town by using a diversion. One of his men remained and spent money lavishly, drawing attention to himself. The duke's man arrested him while your king slipped away in the night. But he didn't get far. He was captured by the duke in a squalid little village on Vienna's outskirts."

"When was this?" Wilfred asked.

"Not ten days ago."

Wilfred shared in his king's frustration. Vienna was less than fifty miles from the safety of Moravia, the territory of King Ottokar's brother. *He almost made it.*

Wilfred drank the rest of his ale bitterly. The trail had gone cold and, although everybody seemed to know that the King of England had been captured, nobody knew where he was now. He tried to put himself in the mind of Duke Leopold. What would that bastard do with a caged lion? It was probably too dangerous to keep him in Vienna but somebody there must know something. He was close, he knew it.

He drained his mug and rose from the table to prepare for bed.

The following morning he pushed on across the plains towards Vienna. It took him five days to reach the city's outskirts. He crossed the river at the ferry point and found himself in a city almost entirely built of wood with no proper defensive walls, despite its vibrant marketplace where Russian merchants traded amber for alpine salt and rich fabrics from Flanders. If Richard had been arrested here, then he would certainly have been taken to a more secure location almost immediately.

Wilfred stabled Jago and then began doing the rounds of the taverns, desperately seeking information as to where the King of England was currently being held prisoner. He threw caution to the wind now, keener to find out where the king was than to keep himself out of danger.

It was as he was leaving a tavern the following day that he felt a heavy hand land on his shoulder. He spun around, his own hand reaching for his sword hilt, wary of being robbed. He wasn't quick enough to stop a mailed fist from slamming into his jaw, knocking him backwards.

Two men rushed him, one seizing his arms, the other his sword. He struggled as he was dragged into a muddy alley between the tavern and its neighbouring building. With a heave, his captor threw him to the mud. He rolled and came up ready to fight with his bare hands but a French voice halted him.

"You ask a lot of questions for a wandering pilgrim," one of the men said. "And this sword. How did you come by it?"

"I'm a knight," said Wilfred.

"One who skulks from tavern to tavern seeking the location of England's king? Who is your lord?"

"The very king I seek."

Then the man switched to English which startled Wilfred, for it had been many months since he had heard his native tongue spoken. "You are English?"

"Yes. And so are you."

"Who are you?"

"Wilfred of Ivanhoe."

"And you swear on the Holy Virgin that you do not wish our king ill?"

"I swear it. I have travelled from Outremer alone for I learned of a plot against King Richard. I have suffered much hardship trying to find him."

"What plot is this?"

"A Templar knight by the name of Bois-Guilbert tried to torture me for information concerning the king's passage home. I told him nothing but was unable to warn the king before he departed."

The two men looked at each other. They were both unshaven and dressed in tattered tunics and muddied cloaks.

"Hmm," said the first man. "I've never heard of you, Ivanhoe, but you seem in earnest. You'd better come with us."

"Who are you two?"

"My name is Reginald of Peterborough and this is Guillaume de Loucelles. We serve King Richard."

"Where is the king?" Wilfred demanded.

"Not so fast," said Reginald. "You might be an Englishman, but there are many of our countrymen who wish our king ill. We must be sure of you first."

Wilfred sighed. He supposed that he had no choice but to trust these men before they would trust him. "Can I at least have my sword back? The king himself gave it to me."

Reginald glanced at Guillaume and then shrugged. "Very well. If you run then we'll know you for a liar."

Sheathing his sword, Wilfred followed them to the same stables he had left Jago. Apparently these two men were just passing through Vienna. When they saw Wilfred's destrier Reginald whistled in appreciation.

"That's a fine horse for so shabby a knight."

"I suited him somewhat better in Outremer," said Wilfred. "I had to sell most of my gear to buy passage to Europe." He realised he cut a poor figure of a knight. He had not shaven since leaving Acre and his blonde beard was heavy and shaggy around his wind-chapped face. His cloak was torn and filthy and he was sure he stank to high heaven.

"Where are we going?"

"To Dürnstein," said Reginald. "Some fifty-odd miles to the east."

"What's there?"

"The rest of our party. Guillaume and I went to Vienna for supplies and information. Looks like we found more than that. We'll see what the others make of you."

They rode all day, stopping only to water the horses and eat a little food. Wilfred was glad of his hosts' generosity and gobbled down the bread and cheese they offered him from their own rations. They followed the Danube west, reaching the city of Krems two days later just as night was falling. There, they spent the night and continued on to the small town of Dürnstein the following morning.

Dürnstein was situated on a bend in the raging Danube and its castle loomed over the town like a monolith from its perch atop a rocky hill. Its walls were sheer and impenetrable. The town boasted one inn but it was a large one that had a second floor of rooms overhanging the cobbled street. Reginald and Guillaume nodded a greeting at the innkeeper and Reginald said something to him in German. Then they climbed the stairs to a room overlooking the street.

There were three men in the room and as soon as Wilfred was admitted, he knew at last that he was in good company. The man sitting by the window was a fair youth and Wilfred knew him as Blondel, King Richard's troubadour who had been with them in Outremer.

"Well, well," said a familiar voice from the corner. "Wilfred de Ivanhoe made it out of Acre after all."

"Furnival!" Wilfred said, pleased to see his fellow crusader. It felt like a lifetime since he and Gerard de Furnival had chased the Saracens out of Jaffa's streets together with the king.

"What road brought you here?" Gerard asked.

"A long one. I was on my way to Marseille when I learnt that the king had turned back and headed up the Adriatic. I followed him as far as Ragusa and then continued over land. It took a lot of asking around in Gorizia and Udine and other godforsaken places but I eventually got back onto the king's track. Too late, it seems."

"There was nothing you could have done had you been with him," said Gerard. "All with him were captured. William de l'Etang, Baldwin de Bethune, Philip de Poitou, Robert de Turnham and his chaplain Anselm are all in the emperor's hands now. Not to mention the Templar knights who rode with him. Those who survived the fight at Udine are also under lock and key."

"You show remarkable loyalty, Ivanhoe," said Blondel. "Most knights have returned home by now and would never have traipsed across half of Europe trying to find their king."

"Before the king left Acre I learned of a plot against him," said Wilfred. "Brian de Bois-Guilbert had his Saracen servants beat me to within an inch of my life, hoping that I would tell them when the king was leaving and which route he would be taking. That false Templar and his like-minded brethren were attempting to waylay him, I am sure of it."

"Because they take their orders from King Philip," said Blondel. "He is the one behind the king's capture."

"King Philip? How can you be sure?"

"Because I have just come from the French Christmas court where I was able to procure a copy of a letter from Emperor Heinrich to King Philip detailing King Richard's capture. The language used in the letter suggests that Heinrich ordered Duke Leopold to do this as a favour for Philip."

"How did you gain entrance to the French court?" Wilfred asked. "Did nobody recognise you as King Richard's troubadour?"

"A troubadour owes no special fealty to any one king. We are travellers and welcome at most hearths. Besides, I am a native of Picardy, and was able to blend in well among Philip's lickspittles."

"This letter," Wilfred asked, "do you still have it?"

"I sent it to my employer, the Archbishop of Rouen."

"Walter de Coutances? He's your employer?"

Blondel nodded. "As the king's acting chief justiciar, Coutances has been frantically searching for the king's whereabouts ever since his ship was sighted off the Brindisi coast. When nothing further was heard of him, it was assumed something terrible had befallen him somewhere south of the Alps."

"Coutances has a wide network of spies and informants," Gerard said. "Blondel here is one of his foremost agents. As a troubadour he is welcome just about everywhere. Even Dürnstein Castle."

"That's where the king is currently held," said Reginald of Peterborough, now free to reveal to Wilfred the real reason he and his comrades were at Dürnstein. "Blondel has made contact with him."

"He is alone but unharmed," said Blondel, as Wilfred gazed at him with awe.

"You actually saw him?"

"Not two days ago. I played the part of a wandering troubadour in search of food and warmth. Dürnstein Castle is almost as grim for its garrison as it is for its prisoners and they were glad of song and news from other parts. Richard was there in the Great Hall, dining with his very captor; one of the duke's lackeys called Hadmar of Kuenring. It was all very civil although I could see the situation has taken its toll on our king's considerable pride. We made eye contact across the hall and I know that he recognised me but thankfully refrained from making it known."

"How large is the garrison?" Wilfred asked.

"I know what you're thinking, lad, and you'd best forget it," said Gerard. "We are not here to plan a daring rescue attempt and we'd never manage one even if we were. Those walls are as sheer as the mountainside itself."

"Well what *are* you all doing here?" Wilfred asked, looking around at the men in the room.

"Awaiting orders," said Blondel. "Furnival is right, there is no way we could rescue the king. For now we play the game by Duke Leopold's rules."

"You mean Philip and Heinrich's" said Reginald bitterly.

"Quite. The Archbishop of Rouen has dispatched letters to England. Queen Eleanor and the ruling council must decide on the right course of action. The emperor and the duke will not get away with this. The pope will excommunicate them for sure, but until we receive word, our job is to sit tight and keep an eye on the castle. It is only a matter of time before Duke

Leopold will hand the king over to the emperor and we must be ready to move with him."

"Make yourself comfortable," said Gerard. "We could be here for quite some time."

"And on the matter of comfort," said Blondel, "You could do with a bath, Ivanhoe. The inn has one, fortunately, for you stink to high heaven."

The next three months were a time of industrious activity for the small group of loyalists lodged in an upper chamber of the inn at Dürnstein. Blondel, who proved to be something resembling the group's leader, wrote many letters to the Archbishop of Rouen and received several replies along with financing which was most welcome for their own meagre supply of coin had dwindled rapidly. In February, the archbishop sent warning that his spies at the emperor's court had news suggesting a deal had been reached between Duke Leopold and Emperor Heinrich. A ransom was to be demanded for King Richard's release it seemed, and Duke Leopold wanted his share. An agreement had been drawn up at Wurtzberg and the handover of the prisoner to the emperor's custody seemed imminent.

At the beginning of March an imperial escort arrived at the castle to take Richard to the emperor's court at Speyer. The cell of loyalists frantically packed up their things, settled their debts with the innkeeper and purchased food for the journey west. Speyer was nearly four-hundred miles away and, although they could hardly tag along with the imperial guard,

Blondel, Wilfred and the others were intent on following it closely to ensure their king arrived at his destination safely.

A hundred miles short of Speyer, they stopped at the small town of Ochsenfurt and the king was lodged at a monastery where he would apparently stay until summoned by the emperor. Wilfred and the others struggled to find an inn that was not full of bishops, knights and other German men of rank. It was clear that something important was going on and it later emerged that the Imperial Diet was to convene at Speyer.

They slept in the stables with their horses and spent their days trying to find out what was going on. Blondel wrote more letters and returned one afternoon with a short, stooped man who, although he was dressed in fine traveling clothes, had bowed, misshapen legs and a face that was fascinatingly ugly.

"This is William de Longchamp, the king's appointed chancellor," said Blondel. "He is to seek permission to speak with the king."

Wilfred gaped at the sight of England's exiled chief justiciar in this backwater German town with no escort but a handful of servants. This was the man whose correspondence had kept the king informed of his brother's treacherous designs while he was in Outremer, the man who had been forced to flee England in disguise due to John's consolidation of power. With the king and his chancellor stuck abroad and in such dire straits, Wilfred wondered what exactly was going on in England.

Blondel was able to wangle better accommodation for the chancellor in the form of an actual bed at the inn and the next day the little man hobbled off in the direction of the monastery which admitted him to see the king.

The days passed and all began to wonder why the emperor had dragged King Richard from the security of Dürnstein to this tiny place on the River Main. More visitors came seeking the company of the king, directed through the Archbishop of Rouen's network. Two Cistercian abbots, as well as the bishops of London and Salisbury who were carrying letters from Richard's family in England, arrived and vanished into the grounds of the monastery.

Longchamp occasionally returned to the inn and kept them up to date on the proceedings. At the end of March, he informed them that there was to be movement at last.

"Emperor Heinrich," he said, as he supped at his ale in the common room while Wilfred and the others listened intently, "has decided to put our king on trial before the Imperial Diet."

"Trial?" Gerard exclaimed. "On what charges?"

"In addition to supporting Tancred of Sicily, he is accused of conspiring with Saladin to allow the Muslims to keep Jerusalem and of having Conrad de Montferrat assassinated."

"But that's arrant nonsense!" said Wilfred. "Lies cooked up by the French! Everybody knows King Philip despised Richard for his support of Guy de Lusignan over Conrad de Montferrat."

"Yes, well, King Philip has the ear of Emperor Heinrich and has been feeding him lies from the beginning. There are even vicious rumours going around that Richard is secretly an infidel. If Philip can persuade everybody that our king is anything of the kind then he can make any charge he wants stick."

Richard was moved to the chapterhouse of Speyer's Cathedral and all Ochsenfurt hurried after him. The trial was held at the palace of the Bishop of Speyer in the shadow of the massive red sandstone cathedral. The town, which was barely large enough to warrant such an enormous monument, was swarming with people and Wilfred and his companions could barely find standing room in the square outside the bishop's palace. There was no hope of getting inside but the emperor had permitted Richard to be accompanied by his chancellor and contingent of English bishops and abbots.

The crowd went wild as the king was brought from the cathedral's chapterhouse to the bishop's palace. Many booed and jeered him. Wilfred and his companions made their own voices heard in support of their king although they were utterly drowned out by the Germans who were already convinced of his guilt.

Wilfred was shocked by how different the king looked. He had lost a lot of weight and his posture seemed stooped as if physically bent by the weight of his burdens. They called out to him, hoping he would hear their words of support, but once again, their voices were as whispers in a hurricane and the king did not look their way.

The trial took all day and the sun was setting over the cathedral's vaulted basilica by the time people began to emerge. Wilfred and the others were gnawing away on some boiled sheep's feet Gerard had purchased from a street vendor when they saw one of the English abbots who had been with the king coming their way. His face was like thunder.

"How went the trial?" Gerard asked him in English. "We've a job finding anyone around here who speaks a language we can understand."

"The king put on a triumphant performance," said the abbot. "He refused to kneel at Heinrich's feet and offered a riposte to every charge thrown at him. He nearly swayed the whole room's opinion of him and there are many German nobles that now see through the lies of the French and the vindictiveness of the emperor. They see now that it was really King Philip who abandoned his oath and proved himself a coward, not Richard. I even think Boniface de Montferrat was convinced that Richard didn't hire the Assassins to murder his brother."

"Conrad de Montferrat's *brother* was at the trial?" Wilfred asked. "Heinrich really did everything possible to see that Richard was condemned, didn't he?"

"But was he successful?" Blondel demanded. "What was the court's verdict?"

The abbot shook his head sadly. "Charges were dismissed but alas, even though the mood of the court turned against the emperor somewhat, he still had his day. He has demanded 150,000 silver marks for the king's release. He also wants the king to contribute to his reconquest of Sicily in the form of fifty ships and two-hundred knights."

There was a brief silence as the group of men digested this.

"He can't be serious!" said Gerard.

"I fear that he is," the abbot replied.

Wilfred and the others were stunned. 150,000 marks? It was an unheard-of sum. The frustration in the air was palpable and none felt it more than Wilfred. Once again, God had seen fit to delay his long-awaited return to England just when he felt he had been so close to it. It was hard to see a way past the emperor's mad demands but there was no avoiding the hard truth of the matter. King Richard was going nowhere and, for the present, neither was Wilfred.

CHAPTER XII

Locksley Chase, November 1193

They were wrapped in their warmest cloaks and furs, their breath steaming on the chill air as the men emerged from the forest, triumphant, the servants carrying a slain deer between them. It was Robert's kill, apparently, and Geoffrey of Stannington beamed with pride. Maud sat patiently in her saddle and made all the right noises as Robert rode over to her, basking in the praise.

Rowena knew that Maud hated partaking in this charade as much as she did. To be hunting in Locksley Chase with Malvoisin, who punished others for doing the same with such ferocity, was not a privilege to be relished. In fact, it felt like the very height of hypocrisy to indulge in such freedom one day and then seek to aid the poor who were forbidden to carry a bow in these woods the next. And Rowena knew she and Maud could not be the only ones who resented being made to take part in the hunt.

She glanced sidelong at Simon of Stannington who slouched in his saddle and took swigs from a wineskin between bawdy jokes with the other men and marvelled at how he could seemingly switch between characters as if he were an actor in a street play. It had been a year since he had revealed his secret to her and still she had trouble believing it. That this boorish rogue who drank far too much and was considered a disgrace to his family should be the hooded bandit known only as 'Hob of Locksley', whose name was praised by the poor and vilified by the rich in equal measure, was a hard thing to swallow.

Malvoisin had warmed to the prospect of Robert of Stannington so much so that Rowena felt she might actually be making some progress in her mission. They had begun to see a lot of the Stanningtons, either at Sheffield Castle or at Stannington Hall and that had given Rowena and Simon plenty of opportunities to talk. She fed him information on who was visiting Sheffield Castle and the dates they would be leaving. Simon and his band of robbers would then accost them on the road and redistribute their wealth to those in more need of it. It was a perfect arrangement but she knew she had to be careful. If every one of Malvoisin's friends got robbed on their way home after visiting him, he would certainly start to suspect that somebody inside the castle was leaking information. Besides, Hob of Locksley was finding more than enough targets on his own.

As the servants began the breaking up of the hind and the feeding of the hounds, Simon rode over to Rowena.

"Do you also find yourself lusting after a man who has recently drawn blood?" he murmured to her. "The way my brother carries on, you would think it was a mating dance."

"I prefer a gentler touch," said Rowena.

"Good to remember."

"I heard Hob of Locksley has begun robbing the sheriff's men collecting the tax for the king's ransom."

"Silver is silver," Simon replied, taking another swig from his wineskin. "I don't suppose Hob of Locksley gives much of a damn what it's intended for."

"Perhaps he should. Robbing fat priors and merchants is one thing, but any delay in gathering the ransom means a delay in the king's return."

Word of the extortionate ransom demanded by the Holy Roman Emperor for King Richard's release had been met with astonishment and outrage before the summer. 150,000 marks? That was around thirty-five tons of silver; far more than England raised in a year!

The queen mother had immediately set in motion the raising of the initial 100,000 marks which would be a down payment. There was a new levy on the lands knights held as well as a new tax on revenues and moveable property. Churches and abbeys were asked to hand over all their gold and silver and, in the case of the Cistercians and other monastic orders sworn to poverty, the proceeds from their wool trade. Rich and poor alike were squeezed for their contributions and it was those who had little to begin with that felt the sting the most.

Rowena had seen the silver pouring into the coffers at Sheffield Castle: barrels of silver pennies and chalices and plates melted down into ingots. There the treasure awaited collection by the sheriff who would convey it to London and add it to the massive stockpile in the crypt of St. Paul's Cathedral.

"Still you pine for our neglectful monarch, Rowena," Simon chided. "The poor need the efforts of Locksley more than ever now that every silver penny is being wrung out of this country to secure his release. People starve while the cellars of Sheffield Castle bulge with silver. If Locksley were to learn when the sheriff would be taking Sheffield's portion of the ransom to London, many poor lives could be made a lot happier."

Rowena knew what he was asking of her but she just couldn't do it. "I know it is a hard thing to accept," said Rowena, "but if that 100,000 marks is not raised, then the king will never come home."

"And what is that to the poor? Do you really think they care who sits on the throne? Nothing will change for them once the ransom is paid. Their lives of toil and hardship will continue regardless."

Rowena said nothing. It was not the first time she worried that her hope for the king's return was a selfish one. Over a year since the king had left the Holy Land and still no word from Wilfred! All the evidence suggested that he was dead and yet she would not let herself believe that. If the king had managed to get himself captured on his way home, then perhaps Wilfred had too? Was he sitting in some German dungeon right now? Perhaps he was even with the king, for it was known that several of Richard's followers had also been captured by the emperor. Oh, to wait year after year and not knowing was more than she could bear! No, there was nothing for it; the ransom *had* to be paid. There was no other way. And, despite her wishes to help the poor, she was determined that the silver in Sheffield Castle went to London, not into the hands of Locksley and his band.

Later that week, they were surprised by a visit from the sheriff and a man of some influence who was known to Malvoisin. His name was Waldemar Fitzurse and he was a tall, spry man with a cunning face that put Rowena in mind of a fox. She knew nothing of him but Constance filled her in.

"He is Count John's advisor," she said, and then added in a whisper as if imparting some tasty gossip; "His father was one of the knights who slew the blessed Thomas Becket upon the orders of John's father."

Rowena didn't wonder that a man of such lineage might find accommodation in the company of the king's rebellious brother and disliked Fitzurse even more with this knowledge.

They were joined at dinner by the captain of Malvoisin's routiers, a handsome but intimidating man called Maurice de Bracy. This was the mercenary Malvoisin had hired with the proceeds of selling some of Maud's inheritance to Jorvaulx Abbey. He and his men were regularly at the castle when they weren't fulfilling some shady errand on Malvoisin's orders. The routiers frightened Rowena. They were rough, scarred men who often hung around the courtyard, drinking, dicing and roaring with mirth at their own bawdy brand of humour. The women of the castle steered well clear of them and there was a shared sense of relief whenever they departed.

The meal was dominated by men's talk as Malvoisin, Hugh de Bardulf, de Bracy and Fitzurse discussed the raising of the king's ransom.

"The sheriff and his bailiffs shall transport the silver in person," said Waldemar, "although they shall require an armed escort. These routiers of yours can be loaned to them, I trust?"

"Certainly," said Malvoisin. "Although I would like to keep de Bracy with me for the time being." He turned to the routier captain. "Your lieutenant can handle guarding a caravan, can he not?"

"Louis de Winkelbrand is more than capable of such a task, my lord," answered de Bracy. "How many men shall I send with him?"

"I should think a dozen would suffice," said the sheriff. "I will have six of my own men, including my two bailiffs who are not to be trifled with. We shall be more than a match for any brigands who think to steal the king's ransom."

"Good," said Fitzurse, "And on the matter of your routier captain, Malvoisin, I have a mind to present de Bracy and his men to the count after Christmas as a token of your loyalty to him."

"You would strip me of de Bracy?" Malvoisin said, his face troubled. "He is a fine soldier and was not cheap ..."

"Cheap?" Fitzurse said with a frown. "Do you seek reimbursement for supporting Count John as you have pledged to do? None of this is cheap, Malvoisin, not for any of us. But I must remind you of the rewards to be had once John sits on England's throne.

Those who showed him the deepest loyalty will find their efforts rewarded threefold."

"Of course," said Malvoisin, looking thoroughly chastised as a servant filled up their goblets with more wine. He drank deeply. "The count shall have de Bracy and any other support I can offer him."

As the ladies retired to Maud's bower, Maud spoke under her breath to Rowena; "Don't you find it odd that Count John's advisor is the one making arrangements for conducting the silver from Sheffield to London? Since when has the king's brother been involved in the gathering of the ransom?"

"I agree that it is strange," said Rowena. "And then there was all that talk of reward for loyalty once John sits on England's throne."

"You two had best curb those thoughts," said Constance, overhearing them. "I am sure Fitzurse is just thinking ahead. King Richard's release is far from certain, even if the ransom is paid. These German barbarians don't know the meaning of the word 'honour'. John may have to step in as king if further calamity befalls Richard. And why wouldn't he be involved in gathering the ransom? He is the king's brother, after all."

Rowena and Maud said nothing more on the matter but Rowena knew that Maud was thinking the same thing she was; that the discussion at table that evening had a distinctive whiff of treason to it.

The following morning the cellars were opened and the silver was carried up, barrel by barrel, to the courtyard where it was loaded onto a wain drawn by two oxen. Fitzurse, de Bracy and his lieutenant,

Winklebrand oversaw the operation while Malvoisin and the sheriff attended to other matters in the Great Hall. As Maud and her ladies-in-waiting took the morning air, Maud led them along the palisade and stopped just above the loading of the wain where the voices of Fitzurse and de Bracy drifted up to them.

"The silver is to be conveyed to Nottingham where the sheriff, William de Wendenal, and his men will convey it to the castle," said Fitzurse.

"Nottingham?" asked de Bracy. "Last I heard, it was London that was receiving all silver for the ransom. What's Count John up to?"

"Don't concern yourself with small details," said Fitzurse. "The document I have presented to Malvoisin is sealed by the Count of Mortain on behalf of the Exchequer of Ransom. It is not for mere routiers to question the count's methods."

"I'm sure," said de Bracy with a grin. "As long as I get paid, I don't care where the silver goes."

"Count John will no doubt be thrilled by your loyalty," said Fitzurse sardonically.

Rowena and Maud shared a glance but said nothing until they were back inside. Constance was sent to fetch some spiced wine while they warmed themselves by the kitchen fire.

"None of this feels right," said Rowena in a low voice. "Why would Count John divert the ransom money to one of his own castles?"

"I agree," said Maud. "And how exactly did Count John get hold of the royal seal? I can hardly believe that the ruling council entrusted it to him."

"No," said Rowena. "John's actions while Richard was in the Holy Land have made him thoroughly untrustworthy. I wouldn't put forging the royal seal past him."

"There must be something we can do, somebody we can warn!" Then Maud struck upon an idea. "If we could get word to the queen mother, she'd listen!"

"But how? And what proof could we offer? We'd be telling her that her own son is a thief and a traitor."

"Queen Eleanor thinks little of her youngest son by all accounts. And you said yourself, John has proven to be untrustworthy. Anyway, if we gave her proof, she'd have to believe us!"

"The letter …" said Rowena.

Maud nodded. "Sealed by John himself. If the seal is forged then Eleanor would have to take action. We need to get that letter! Malvoisin's solar will be empty now."

She was halfway out of her chair when Rowena stopped her. "I'll go. It'll arouse less suspicion."

"Very well. But be careful, Rowena!"

She snuck off before Constance got back with the wine and passed through the Great Hall where Malvoisin and the sheriff were still discussing the enforcement of law and order. She made for the stairs and headed up to the solar. Lady Malvoisin was currently staying with a cousin in York so the chamber should be empty. Rowena just hoped there were no servants still about.

The door to the solar was ajar and Rowena pushed it open further with the toe of her shoe. *Good.* The room was empty. A fire burned low in the grate and the servants had made the bed. She slipped in and hurried over to the table which was strewn with documents.

The topmost document was some sort of official letter sealed with a large red disc of wax imprinted with the image of the king on his throne. Around the rim ran the Latin text identifying him as 'Richard, by the grace of God, King of the English'.

Rowena seized the letter and folded it up before hiding down the front of her dress. She made her way over to the door and froze. She could hear Malvoisin's voice in the stairwell! He was on his way up to the solar!

She desperately looked around for somewhere to hide but knew it was hopeless. There was nowhere that would conceal her.

But there was a second voice in the stairwell; a female voice that sounded like Maud's. She was speaking to Malvoisin, distracting him so Rowena might have a chance to escape the solar. *Good, Maud!*

Rowena snuck out of the solar, taking care to leave the door ajar, just as she had found it, and hurried over to the window alcove between the door and the stairwell. She couldn't hear what Maud was saying but apparently her diversion had run its course and Malvoisin's heavy footfalls could be heard on the stairs.

Making sure the hem of her skirt was tucked well behind her, Rowena held her breath as Malvoisin passed the alcove and entered the solar. Breathing a sigh of relief, she silently made her way down the stairwell where Maud was waiting at the entrance to the Great Hall.

"Did you get it?" Maud asked excitedly.

Rowena nodded and patted her chest. "It was a close call but your quick thinking saved me."

"I saw him heading for the stairwell and quickly thought of something to ask him. Well done for being so brave! Now we have the proof of Count John's treachery."

"But how do we get it to Eleanor? We can hardly ride to London ourselves. There has to be someone we can send, a man of letters whose word would be beyond reproach."

They both thought for a moment and then, in simultaneous realisation, spoke a name in unison; "Brother Broch!"

"There you two are!" said Constance, as she approached them. They both jumped for fear that she had overheard their conversation but she didn't show any suspicion. "Come, your wine is getting cold."

The grange at Copmanhurst had come along very nicely in the past year. Brother Broch had borrowed seven lay brothers from Fountains Abbey to help him till the earth and plant seed. By August, after many months of weeding and bird-scaring, they had a crop of barley to harvest. Brother Broch had even constructed several hives of beechwood boards smeared with dung and ash for the keeping of bees.

By early December, the fields were bare and the lay brothers had returned to their abbey. Brother Broch remained at the grange and spent the winter months brewing mead from the October honey. Rowena found him in the small brewery that had been constructed, engulfed in steam from the cauldron in which he was boiling honey and water. The two hounds he had acquired to keep him company during the solitude of winter basked by the heat of the cookfire and raised their great shaggy heads to investigate Rowena as she entered. With a pang of homesickness, she remembered Gurth the swineherd and his latest hound, Fangs, whom she believed came from the same litter as these two.

"Lady Rowena, my dear," said the monk, as he replaced the lid on the cauldron. "I had not thought to see you this side of Christmas. What brings you to Copmanhurst when everyone else is indoors by their hearths?"

"This letter brings me here," she said, removing the sealed document from her dress and handing it to him.

"What's this?" said Brother Broch, as he examined the letter.

"We think that Count John is using a forged copy of the royal seal to divert payments of silver in the name of the Exchequer of Ransom."

"Diverting them into his own coffers, I shouldn't wonder!" said Brother Broch. "Enriching himself while making sure the king remains a prisoner. By Saint Dunstan, the bugger really is trying to steal his brother's throne!"

"This letter needs to reach Queen Eleanor," said Rowena. "It is urgent that she learns of her youngest son's attempt to keep the king a prisoner."

Brother Broch rubbed his chin as he considered the task. "All my lay brothers have returned to Fountains for Christmas," he said. "And I'm not sure I'd trust any of them with such an important task anyway. Not that I doubt their loyalty to our king, certainly not, but it is a long journey to London and few of them have ever left the West Riding. No, I shall have to go myself."

"When will you leave?"

"As soon as I can arrange for one of the lay brothers to remain here and look after the bees," he said. "I will ride to Fountains Abbey tomorrow."

Rowena was pleased. It might take a week or a month for the letter to reach Queen Eleanor but it didn't matter. The silver from the vaults of Sheffield Castle would never reach Nottingham. It had been arranged. Rowena had renounced her previous conviction that the silver would never fall into Locksley's hands and Brother Broch was not the only one her and Maud were calling on for help. The day she had stolen the letter from Malvoisin's solar, Maud had dispatched Rowena on an errand to Stannington Hall.

At the end of the month, Christmas arrived, and so too did the guests which consisted of Malvoisin's usual circle of unsavoury characters. Prior Aymer was there, along with Hugh de Bardulf. They were also joined by Reginald Front-de-Boeuf who frightened Rowena more than all the others combined.

He was a massive man with a great gut that defied his twenty-odd years. His face was broad and scarred for he was a quarrelsome man quick to violence. It was his voice that Rowena found most intimidating, for it was a deep brass horn that regularly uttered oaths foul enough to bring colour to the faces of even the hardiest men.

This unappealing crowd was at odds with the colourful backdrop of the Great Hall bedecked with its festive ornamentations of holly, ivy and bay twigs. The yule log blazed in the hearth and the tables groaned under their bounty of pies, jellies, roasted pheasants, smoked eels and the great boar's head that served as the centrepiece at the head table.

It had been an eventful year and there was much to discuss over the food and wine. Despite Count John's efforts, the king's ransom had finally been raised and, five days ago, Queen Eleanor had set sail for Emperor Heinrich's court with the 100,000 silver marks and sixty-seven political hostages. For most of the country, the sense of relief was palpable. If the queen mother made it to Germany with the payment, then the king would finally be released. An end to the crippling taxes and widespread disorder and corruption was in sight. But the feeling over the heads of those prominent men who dined in the Great Hall of Sheffield Castle that Christmas was not one of relief but of impending doom for their own sins.

Things had not gone to plan for Malvoisin and his circle, even less so for their lord, the Count of Mortain. The silver he had tried to embezzle had been robbed by Hob of Locksley en route to Nottingham and the count's forgery of the royal seal had been revealed by a secret letter to Queen Eleanor. Count John was in disgrace and his position incredibly precarious in light of the king's imminent release.

After the eating was done some travelling mummers put on a play depicting King Herod and the Massacre of the Innocents. Rowena found little to enjoy about such a macabre story and the mood of the men had not been improved much despite the vast quantities of wine they had imbibed. The poor mummers realised they were not particularly welcome and cut a hasty retreat after they had been fed.

Dancing followed and the men let the women down as Malvoisin called de Bracy, Bardulf, Prior Aymer and Front-de-Boeuf to a private counsel in his solar. Evidently there was something urgent he wished to discuss, the importance of which overrode trivial festivities.

"What do you suppose they have to discuss that is so important?" Maud asked Rowena, as they watched the remainder of the men in the hall being mobbed by women who wished to dance.

"I don't know but I can imagine it has something to do with what they are going to say to the king when he returns. They have some plans to make if they are to wriggle out of the trap they've made for themselves. The king may spare his own brother's life but he may not be so lenient with his followers."

"How long do you think they'll hold out once the king has returned? Do you think there'll be an actual rebellion?"

Rowena shrugged. "If they feel they have nothing to lose then perhaps. Count John still holds several castles."

"What do you say we have a listen?" asked Maud. "I'm dying to know how they're planning on explaining themselves. Or, if they are planning on further treachery, we might be able to warn somebody."

Rowena glanced around at the merrymaking in the hall. Few were paying them much attention but Constance was nearby and she would definitely notice if the two of them snuck upstairs together.

"Wait here," said Maud, flashing Rowena one of her mischievous grins.

Rowena watched as she hurried into the crowd as the current carole came to an end and began speaking to a handsome young knight who looked terrified that his lord's ward was speaking to him. A look of relief seemed to wash over him when she pointed over at Constance.

Constance hadn't seen and Maud bustled back to Rowena as the next dance picked up. The young knight made a bee-line for Constance and asked her to dance. Constance flashed a panicked look at Maud and Rowena and Maud gave her an encouraging wave. Rowena stifled a giggle as Constance was whisked off into the next carole.

"Well, that should keep her busy for a while," said Maud. "Come on, let's head upstairs."

They skirted the whirling circle of dancers and made for the stairwell. Once they were outside Malvoisin's solar, they pressed their ears to the wood and listened to the conversation going on within.

"Sires," said the voice of Malvoisin. "I think we all know that, as it stands, Count John's plan has failed and that his brother will indeed return to England. Even the French have not been able to keep that devil contained. This will spell bad news for John but even worse for his followers. We are therefore forced to take drastic action if we are to keep our heads on our shoulders."

"What action could we possibly take now?" asked Hugh de Bardulf. "Queen Eleanor is already on her way with the ransom money. Any chance we had at stopping her has passed."

"There you are wrong, sheriff," said Malvoisin. "The queen mother is indeed on her way, with 100,000 marks in her train for which she is responsible. If the silver does not reach Emperor Heinrich, then Richard will not be released."

"What are you suggesting?" asked Prior Aymer. "That we send brigands to waylay the queen mother and the silver?"

"We have no need to send anyone," said Malvoisin. "Agents loyal to our cause are already in Germany awaiting her arrival. A Templar knight who is a friend to Front-de-Boeuf here, has been keeping a close eye on the movements of the king and his allies."

"A Templar?" asked de Bracy. "They have shown their support of Richard in the past. What makes you think you can trust one of their brethren?"

"What makes you think we can trust a mercenary like you?" Prior Aymer asked, pointedly. "You'll follow whoever offers the highest fee. At least the Templars fight for a higher cause than money."

"Indeed my Templar friend has no interest in coin," came the unmistakable growl of Front-de-Boeuf. "And he is no friend to Richard. He follows Lucas de Beaumanoir, who has recently returned to England and, were it not for Richard's meddling, would be the Grand Master of the Knights Templar. There are many who do in fact consider him to be such and will gladly support John if it means Richard remains under lock and key."

"And what will we have this Templar friend of yours do?" asked Bardulf. "Steal the silver?"

"Aye, and hand it over to Emperor Heinrich not as a ransom, but as payment for keeping Richard where he belongs; in a cold, dark dungeon!"

Maud and Rowena shared a look of horror. The treachery of the men in their midst knew no bounds.

"Hush, Reginald," said Malvoisin. "Your voice doubles in volume when you are addled by drink. The reason I have called you to my solar is that I fear there is a spy in the castle."

"A spy?" thundered Front-de-Boeuf. "Hang him from the castle walls by his own entrails!"

"If I knew who it was, then I might put on such a colourful event."

"What has this spy done?" asked de Bracy.

"Put it this way," said Malvoisin, "Few knew that the silver from Sheffield was being diverted to Nottingham Castle. And it was on the road to

Nottingham that the bandit who calls himself Robert de Locksley and his followers ambushed Bardulf here and made off with nearly a hundred marks."

Robert de Locksley, thought Rowena with scorn. The French-speaking portion of the English population had no idea what the Saxon word 'Hob' referred to and thought it was a shortened version of the name Robert.

"The bastard tied my men and I up and left us for the wolves!" exclaimed the sheriff. "God be thanked that a vintner travelling north from Nottingham found us for I dread to think how long we might have sat trussed up otherwise. But the silver, which Count John was depending on to protect his interests has vanished. I even have my suspicions that this Locksley has distributed at least some of the wealth with the villeins of the Chase of all people. They hold him up as a protector of the weak and damn near a saint."

"Somebody within this castle informed him that the silver was headed to Nottingham," said Malvoisin. "And that's not all. The day the silver left, the letter sealed by the Count of Mortain vanished from this very solar."

"Do you suspect this spy stole the letter and was the one who told the queen mother of Count John's forgery of the royal seal?" asked the sheriff. "There was an ungodly uproar in London about that business, by all accounts."

"It seems probable," said Malvoisin. "There has been altogether too much coincidental about all of this. My only conclusion is that a spy within these walls has been in contact not only with the queen mother, but also that godless rogue Locksley."

There was a silence as the members of the informal council considered these words. Then, Prior Aymer spoke with a sudden urgency.

"That damnable Brother Broch of Copmanhurst!"

"Who?" demanded Front-de-Boeuf.

"There is a monk of my order, although not of my abbey for I'd have defrocked him long ago, who has set himself up as a healer of the poor down at Copmanhurst. He's an incorrigible oaf who thinks he's holier than his superiors. Such are the monks bred by Abbot Ralph of Fountains Abbey."

"Why do you suspect him?" Front-de-Boeuf pressed.

"He has been in and out of this castle on various errands. Isn't he the pet project of your ward, Malvoisin? Her and her ladies-in-waiting seemed to be on very good terms with him last I visited."

"Well, yes," said Malvoisin. "It was the lady Maud who demanded that I sell a portion of her lands to Fountains Abbey so that this monk could build his grange. She damn near blackmailed me as a matter of fact …" He trailed off as his suspicions began to deepen. "But this Brother Broch, could he have travelled to London and gained an audience with the queen mother?"

"In fact," said Prior Aymer, "one of my own lay brothers has regular dealings with the lay brothers of Fountains Abbey. He spoke to one of them who had worked on that grange at Copmanhurst during the summer harvest. He said that he had to return to the grange in order to look after its bees while Brother Broch took a trip to London. This was earlier in the month."

"Just after the letter was stolen," said de Bracy.

The room had fallen silent. Rowena and Maud looked at each other, their faces pale as the realisation that Malvoisin might be considering their own guilt dawned on them. There was the sound of a chair's legs scraping as somebody rose.

"If you'll excuse me, sires," said Malvoisin. "I must get to the bottom of this immediately."

Maud and Rowena knew they had to get out of sight and they hurried towards the stairs just as the door to the solar opened but they were too late.

"And just what business does my ward and her lady-in-waiting have outside my solar?" Malvoisin barked.

Maud and Rowena froze at the entrance to the stairwell. They turned sheepishly to face Malvoisin. The faces of his comrades appeared in the doorway behind him, overcast with suspicion. It was no good. There was no plausible explanation for their presence outside the solar. They had been caught eavesdropping and now there was no doubt about their guilt.

CHAPTER XIII

Stannington, December 1193

There was, Simon was rapidly coming to the conclusion, such a thing as stealing too much. He replaced the last stone, concealing the bags of silver within the wall of the bridge. The mud beneath his feet was frozen hard and the black water flowed beneath the bridge sluggishly. It was a great hiding place but it would take him forever to spend up that cache. Still, little by little, it would all go to a good cause; right back into the purses of the people who had worked for it.

When Rowena had visited him at Stannington Hall to tell him that the sheriff would be accompanying a wain of silver on its way to Nottingham, he knew it was too good an opportunity to pass up, despite the lateness of the season. His band of robbers had already settled down for the winter at Harthill Walk when he had ridden into their camp and roused them from their cookfires and pallets with promises of more silver than they had ever dreamt of.

The band had grown to over twenty in the past year. The high taxation had only increased in the desperate attempt to gather King Richard's ransom while the unjust trials, the corruption and the cruelty had continued, leaving many with no other option than to vanish into the Chase and live off the vert and venison that was so strictly forbidden. The camp had begun to resemble a crude village with stables, blacksmith, bakery and tannery. It was more or less self-sufficient as they had little need to venture into the villages except to distribute stolen money to the poor and to barter skins and meat for flour and arrows.

The robbery had gone off without a hitch although they had struggled to intercept it in time. The sheriff and the silver were deep within Sherwood by the time the robbers caught up with it. The routiers Malvoisin had sent as an escort had put up a noble fight and three were dead by the time they threw down their weapons and surrendered.

The robbers had taken great pleasure in tying up the sheriff and his men and many jokes were made at the expense of one who had tried so hard to find and capture the hobhoods of Locksley Chase.

The silver had presented a problem the moment it had passed into their possession. It would take them an age to distribute such a gigantic sum to the poor. They had buried the bulk of it at Harthill Walk but Simon was determined to put some of it to more immediate use. There were several businessmen known to him who had taken out large loans from Jewish moneylenders. With the king's ransom sucking England dry, the moneylenders were calling in old debts. That meant that honest, hardworking folk like Stephen the draper and Alfred the pewterer faced ruin. Simon was determined to prevent that from happening and had hidden his share of the loot under Miller's Bridge.

It was the only place he could think of that was close enough to Stannington Hall so he could easily retrieve it. He didn't dare conceal it at the hall itself for there were far too many servants poking about but Miller's Bridge was deserted at night, overlooked only by the manorial mill with its great creaking water wheel.

He and John often crept under the bridge at night and made small withdrawals from the cache. Simon had already bailed out three businesses over the Christmas period with the very same silver that had been squeezed out of them by the moneylenders and the sheriff's bailiffs. It was a good scheme, if a little closer to home than he was comfortable with.

It was halfway through the twelve days of Christmas and they were to celebrate the feast of Saint Sylvester at Sheffield Castle that evening. It pleased Simon to see Rowena again but when they rode into the bailey, it was clear that the mood in the castle had soured since their last visit. Everybody seemed to be on tenterhooks for some reason and Simon put it down to the news that the queen mother was now en route to Germany with the ransom that would set King Richard free. Everybody knew that Malvoisin was a supporter of the king's treacherous brother John, and Simon did not doubt that the king's imminent return was giving Malvoisin more than the occasional sleepless night.

While Simon and his family were making their way around the hall, exchanging compliments of the season with acquaintances, Rowena hurried over to him. Simon's father's back was to them and they were afforded a brief conversation in private.

"Thank God you came," she whispered.

"Well that's the best greeting you've given me," said Simon with a grin. "Perhaps you are falling for my charms after all."

"Oh, don't be silly. Something terrible has happened and I need your help."

"What's the trouble?"

"Malvoisin found out that Maud and I have been feeding Locksley information. He doesn't know the extent of our activities or Locksley's true identity for we both held strong even through his severest interrogations, but Maud and I are little more than prisoners in the castle now. We are forbidden from leaving the Great Tower, even to take the air in the bailey! Constance is now our gaoler on orders of Lord and Lady Malvoisin."

"Damn them!" said Simon. "Do you want me to get word to Cedric? He'll have you out of this mess in no time."

"No, I'm sure my days at Sheffield are at an end anyway. Malvoisin will surely dismiss me after Epiphany. But I have an important errand for you." She glanced around to make sure nobody was watching them, then reached into her dress and passed him a small letter. "You must take this to the one they call the Clerk of Copmanhurst. He was the one who carried our message to the queen mother earlier this month."

Simon frowned but took the letter and hid it within his own robes. "I'm not a messenger boy."

"Simon, it is vital that this letter reaches London and lands in the hands of the ruling council. The reason Maud and I are under house arrest is that we overheard Malvoisin and his cronies discussing a plan to waylay the queen mother and the silver before it reaches the emperor's court. Some Templar who is a friend to Front-de-Boeuf is already in Germany awaiting its arrival. I know you don't much care about our king, but do this please, if only for me."

She was right. Simon didn't much care about the king, but there were tears in Rowena's eyes now and he saw how important it was to her that the king was released and returned to England along with that Wilfred of hers, the lucky fellow.

"Very well," he grumbled. "Who is this Clerk of Copmanhurst?"

"His name is Brother Broch and he runs a small grange for the good of the poor. If you don't find him there, look to the ruined chapel to Saint Dunstan which lies a little off the road north of Copmanhurst."

"I'll find him," said Simon.

The chapel to Saint Dunstan was a sad, dilapidated thing with a sagging roof and ivy crawling up one side of it. It was a relic of the days before the Norman Conquest and its Saxon architecture was weather-beaten and crumbling. The belfry above the porch still stood proudly and within could be seen a bell that was green with age.

The clearing that surrounded the chapel also contained a bubbling spring which, over the course of many centuries, had worn a basin into the rock. Near to this, leaning like a drunkard against a large rock, was a crude shelter of rough-hewn logs with the crevices padded with moss and mud. A cross cut from tree branches stood at its entrance and told Simon and his companions that they had come to the right place.

He had only brought John and William with him on this frosty January morning. He didn't want to intimidate the monk by bringing his whole band to his doorstep for he was an irascible fellow by all accounts.

As they approached, two enormous wolfhounds came bounding out of the hovel, barking their outrage at the presence of strangers. Simon drew his sword while John and William nocked arrows to their bowstrings.

"Halt!" bellowed a voice, and the hounds immediately sunk down onto their haunches, their barks reduced to reluctant growls.

The man who emerged from the hovel cut a sturdy figure of the type whose face is always ruddy and on the verge of perspiration. He was not fat exactly; there was a good deal of muscle in his arms borne of years of labour and he had an air of health and vitality about him. In his hands he carried a stout club of knotted wood.

"If you think to rob a poor monk then you'll see a deal of trouble for your efforts," he said. "My hounds and I are more than a match for three godless brigands who dare not even show their faces."

Simon lowered his hood and removed the black mask that obscured his face. John and William followed suit. It was unlikely this monk would recognise any of them and equally unlikely that he would see their faces again. Besides, Simon needed the trust of this monk if he was to deliver Rowena's letter.

"You are the one they call the Clerk of Copmanhurst?" Simon asked him.

"I am blessed to be called that, yes."

"You do much good work here, monk. Your charity is a godsend to the poor of the Chase."

"I do what good I can," said the monk. "It is a shame that others don't. While I and my brethren labour to sow crops and build shelters for those who are homeless and hungry, villainous rogues like you only add to the misery in the Chase."

"Villainous rogues?" asked Simon, insulted by this unsympathetic characterisation of him. "We only rob those who can afford to be robbed."

"Well, I have nothing, as you can see. But if you wish to test your mettle against my own, you'll find that not everybody will yield to thugs like you."

"Thugs now? Very well, Brother. If you wish to prove that you are of sterner stuff than every other churchman we've robbed, then let us have a contest to see which of us is easiest overcome. What shall it be? Wrestling? Archery?"

"In my youth I was known for my skill with the quarterstaff."

"Fine," said Simon. "Quarterstaffs it shall be."

"What's the point of this?" John asked in Simon's ear, as he unfastened his brooch and removed his cloak. "We came here to enlist this monk as an ally, not beat his brains out."

"Oh, it's just a friendly competition," said Simon, handing him his cloak. "This monk is a trifle rude for my liking. I want to gently knock him into his place that's all. He'll be less quarrelsome once he recognises me as his superior."

The monk had hurried off to find two branches that could be quickly shaped into staffs. Once this task was complete, he handed one to Simon.

"Now then, you young rogue," said the monk. "I'm going to show you that not every man of the cloth is meek and mild."

"First, tie up those hounds," John demanded. "They'll rip us limb from limb once they start seeing violence done to their master."

"Very well," said the monk. "If it will set your minds at ease. Though I doubt they'll feel the need to come to my defence."

He tied up the hounds and ruffled their ears. Then, he hitched up the hem of his habit and tucked it into his belt of woven rushes before retrieving his quarterstaff. The sight of his thick, pink legs in their well-worn sandals elicited guffaws from the robbers as he gave his weapon a twirl.

"Whenever you're ready, *Brother Tuck*," said Simon with a grin.

The attack came suddenly and with surprising quickness. Simon just had time to bring up his own staff and block the downwards blow, wincing a little as the whack of wood on wood made his arms tingle up to his elbows.

He launched his own attack by swiping at the monk's ample middle but his opponent leapt out of the way with surprising nimbleness. Another blow came swinging its way towards Simon's left side which he only just had time to block.

Simon's companions roared encouragement while the monk's hounds watched with mild interest as the fight hit its stride. Wood smacked and slithered and sweat began to bead on the foreheads of both men as they struck, blocked and counterstruck. Simon began to worry that he had underestimated his opponent for the monk's abilities defied his figure and profession.

He yelped with pain as the monk caught him a blow on his knuckles and had to duck as the other end of the quarterstaff whistled over his head. Seizing an opportunity, he thrust at the monk's middle with the butt of his staff only to find it blocked by his opponent's lightning reflexes. *Who was this monk?*

Then, as if he had only been toying with him until now, Brother Broch unleashed a barrage of ferocious blows designed to wear Simon down and beat him to the ground. Simon struggled to block each of them and he managed a fair attempt but it was ultimately futile. The monk was a far better fighter and within moments, Simon was flat on his back, the monk standing over him, triumphant.

"All right, that's enough!" cried John. "We didn't come here to measure cocks, monk. We have an important favour to ask of you."

"Indeed?" asked the monk, as he cast aside his staff and headed towards the bubbling spring. He stooped over it and splashed his face and neck with water before drinking deeply. "What favour would hedge robbers ask of a holy man?"

"I had hoped to teach you some manners," said Simon, getting to his feet and wincing at the protests of his bruised body. "But it seems that I have met my match in a man of the cloth. That's all right. I'm man enough to know when I'm beaten. But we are no simple hedge robbers. You are a charitable man yourself, perhaps you will think better of me when I tell you that I am the one known as Hob of Locksley."

"Hob of Locksley," said the monk. "That is a name given much praise in the Chase. Yes, I had a mind that you were him."

"Then surely you can see that we are men with the same mission in life. Why were you so insistent on insulting us if you suspected that I was Locksley?"

"Robbery is robbery, and a sin, no matter your intentions."

"How else are we to persuade the rich to share a little of their wealth with those who have less?"

Brother Broch chuckled as he untied his hounds. They no longer seemed to consider the strangers a danger. "True, that is a hard task. But it doesn't hurt to remind a fellow once in a while that not everybody will be threatened into handing over their purse."

"Doesn't hurt?" said Simon with a sheepish grin. "I beg to differ. I only wish that you'd chosen archery. Come, Brother Tuck. Let us put this silliness behind us and turn to our business here and what could be the start of a most beneficial partnership."

"I'll be no robber if you think to recruit me," said the monk. "And you'll call me Brother Broch unless you want me to curb your insolence once more."

"We only require a favour of you, or rather, the Lady Rowena of Rotherwood does."

"Rowena?" said the monk, turning suddenly to them. "You've not got her mixed up in your villainy, have you?"

"Rowena mixes herself up in whatever she chooses. And this time it has landed her in hot water. She overheard Malvoisin and Front-de-Boeuf discussing a plot to steal King Richard's ransom money which is currently on its way to the emperor's court. They have a Templar turncoat waiting for it in Germany. It's all in this letter."

He handed Rowena's letter to the monk. Brother Broch accepted it and glanced at the seal.

"Rowena said that you conveyed important information to London before," said Simon. "Now she calls upon you to do so again."

"But Queen Eleanor has already left with the silver," said Brother Broch. "We do not have much time."

"No. Can you leave immediately?"

"I will do my best. Can you lend me a fast horse?"

"The fastest I own," said Simon. "You'd better pack for your journey."

"I would offer you fellows some hospitality but I am sworn to poverty …"

"Fortunately for you, we are not," said Simon. "You may come to our camp. It is on your way and you can set out for London in the morning. Tonight we'll give you the finest banquet the greenwood has to offer. Venison, ale, bread of the finest flour, not to mention a pipe or two of Gascon wine that some careless vintner mislaid on his journey to Sheffield."

Brother Broch smiled from ear to ear. "Locksley," he said. "You may be a villain and a sinner, but God forgive me if I don't find myself warming to you."

CHAPTER XIV

Speyer, January 1194

Wilfred let his mind drift to memories of Rowena as the delicate notes plucked from the lute by Blondel's fingers resonated in the tapestried room. The fire in the grate crackled as the rain pattered against the wooden window shutters.

It was several days after Epiphany and the Christmas celebrations had wound down at last. Twelve days of feasting and celebrating in a court as wealthy and extravagant as that of the Holy Roman Emperor could be quite exhausting but Wilfred knew he couldn't complain. He had spent his previous Christmas in a barn in Gorizia, cold, hungry and alone as he had searched for the king. At least this Christmas he had been with his king and other good company besides.

It had been an eventful but frustrating year. Not long after the trial they had been permitted to see the king. It had been a joyous reunion and Richard, still buzzing from his triumph before the Imperial Diet, positively beamed at seeing some of his loyal followers who had traipsed across half of Europe to find him.

He had grasped Wilfred in a bearhug most unbecoming of a king and pounded him soundly on the back. "Ivanhoe! God's legs but it is good to see you again! Longchamp has told me of your loyalty, of how you tracked me through the Alps, all the way to Dürnstein."

"I would never have found you, sire," said Wilfred, "had not Blondel and his companions found me first."

The king's face turned suddenly serious. "The reliquary, Ivanhoe. Do you still have it?"

"I do." Wilfred patted his tunic where the lump of the reliquary containing the fragment of the true cross lay nestled against his breast bone.

"Thank Christ I gave it to you before I left Acre. Leopold's men stripped me of everything when they took me to Dürnstein. If that most holy of relics had fallen into that Austrian bastard's hands I may well have given up on life there and then. Keep it for me, Ivanhoe. Keep it safe until I am out of this damnable mess."

"I will, sire."

They had remained with the king at Speyer for all of Lent but Emperor Heinrich, true to his fashion, betrayed Richard and his own Imperial Diet immediately after Easter. One cold morning, the king was whisked off to some unknown location and Richard's followers feared the worst. The Emperor was still clearly keen to squeeze a fortune out of the situation and now apparently intended to keep Richard hidden from public view until his ransom demands were met.

It was Longchamp who finally found out where the king had been taken. By pressuring members of Heinrich's court, he learned that the king had been squirreled away in the most desolate and dreaded of prisons in the Holy Roman Empire: Trifels Castle.

Wilfred and the others accompanied Longchamp to the town of Annweiler which lay in the shadow of the imposing castle. They waited patiently while Longchamp gained entry to Trifels and returned with grave news.

"The king is kept manacled in one of the worst cells like a common criminal!"

There was considerable outrage at this and many oaths sworn against the emperor. After much negotiation with the castellan, Longchamp was able to secure better accommodation for the king whose time in the dungeons had brought on another bout of quartan fever. Apparently fearful that his prized prisoner might die in his custody, the emperor was eventually convinced to remove Richard to his imperial palace at Hagenau where Wilfred and the others were reunited with him once more.

It was a vast improvement over Trifels but, as the weeks stretched into months, frustrations ran high. Every day the king remained a prisoner was a day his enemies ate away at his influence and lands. King Philip had launched another invasion of Normandy and several of Richard's Norman vassals, their backbones apparently softened by the king's imprisonment, had surrendered important castles to the French king who was able to march right up to the gates of Rouen itself.

There was some good news, however, as the king's companions who had been arrested during his desperate flight through the Alps were released and came to him at Haugenau. After Richard had reluctantly agreed to the terms of his release, he had been afforded a surprising degree of freedom. He was allowed to surround himself with his friends and there were constant visitors from England who carried news and letters to and from the king. He was even allowed to send to England for his favourite falcons and often went hunting.

The emperor carted his captive king around with him from court to court as if he were a prized palfrey. They had spent most of the summer at Worms before returning to Speyer as the season turned once more. Had it been a year since they had left Acre? It was hard to believe. Time had moved fast and yet, the precariousness of the king's position felt like it had gone on for a lifetime.

Longchamp had returned to England to assist the queen mother in gathering the ransom and the hostages the emperor demanded. Blondel was still in regular communication with the Archbishop of Rouen and it was on that rainy January afternoon that news reached them that Queen Eleanor had set out with the silver and hostages.

There was a modest celebration and wine was drunk in toast of the king and his resourceful mother. Relief pervaded the king's chamber as the realisation that the nightmare was coming to its end. The ransom, extortionate as it was, was going to be paid and they would all return home.

Home to Rowena, Wilfred thought wistfully as Blondel's song came to its end. By Christ and his saints, it had been a long three and a half years! He half dreaded what he might find when he returned home, the immediacy of the unknown suddenly filling him with more dread than it had before. What if his father had married her to somebody else? Impossible! Rowena had said she would wait for him, that she'd never love another. And yet, what did love have to do with it? They weren't characters in one of Blondel's songs. They were real people bound to the cruelties of fate and the whims of others. His father was a stubborn and persuasive man. *What if he had managed to twist her mind …?*

The evening rolled on and Blondel left to talk with one of the Archbishop of Rouen's messengers who had something for him. He returned with a grave face.

"Sire," he said, addressing the king, "I fear that there are ill plans afoot."

"What is it?" demanded the king. "With my ransom on its way and my freedom a matter of days away, what news can be so ill as to steal the flush of good drink and song from the face of my dearest troubadour?"

"The peril facing the transport of your ransom, sire, not to mention your good mother."

"What have you heard?"

"News from England. Various supporters of your brother seek to prevent your return and have concocted a scheme to ambush the queen mother's ship and make off with the silver."

"Damn their souls!" the king roared, upsetting his wine goblet as he rose from his seat in a rage. "Which supporters are these? Tell me their names and I'll have their heads on spikes upon my return!"

"The letter did not give names," said Blondel, "only that they have a contact somewhere here in Germany, possibly in the imperial court itself, who is to arrange the theft. He is said to be a Templar."

"One of Beaumanoir's serpents, no doubt," said the king. "They have never forgiven me for dashing his hopes to be Grand Master."

Wilfred felt a cold shudder at these words. Had it not been for his brutal interrogation at the hands of Brian de Bois-Guilbert, then he would most likely be home and in the arms of Rowena by now. It had been the knowledge that Beaumanoir's Templars had been so keen to learn the details of the king's journey home that had spurred his own journey through the Alps to find the king and protect him if he could. Now, here they were a year later. Could Bois-Guilbert still be out there too, waiting, watching? Surely he had returned to his home now? But then, just as the king's followers would stop at nothing to ensure his safe return, surely his enemies would stop at nothing to prevent it?

"A similar letter was delivered to your mother too, sire," Blondel continued. "She is currently at Cologne, according to the messenger who brought me this. She is warned and they are planning a decoy so that both she and the silver will be brought to the emperor safe and sound."

"A decoy?" Richard asked, one eyebrow raised. "That sounds like my mother's cunning sure enough. What's the decoy?"

"The silver is to be unloaded at Bonn and the ship will continue upriver where it will be attacked by this Templar and whatever men he has. It will be to no avail for by then the silver and the queen mother will be heading down the old Roman road that connects Cologne to Mainz."

The king was hardy put at ease by this. "If anything happens to that silver then I will remain in captivity for the rest of my life," he said. "And if anything happens to my mother, I will never forgive myself. There must be some way we can find out who this Templar is and where he intends to attack my mother's ship. I would sleep a lot better knowing that whatever plot my enemies have formed has been nipped in the bud."

"There are some Templars here at court," said Blondel, "but none I can think of that might wish you harm. For a Templar to get caught up in such a scheme, it would have to be something personal. They are not mercenaries."

"Brian de Bois-Guilbert," said Wilfred. The room looked at him.

"Now there is a man who fits the bill," said Richard. "One of Beaumanoir's staunchest supporters. I still haven't forgotten how you swept him out of his saddle at Acre, Ivanhoe." He gave a small chuckle, despite the gravity of the situation. "If only we could deal him such a blow now. But where is the bugger, that's the question!"

"I will use every contact I have," said Blondel. "If he is here, then he will not stay hidden for long."

Blondel's network of informants and contacts proved itself once more as within two days they knew where the Templar was.

"Jacob is a young lad I have used before to follow people and gather information," said Blondel. "He's a trustworthy lad but I've never sent him on such a dangerous mission before. He was able to locate a Templar knight of Norman stock who has been seen both here in Speyer and in Haugenau. I told him to work his way into the service of this man and he has done so, running errands in the guise of a page."

"Is it Bois-Guilbert?" Wilfred asked.

"He does not know the name of the man he serves but there is no doubt that this is the Templar we seek. He and a company of routiers are currently at Koblenz. They intend to ambush the queen mother's ship as it approaches the bend of the Rhine northeast of the town."

"When?" asked Gerard.

"In three days' time."

"Then we can still stop them," said Gerard. "We can just about make Koblenz in time and give that Templar bastard something else to think about than robbing the queen mother!"

When they presented their news to the king, he was pleased but sighed in frustration all the same. "If only I could ride out with you," he said. "To sit here and do nothing while my enemies do all they can to ensure I remain a captive is almost more than I can bear. Godspeed, my loyal men. Strike all the harder for my absence for I shall be with you in spirit if not in body."

They rode hard and fast, following the Rhine northeast until the rooftops of Koblenz could be seen on a bend in the river two days later. The weather was dismal; alternating between sleet and heavy rain and they were soaked through by the time they found lodgings.

"The Templar and his men are staying at the *Goldener Löwe*," said Blondel. "I have written ahead and told Jacob to meet us outside. Ivanhoe and Furnival, you go and fetch him back here. Once the Templar and his men ride out, we can ambush them on the road and put an end to their treachery."

The rain had not let up and Wilfred and Gerard pulled up the hoods on their riding cloaks as they stepped out into the night. The streets were muddy and deserted. Only the glow of hearth fires and candles from windows and doorways indicated that there was anybody in Koblenz at all.

Even the *Goldener Löwe* seemed to be devoid of the raucous laughter and song one normally found at inns. They took shelter under a nearby archway from where they could see the door and they waited.

An hour passed. Nobody went in or came out.

"Damned strange," said Gerard. "This place isn't exactly a hamlet and our own inn has plenty of business. What's up with this place?"

"Something could have gone wrong," said Wilfred. "Blondel said this lad was supposed to meet us outside."

"Might pay to have a quick look inside," said Gerard. "They won't be expecting us."

"No, but we should keep a low profile nevertheless. Speak only German."

Wilfred had picked up a smattering of the tongue over the past year. Not enough to pass as a native, but he could ask a few questions.

They hurried through the rain to the door of the inn. The warmth of the fire was a comforting embrace. One or two small groups sat apart from each other, nursing jacks of ale. The innkeeper was bringing a roast chicken out of the oven and placing it on a board with a couple of loaves.

"Any beds for the night?" Gerard asked him in his best German.

The innkeeper squinted at him. "Aye, more than usual. You fellows are in luck. You can have a room to yourselves."

"Why is business so slow?" Gerard asked. "Other inns in this town seem to have enough guests."

The innkeeper rolled his eyes. "We've had some rough company of late. Some foreign knight and his friends have taken a room for themselves. Been here five days and have all but emptied my larder leaving me with naught but a promise that they'll settle their tab when they leave. It's not that I don't trust them, but they have a tendency to frighten off my other customers. They're a boisterous lot and like to drink."

"Is there a boy with them?" Wilfred asked.

"Aye, they have a page that runs in and out, fetching them things."

"Is he upstairs now?"

The innkeeper nodded. "Him and two of the others."

"Are you saying the rest of them have gone out?"

"Rode out this morning."

Wilfred and Gerard shared a glance as the innkeeper carried the chicken and bread over to a group in the corner.

"Something's up," said Wilfred under his breath. "Else that lad would have kept his appointment."

"Aye, it sounds like the Templar and the others left him under guard here. I hope we're not too late."

"Come on, let's take a look upstairs."

They headed up to the upper story, waving aside the innkeeper's concerns. "Just checking if the rooms are suitable," said Gerard.

They went from room to room, trying the doors. Most were empty. The one facing the stairs seemed to be bolted. Gerard rapped on it with his knuckles. There was the sound of footsteps within and then it creaked open a fraction. A scarred face peered out and said something in German.

With a stamp, Gerard booted the door open and knocked the man backwards. Wilfred and Gerard shouldered their way in, drawing their swords. The man Gerard had knocked down rolled out of the way as a second man charged them from the corner of the room, blade raised.

Gerard parried the blow with a deafening clang and then swung his own blade into the side of his assailant, smashing his ribs and cutting deep into the flesh.

Wilfred swung at the first man but cut only empty air as he moved out of the way, drawing his own sword in the process. Wilfred ducked as the blade whistled overhead and thrust his sword into the man's belly.

The man cried out and the sword slipped from his grasp to clatter on the floorboards. His face a mask of agony, he leant backwards. Wilfred ripped his blade free from the man's guts and swung it down onto his neck.

Wilfred and Gerard checked the room for any other threats and found a boy lying on a straw pallet, his face so horribly bruised that at first Wilfred thought he was dead.

"Are you Jacob?" he asked the lad in German.

The boy mumbled an affirmative through his pulped lips, his eyes gazing at them, wide and white. "I did not mean to betray King Richard, I swear it!" he managed.

"What happened?"

"The Templar got suspicious of me. He questioned me. I slipped up and he knew me for a spy. Then ... he tortured me. I tried not to say anything but they kept beating me, telling me what they were going to do to me ... before they would kill me. God forgive me!"

"What did you tell the Templar?" Gerard demanded, seizing the youth by the front of his tunic.

"I told him that the ship was a decoy, that the silver was being taken by road."

"Damn!" said Gerard, releasing the boy roughly. "They'll be on their way to ambush the queen mother as we speak!"

"Come on," said Wilfred. "We have to get back to Blondel and the others. Help me lift the boy."

Despite his frustration, Gerard could see that the boy had been cruelly mistreated. His ribs were broken and there looked to be the burn marks of a hot iron on his body. Together, they lifted him off the bloodied pallet and carried him downstairs. The innkeeper and the few customers gazed at them in horror. None had dared follow them upstairs.

"You won't have any more trouble from that knight and his men," Gerard told the innkeeper. "And you can rent out the room again. Once you clean it up, of course. Bit of a mess I'm afraid."

When they got Jacob back to their own inn, Blondel saw to it that he received medical attention and a bowl of hot broth.

"Poor lad held out as best he could," said the troubadour. "I shouldn't have let him know so much. It has endangered everything."

"Had he known nothing, he would have been tortured to death," Wilfred said.

"True. There are no safe ways to play this game of spies. Come, we must ready our horses. The Templar will already be lying in wait as Queen Eleanor and the silver make its way towards them."

As they followed the Roman road northeast, they picked up the Templar's trail. A merchant heading towards Koblenz told them that he had passed a group of twenty or so riders wearing no sigils; a sure sign of routiers. They proceeded cautiously and Blondel sent one of the men to scout the road ahead. He returned bearing news that the routiers were camped at a spot where the wooded slope of the Rhine Valley encroached upon the road.

"We must come up with a plan," said Blondel. "We are six. No match for twenty routiers."

"The queen mother surely has a large escort," said Gerard. "Together we might be enough to take them."

"What do you propose?" asked Blondel. "Wait for them to ambush the queen and then ride in to help? Too risky."

"If we could warn the queen of the ambush and persuade her to send her escort on ahead, we might be able to surprise the routiers and pin them between us," suggested Wilfred.

They considered this.

"That might be the best we can do," said Gerard. "But how are we to get past the Templar to warn the queen?"

"One of us could cut across country," said Blondel. "Skirt the routiers and reach the queen before she falls into the trap."

"It had best be Wilfred," said Gerard. "He has the fastest horse."

"Agreed. Wilfred, you must make for the top of the valley and follow it along to where the queen mother is making her progress. Convince her to lend you her troops and then lead them to where the routiers are lying in wait. Once battle is joined, we will fall upon their rear and, God willing, we will be able to defeat them."

Wilfred did not like the idea of abandoning his comrades to go chasing off into the countryside in search of the queen mother but knew it was the only way. As Gerard had said, Jago was the finest and fastest destrier among them and it had been his idea after all.

As he galloped up the slope of the valley he wondered how in God's name he was going to be able to see the road from up high. The valley slopes were thickly wooded, the branches of the trees laden with snow. The going was slow, no matter how hard he pushed Jago. He came to a tributary of the Rhine, the water moving sluggishly beneath the crust of ice which shattered as he tried to ride across it. Jago whinnied his protests and Wilfred felt for him as the icy water rose up around his thighs. Still, they pushed on.

Once he was confident that the Templar and his routiers were well behind them, Wilfred cut back to the road and gained more time as he galloped along the broken highway. Eventually, he could see a cluster of horsemen up ahead and reined Jago in as they spotted him. For a moment he was worried that he had returned to the road too early for these men wore no sigils. Then he realised that the queen mother was attempting to travel incognito and her escort would likely be disguised as routiers. Just to be sure, he addressed them in French as they approached him.

"I am a knight of King Richard. I must see Queen Eleanor immediately. It is vital."

To his relief they replied in French although they remained suspicious. "What makes you think Queen Eleanor rides this road?" their captain asked.

"Why else would a company of French-speaking knights be on this road?" Wilfred replied. And then, just to prove himself a little further, he added; "Is there any one among you who speaks English?"

"Aye, I do," said one of the knights in a south-west accent. "So, you are an Englishman all right. That doesn't prove a damn thing. The king has many enemies, from England and abroad."

"Let me see Queen Eleanor, I beg you," said Wilfred. "A company of routiers lie in wait but a few miles down the road."

That had their attention and, suspicions or no, Wilfred was accompanied up the road to a column of carts, wains and carriages. There were no banners, shields were covered and there was little to suggest that the convoy was anything but a band of merchants travelling together for the sake of safety with a contingent of routiers. Wilfred was conducted to a carriage at the rear of the column and made to wait while the captain of the vanguard stepped up to speak with someone behind its curtains.

He climbed down and the curtain was pulled aside by the carriage's occupant. Wilfred found himself looking up into the face of an elderly woman wrapped up in furs against the cold. Queen Eleanor had passed her seventieth year but had lost none of the steely resolve and command that had made her so famous as the wife of two kings. She gazed down at Wilfred with a cold curiosity.

"You came to give me a warning, I am told," she said in her Occitanian accent which Wilfred recognised in the voice of her son.

"Yes, Your Grace," said Wilfred. "I am Wilfred de Ivanhoe. I was with your son the king in the Holy Land and have spent the past year with him during his captivity. Not five days ago, we learned from the Archbishop of Rouen that the king's enemies plan to rob you of the silver intended for his ransom."

"As did I," interrupted the queen. "Only somewhat earlier than five days ago."

"We were told that the silver was to be unloaded at Bonn and taken by road to Speyer," Wilfred continued. "But during our preparations to thwart the plotters, we found out that they had learned of the decoy and intend to ambush you on this very road not ten miles away."

Queen Eleanor regarded him closely. "And your purpose in coming to me was to warn me of this? I can hardly turn back now. This silver must reach the emperor or my son will never be freed."

"My comrades wait beyond the ambush but we are few in number. If you could lend me your escort, we could surprise the bandits and clear the way for you."

"What should make me believe that you are not one of these bandits sent ahead to rob me of my escort and lead them into a trap?" the queen demanded.

Wilfred had been afraid that this would be her reaction. "Your Grace, there is nothing I can say that will convince you. I only appeal to your trust as your son's loyal servant." He reached inside his gambeson and pulled out the reliquary, holding it up so that the queen might inspect it. "This reliquary contains a splinter of the holy cross. Your son gave it to me for safekeeping before he left Acre. I bear it for him still, as I bear my loyalty."

Queen Eleanor's eyes widened and she leant out of her carriage to look at the reliquary that was still chained around Wilfred's neck. He stood on tiptoe and was acutely aware of how close the queen's face was to his. He could see every wrinkle in that august face, won by years of responsibility, imprisonment, dedication to her family, and the grief of loss and betrayal by those she loved. She blinked once and then released the reliquary, looking away suddenly.

"It could be a falsity," she said. "But I feel it in my bones that it is not and that you do indeed carry a piece of Christ's cross around your neck. Your story rings true, Wilfred de Ivanhoe. God forgive me if I am wrong in my judgement of you. And God forgive you if you play me false for I will not. You may take my escort and surprise these brigands. Clear the road for me, Ivanhoe. I am cold, tired and eager to reach my destination."

Nothing further passed between them and Wilfred was led back to Jago while commands were shouted up and down the column. Presently he found himself at the head of a company of twelve mounted knights and ten men-at-arms. They moved out and Wilfred glanced back to catch a glimpse of Queen Eleanor peering out of her carriage at their departure. Not a single soldier remained by her side. *We've got to win this*, he thought.

The bend in the road as it followed the curve of the river was closer than Wilfred thought and he realised with a sickening feeling that he had reached the queen in the nick of time. If he had been much later then the ambush would have been sprung.

"The routiers are hiding behind that clump of trees," said Wilfred to the captain of the vanguard. "Be ready."

Attacking the vanguard would be the obvious move to Wilfred's mind. But the Templar wouldn't expect the vanguard to be reinforced with every available soldier from the queen's column. Indeed, the routiers seemed to realise this as they charged, for their horses faltered as they rounded the clump of trees and uncertainty showed on their faces.

Crossbows thudded and horses were kicked into a charge as the two companies met. Spears scraped against shields and swords hacked at mail and glanced off helms. Two of the routiers had been skewered in their saddles which gave Wilfred hope that the day would be theirs. He glanced around for sign of a Templar knight but could see only the mad press of mounted figures pushing against one another, the screaming of wounded men and horses deafening his ears.

It had been over a year since he had last been in battle. He remembered the stench of fear and blood all too well and tried to ignore it as he faced down an opponent. He tried to slip back into the part of a warrior as if it were no more than putting on an old gambeson, worn and soft, and he found it strangely easy.

He deflected a blow from his opponent's sword with his shield and stabbed the man through the gut.

As the man toppled from his saddle, Wilfred finally saw him.

Astride a large black destrier sat a tall man with a great helm obscuring his face. He wore no white tabard with a red cross or anything else that identified him as a Templar knight but on either side of his helm had been fastened the wings of a raven. By his side fought two swarthy men whose dress, while modified for a colder climate, had the unmistakable Saracen flavour to them.

Brian de Bois-Guilbert.

There was no doubt in Wilfred's mind that his old foe was the one they now faced. He spurred Jago forward, determined to fight Bois-Guilbert one last time and to finish him for good.

He almost made it. Jago let out a snort of pain and his legs buckled as a routier's spear punctured him behind the shoulder. Wilfred cried out in anguish as Jago went down and he was thrown forward to land on his back. He was sure that he would die then and there for his head spun and he was weighed down by his gambeson while men on horses towered over him.

More horses suddenly entered the fray and pushed the others back. From the ground, Wilfred recognised Gerard as he rode over him and knew that the rest of his comrades had joined the battle.

It was over for the routiers. By the time Wilfred had got to his feet, the battle was done and the queen's men were pursuing them up the wooded slope of the valley. Blondel, Gerard and the others were wheeling their horses around, waving bloodied swords in the air and cheering wildly. Wilfred looked down at

Jago and saw that his magnificent destrier who had been with him through so much, was breathing his last. His great black eye rolled in its socket as it gazed questioningly up at his master.

Wilfred knelt down, patted the beast's glossy neck and wept.

The day had been won and the king's ransom arrived at Speyer on January the 17th. Brian de Bois-Guilbert and what was left of his mercenaries had vanished into the German forests and Wilfred was not the only one who lamented their escape. But the disappointment was momentary for the job was done and the ransom delivered.

Emperor Heinrich took his time, of course, removing Richard to Mainz and making all concerned wait until after Candlemas. The reason for this delay eventually became apparent. The emperor had received an offer from King Philip and the Count of Mortain to match the ransom if he kept the king imprisoned. Clearly tempted by the idea of not having to share such an extravagant sum with Duke Leopold, the emperor was eventually convinced to reject the offer, both by the disgust of his own German lords at such treachery and the realisation that Philip and John had not a hope of raising such a sum even between them. It was decided at last and, on the fourth of February, Richard was released.

Wilfred, still mourning the loss of Jago, allowed himself to partake in the celebrations. It was over at last. They were going home.

CHAPTER XV

Sheffield Castle, February 1194

Contrary to Rowena's expectation, she had not been dismissed from Maud's service after Epiphany. Whatever Malvoisin's suspicions were, he did not seem to place the blame squarely on her shoulders. Their situation had not improved however, and she and Maud were still under house arrest and under the watchful eye of Constance.

It was a dull and isolated existence. They hadn't met with the Stanningtons recently and, having not seen Simon in over a month, Rowena was beginning to feel increasingly cut off. She couldn't even visit Brother Broch and he had even been turned away when he tried to visit them at the castle.

In mid-February, the sheriff visited Malvoisin. There had been a noticeable rise in panic among the Count of Mortain's supporters as the news of King Richard's release swept the country. The king was returning and that spelled doom for his enemies. Every day Rowena thought about Wilfred's fate. Would the king know what had happened to him? Was he in the king's entourage maybe? The thought that they might be reunited within a matter of weeks was almost too joyous for her to bear and she forced herself not to be overly hopeful.

"The Count is arranging a tournament at Ashby-de-la-Zouch next month," the sheriff told Malvoisin.

It is his way of showing that he is still in control of at least a part of the country. If he can show off the might of his allies then he may muster more support."

"God willing it will be enough to thwart Richard should he make it to England," said Malvoisin, as he stared into the contents of his wine cup.

Rowena and Maud shared a glance. It was alarming how openly the king's enemies spoke of treason these days. It seemed that they were now fully committed with no chance of turning back.

"And speaking of maintaining control," the sheriff said with a little more hope in his voice. "I am close to capturing the villain Robert de Locksley."

Rowena's eyes darted in the sheriff's direction.

"How so," Malvoisin asked, "after he has eluded you this far?"

"I have one of the brigand's associates now in custody. Simon de Stannington."

Malvoisin frowned. "Geoffrey's drunken knave of a son? But what has he been doing consorting with robbers?"

"Filling his own pocket, no doubt," said the sheriff. "He was found to have a cache of silver hidden beneath Miller's Bridge; the very same silver that was robbed from me on its way to Nottingham Castle. I took him to York in chains last week to await trial at the next county court but he's refusing to name his associates."

"I'm confident you'll break him, sheriff. I want the location of Locksley's camp from Simon's lips or his head in the noose instead!"

Panic gripped Rowena. *Simon taken?* The foolish oaf of a sheriff had no idea that he had the real Hob of Locksley in his custody but how long would that last? What would they do to Simon in order to get him to talk? And if he didn't talk, he'd be hanged anyway. It was all too terrible to bear and even more so because she was powerless to do anything about it.

Later that evening, Malvoisin came to Maud's bower. He spoke to them both but kept his eyes fixed on Rowena.

"Well, it seems that I now know at last whom you have been feeding information. I had my suspicions that it was that idle monk from Fountains Abbey and perhaps he too is mixed up in all of this, but Simon de Stannington? I was a fool not to see it. While our attentions were on Maud and the elder Stannington, her lady-in-waiting was conniving with the younger brother behind our backs!"

Rowena and Maud said nothing. There was no defence; they were more or less guilty of what Malvoisin accused them. The only question was what would happen to them now.

"I don't know how guilty the young Maud is in this damnable scheme," Malvoisin continued. "But of your guilt, Lady Rowena, there is no doubt. I had noticed your familiarity with Simon de Stannington but put it down to the flirtations of a wanton maiden. Now I know the truth; that you were feeding this spy information about the movement of wealthy targets for Locksley to rob! My very friends! And not to mention the contributions of three manors to the king's ransom. Have you no shame, Rowena?"

Rowena was silent. There was a deal she would like to have said in reply, something to do with Malvoisin's tyranny being the reason for a man like Locksley to help the poor and not least the fact that the 'ransom contribution' had been intended to be used *against* the king, but she kept her mouth shut, knowing it would do no good and likely worsen her situation.

"I think I can safely say that you have worn out your welcome, Rowena of Rotherwood," said Malvoisin. "Tomorrow you will be escorted back to Cedric with a full report of your actions here at Sheffield."

"It wasn't all Rowena's fault!" spoke up Maud. "I knew about it too! We were in on it together."

"If I were you, my lady," said Malvoisin, turning to his ward, "I would keep my mouth shut. I have decided that you have played no part in this treachery for the good of your name which, thankfully, remains untarnished. I have arranged with the Furnivals that you will marry Gerard the younger. We can forget the Stanningtons, they are clearly unsuitable considering the company their youngest member keeps."

"You can't decide who I marry!" Maud exclaimed. "Only the king can do that!"

Malvoisin smiled. "It *will* be the king who decides. When Richard fails to return, his brother John will be crowned and then many things will change."

He left them then and Constance slunk out of the room after him, turning to lock the door behind her. Maud and Rowena hugged each other, tears in their eyes.

"I am so sorry, Rowena," said Maud. "You have been such a good friend these past few years and all it has brought you is trouble."

"Oh, don't think about me, I'll be all right," said Rowena, as she palmed away a tear. "I'm the one who should be sorry. It was me who started all of this. I was the one who stole from the castle kitchens and I was the one who struck up an acquaintance with robbers. I fear I have led you astray, my lady."

"Nonsense! Before you came to Sheffield, I was lonely and bored. Since you've been in my service, I haven't had such fun in all my life! And we helped people, didn't we? I mean really helped them. And we warned the queen mother of treachery. Twice."

"Yes, I suppose we did," said Rowena. "For all the good it did. If John becomes king things will only get worse."

"I don't care what Malvoisin says," said Maud resolutely. "The king *will* be home soon and your Wilfred too. It will be all right, you'll see."

"I hope you're right," said Rowena. "But then you'll be married anyway. The king's return won't bring you much happiness."

"I suppose it won't. It's strange that the one thing we have tried so hard to make happen is the one thing that will result in what I fear the most."

"It will probably still be Gerard de Furnival that you'll marry," said Rowena. "His father was with the king in the Holy Land. He's not so bad, you know?"

Maud managed a little laugh. "No, he's not. And bless you for trying to make me feel better. I will just have to make do with the situation and pray that I will learn to love my husband as Lancelot loved Guinevere and as you love your Wilfred. He *will* return, you know? Safe and sound and then you will marry him."

"Thank you," said Rowena, fresh tears spilling from her eyes at the awful unfairness of the world.

"Promise me that when you do, you'll love him for the both of us?"

"I promise."

Early the next morning, two soldiers wearing Malvoisin's sigil escorted Rowena from Sheffield Castle towards Rotherwood. Her parting from Maud had been a tearful one and even Constance seemed sad to see her go. All in all, her time at Sheffield had not been a total waste, not to her anyway. But it was the thought of Simon in some gaol at York that occupied Rowena's mind on the ride north.

If there was one person in this whole business who had surprised her the most, then it was Simon of Stannington. At first she had thought him a boor and a letch and perhaps he had been. But beneath that devil-may-care bravado, there had been a kernel of goodness. Somehow, over the past three years, that kernel had sprouted, bloomed and taken him over and Rowena felt like there wasn't a finer man in all of the West Riding.

The poor praised the name of Hob of Locksley without even knowing who he really was. Who would help them once Simon of Stannington had been executed? As they neared Rotherwood, Rowena came to a decision. She was no longer Malvoisin's prisoner. She could do something to help Simon. It might be a futile gesture, but at least she could *do* something.

She tugged on her reins and turned her horse around. Her escort swivelled in their saddles in confusion and then struggled to give chase as Rowena kicked her mount into a gallop.

She rode back south and left the road for the wooded trackways that skirted Sheffield. The cries of her guards could be heard behind her as she urged her horse on and on, desperately trying to lose them. Their voices drifted away as the trees whipped past her and she veered south towards Copmanhurst.

Brother Broch and his hounds were sitting at the steps to the ruined chapel of Saint Dunstan, enjoying the morning sun despite the chill in the air. The three of them glanced at her in surprise as she rode into the clearing and drew up, her palfrey foaming at the mouth.

"Lady Rowena!" the monk cried. "I have not seen you in a long time. You look as if you have outrun the devil himself!"

"Long story, Brother," Rowena said, as she slid down from the saddle. "I have an urgent favour to ask."

"Whatever it is, I hope it doesn't involve another trip to London," said the monk. "Two such trips have left me with unspeakable saddle sores. But whatever I can do, I will do, God willing."

"It's Simon of Stannington. Hob of Locksley, rather." She didn't know if Brother Broch was aware of Locksley's true identity but it didn't matter much.

She trusted Brother Broch with her life. "He is being held prisoner at York and they will execute him for sure. You know where his band's camp is, don't you?"

Brother Broch coughed nervously. "Well, they did take me there before I set out for London that second time …"

"Oh, I don't need you to tell me where it is; the few who know the better. But you must get word to his men. They *have* to rescue him, Broch, they simply must!"

"Calm yourself, child," said the monk. "I will ride to their camp and see what can be done. They may already be planning a rescue attempt, though how such a thing can be pulled off with him in some dungeon in the city is more than I know."

"Please convince them. You know how much he means to the poor of the Chase."

As Brother Broch began to pack his things for his journey to the robbers' camp, Rowena refreshed herself at Saint Dunstan's spring before mounting her horse and riding back north.

She caught up with her guards along the way and, although they were extremely grumpy for having been given the slip, they seemed relieved enough to be reunited with their charge and Rowena let them conduct her all the way home to Rotherwood.

CHAPTER XVI

York, February 1194

The prison cells at the end of the Ouse Bridge were tiny, dank little holes near the waterline. Through the small grille above his head that let in the only light, Simon could hear the lapping of the river against the stone and the cries of the dockworkers as they unloaded merchant vessels further along the river bank.

He felt awful. His left eye was badly swollen and his nose felt like it was broken. He couldn't remember when he ate last. In fact, he wasn't sure how long he had been here. Had it been a week already since the sheriff had come for him?

He had been such a fool. He should have listened to the others, to John and Rowena. They had tried to warn him. His ambition had become his downfall. Somebody had evidently seen him going to and from Miller's Bridge and, after poking about down there, had found the cache of silver. Now, they would hang him.

The sheriff and his men had tried to wring the names of the rest of the band from him, as well as the location of their camp but he had held fast, refusing to betray the people he had already placed in so much danger. He managed a small grin in the darkness, ignoring the pain this caused his cracked lips. That fool of a sheriff didn't even know who he had in his custody. Simon would die on the scaffold and the authorities would never learn the true identity of Hob of Locksley. There was a small bit of satisfaction to be had from that.

A key turned in the lock and the door grated open on its rusty hinges. Two men in mail reached into the tiny cell and hauled him to his feet.

"Come along, you," said one of them. "It's time to face the king's justice."

"And what exactly does that mean these days?" Simon asked, as they pulled him out of the cell and up the spiral stairwell to the guard room atop the bridge.

The daylight burned his eyes as he was led out. He was aware of many people watching him, diverted from their errands to gawp at a prisoner being removed from the cells. A haycart awaited him and he was lifted up into it, his manacled legs unable to manage the step up. As the cart trundled off, Simon squinted at the city of York in all its splendour and squalor. Downriver, he could see the newly rebuilt wooden keep of York's castle which had been burned down during the riots against the Jews following King Richard's coronation. Up ahead, the city unfolded before them on either side of its main street which was clustered with houses and shops.

People scuttled out of the way as the driver of the hay cart yelled at them and brandished his whip. The other guard stood in the cart with Simon, watching him with a cold smile.

"You, there!" barked the driver at another cart that was blocking their way. "Move aside! We are escorting a prisoner to the common hall!"

The other cart was piled high with empty poultry crates and broken barrels. Its driver was a small figure in a tattered old cloak. He seemed to be having trouble with his horse which was an old nag of a thing barely capable of pulling its load.

"I said move aside!" the driver yelled again. "Get that old junk out of the road!"

A crowd had begun to gather around the spectacle and there was much mirth at the situation. Simon looked at the faces in the crowd and suddenly started when he recognised one of them. *Was that … William of Studley?*

Impossible. William and the others would be keeping their heads down back at Harthill Walk, hoping against hope that their captured leader would not betray them. He must be delirious, half-starved and unused to daylight.

"Go and get that idle bastard to shift his cart," the driver of the hay cart said to the guard by Simon's side. "This scum will be late to his own trial at this rate."

The guard grumbled and got down from the cart. As he pushed his way through the crowd, they seemed to envelop him so that only his iron helm could be seen through the press of people.

"Stand back from him!" the driver bellowed. "Can't you see we are on important business?"

There was something very odd about this whole farce, Simon decided and, had he not been on his way to his own judgement at the county court, he might have laughed at the absurdity of it all.

Hands seized him from behind and, before he knew what was happening, he was being pulled down from the hay cart. The driver turned around and saw what was happening. He roared an oath and stood up, reaching for the sword at his belt.

Somebody gave the cart a hard shove. The guard cried out as he lost his footing and tumbled into the crowd amid further laughter and confusion.

Simon struggled to keep his feet as he was hustled down a side street and a hooded cloak was draped over his shoulders.

"We got him, lads!" hissed a voice Simon recognised.

"What of John? Did he get away?"

"Aye, he's driving his cart off now. The rest of our boys are still giving those guards a hard time."

Simon peered at his abductors in the gloom of the alley. "Thomas?" he said. "Ulrich? And William! Then I *did* see you!"

"Do you think we'd leave you here to be hanged?" said Thomas the miller with a grin. "But it's the Lady Rowena you have to thank for this bold rescue. It was her who sent Brother Tuck to us with the news that you were to be tried at the next county court."

"Enough talk," said Ulrich. "We've got to get those shackles off his feet or we'll never get through the city gate."

Simon felt light-headed with elation. His loyal men had come for him, snatching him from the jaws of death at great peril to themselves. Could anyone ask for better friends? And the Lady Rowena ... She had been behind it all! The knowledge that she cared so deeply for him was almost more than he could bear and the light-headed sensation seemed to flood his entire body. The world swam before his eyes and he felt himself slipping off into unconsciousness.

He awoke upon several cushions, gazing up at a beautifully painted ceiling. The smell of perfumed oil from a nearby lamp made him feel as if he had awoken in some exotic den of the east and for a moment, he wondered if he had died and was now in the Kingdom of Heaven, despite the reservations he had about the quality of his soul.

There was a woman in the room, dressed in a long, silver gown and, as she turned to him, Simon realised that she was but a girl and an exceedingly beautiful one at that. From what he could see of her hair, it was black and curled and, although her face was smooth as cream, there was something of the foreign about her.

"You are awake at last," she said, noticing that he was staring at her. She reached out a delicate hand and felt his forehead. "The fever has broken."

"Where am I?" Simon asked, purely out of interest for as far as he was concerned, wherever he was, it was all right in the company of such a beautiful maiden.

"In York and safe for the time being," she told him, cryptically.

"Rebecca, why are you unveiled when you speak to a gentile?" asked the voice of a man who had just entered the room.

"So that our guest can see my face and is not afraid," said the girl as she covered her face with her silken veil.

Gentile? A shudder of horror and revulsion rippled through Simon's body. He was in the house of a Jew! One of those heathen cabalists who dabble in necromancy! It was said that the Jews abducted Christian children and sacrificed them in their blood rites. What diabolical business had these two unbelievers with him and how had they got hold of him?

"Why ..." he stammered. "Why am I here?"

"You were brought to us because you needed medical attention," said Rebecca. "Your friends paid my father handsomely for the risk he took in accepting you into his house. It was quite clear by your shackles that you had been imprisoned."

Simon remembered now. William of Studley, Thomas the miller and others had snatched him from the hay cart on his way to his trial. He must have collapsed and they had brought him here. His shackles were gone even though the chafe marks remained.

"Where are my friends?" he asked. "And why did they bring me to a Jew's house?"

"For I am a healer," said Rebecca. "A pupil of Miriam, daughter of the Rabbi Manasses of Byzantium. She instructed me in herblore and medicine. I am Rebecca and this is my father Isaac. Your friends are nearby and await your recovery.

When they left you with us, they said you were a poacher called Dickon brought to York to stand trial."

Good for them, thought Simon, *for not revealing to these Jews my true identity.* "Ah. Yes, well, that I am. Dickon Bend-the-Bow they call me, for there is no finer poacher to be found in Locksley Chase."

"Then you must hasten back there as soon as you are fit to do so. I will carry word to your friends when you are recovered. In the meantime, drink a little wine and have some broth. Your time in gaol has been hard on your constitution."

Simon accepted the food and drink, feeling he had no other choice. It could be drugged or poisoned, yet the Jewess's story rang true. But why had his friends left him the hands of the heathen? Perhaps in their desperation, they too had felt they had no other choice.

Three days passed and Simon began to feel his strength returning thanks to Rebecca's balms and broths. All the while, her father Isaac ducked in and out of the chamber, assuring himself that nothing untoward was going on between the gentile patient and his daughter. He constantly wrung his hands with worry but Simon was not fooled into thinking it was on his account. The old Jew was probably terrified the sheriff's men would break down his door at any moment looking for the fugitive he harboured.

On the fourth day, Simon was up and about, dressed and thinking about how he was to escape York and return to Locksley Chase. The Jew's house was an extravagant stone townhouse built in the modern style with Norman arches looking out onto an enclosed garden. As Simon moved from room to room, he saw that, aside from the chamber in which he had regained his strength, it was a house that was in the process of being emptied. Isaac's servants were wrapping up silver finery in cloth and tapestries, chests were being packed and bookcases being emptied.

"Are you leaving York?" he asked Rebecca.

"We must," she replied. "My people are welcome nowhere in England but we had been among friends here in York. Alas, we have no friends left here, not since the violence following the king's coronation took so many from us."

Simon looked at the floor, feeling some sympathy for the girl and her father, unbelievers though they were. The riots and murderous violence that had broken out four years ago, stoked by the fervour of the king's departure to reclaim Jerusalem from the infidels, had appalled even the staunchest critics of the children of Israel.

"How did you and your father survive when so many of your people perished?" he asked Rebecca.

"When the worst of the violence broke out," said Rebecca, her voice faint as she recalled that awful night, "my father and I knew it would only be a matter of time before they looted this house and so we packed up our most valuable belongings and sought shelter with my teacher Miriam.

"Most of York's Jews thought to find safety in numbers and headed to the castle to seek refuge from the mob. My father thought that a fool's errand and did not trust the castle's constable to protect them. He was right, of course, in the end.

"We hid in Miriam's cellar which had a secret door. When we thought the mob's attention was fully focused upon the castle, Miriam went out to see who was left of our community. A roving band of rioters saw her and knew her for a healer. As Nazarenes so often do, they mistook her skills in medicine for witchcraft and they burned her alive in the street."

Simon frowned. Despite his own suspicions of Rebecca's people and their ways, she had healed him after all, and she now painted a sobering picture of a people burdened by the prejudice of others.

"The rest of York's Jews fared little better," Rebecca went on. "The wooden keep they had sought shelter in burned down with them inside it. At first we thought the mob had set torches to it but it has since been revealed that my people had murdered themselves to avoid being forced to convert to the Nazarene path. They set fire to the building around them to prevent their bodies being mutilated after death. Such is the dedication of my people to their faith."

"Where will you go now?" Simon asked.

"We go to Ashby to stay with a friend of my father's. There is to be a tournament there in a few weeks held by the king's brother with whom my father has many business dealings."

"I don't doubt it," said Simon, forgetting his previous sympathy for a moment. "It is well-known that money rules a Jew's heart instead of a conscience."

Rebecca's eyes flared with anger at his words. "You speak so of my father who has given you refuge in his own house at great peril to his safety?"

"You yourself said that my friends paid him well," said Simon. "And how else should I speak of a man who shelters an enemy of Count John while simultaneously financing that traitor's schemes?"

"Perhaps you should consider the options left open to a Jew in England," said Rebecca, the fire still in her eyes. "Money lending is the only trade my people are allowed to ply, though it earns them nothing but scorn. Men like my father cannot afford to be political. The gentiles will readily borrow money from a Jew, even threatening them into lending it to them, but when the debt is called in, it is the Jew who is the bloodsucker. Not content to merely abuse those to whom he owes money, the gentile fabricates outrageous lies about the Jewish faith. I've heard them all; that we crucify Christian children in the cellars of our houses, that we use their entrails in divination rituals and their blood in our unleavened bread during Passover. And all of this said of a people without whom the gentiles would be unable to finance their businesses and their wars! Is there a single race on God's earth that is at once so detested and yet so required as the children of Israel?"

There were tears in Rebecca's eyes now and her outburst left her shaking and heavy of breath behind her veil. Simon, although not entirely stripped of his suspicions regarding the Jews, felt that he had never met anybody quite so strong and determined in their convictions as Rebecca.

Except perhaps Rowena.

Yes, there was a similarity there and not just that they were both beautiful. Rebecca shared some of the fiery spirit Simon had come to love in Rowena and it was the last thing he had expected to find in the heart of a Jew. Perhaps they were a misjudged people after all, and, while he did not feel quite ready to dismiss everything said about them, Rebecca had indeed drawn some sympathy from him for her people's plight.

Isaac, alarmed by the passionate tone in his daughter's voice came hurrying into the room. Upon seeing Simon dressed and out of bed, he said; "You appear to be well healed, Dickon Bend-the-Bow. Will you be leaving us now?"

"Yes," said Simon. "And … thank you. For your hospitality."

"We Jews are known for our hospitality and charity to our own people even if we rarely bestow it upon gentiles. Nevertheless, my people also know the chafe of shackles all too well. Criminal you may be, but if poaching the king's deer is your crime, then perhaps you do not deserve so harsh a punishment. You are of Saxon stock, are you not?"

"I am," Simon replied.

"Few poachers are not and, by the God of my fathers, if there is one people that the Jew should look upon with some sense of fellowship, it is the Saxons of England."

"What do you mean?" Simon asked, not entirely liking the association.

"How could we not have a fondness for a people robbed of their homeland and forced into servitude? Wherever a Norman castle now stands, there once stood a Saxon hall."

Simon smiled. This Jew was sounding remarkably like old Cedric of Rotherwood and he wondered what that old warhorse would think of such a comparison.

"Rebecca, would you please go and rouse this man's fellow from his idle slumber at the inn across the road?" said Isaac to his daughter. "And you, Dickon, I will give you a last meal in the kitchen before you depart. It is a long ride to Locksley Chase."

As Rebecca donned her shawl and headed out into the street, Simon was led by a servant into the kitchen and given wine, bread and fish. Isaac slipped out into the garden and was gone for some time.

Simon, left alone in the kitchen, got up after finishing his meal and went over to the arched windows that overlooked the garden. There, beneath an apple tree, was a stone portal leading to some underground chamber beneath the house. As he watched, Isaac emerged from the portal, a sack in his hand. He turned to close the door to the portal which was in the form of a large stone Simon judged to be on rollers by the ease of which the old man moved it back into place. Once closed, the portal was invisible to the naked eye and resembled a natural rock.

Simon returned to the kitchen as Isaac re-entered the house, unaware that he had been spied upon. He placed the sack upon the table where it rested with a heavy 'clink'.

"You came here in naught but your clothes," said Isaac. "And you will need a fast horse to speed you on your way. I have no such horse that I might lend you, but here is one silver mark with which you can buy one."

"You are most generous," said Simon, glancing at the sack. "You really didn't have to do that. You have fed and sheltered me already."

Isaac winked. "Your friends paid me to do that so let us call this a small refund on that transaction. Besides, it is not just your safety I think of but my daughter's and my own. The sooner you are out of my beard the better."

There was a knock at the door and one of the servants hurried to open it. Rebecca entered while a man waited on the doorstep. Simon grinned when he saw that it was John.

"Fighting fit again?" John asked him, as Simon grasped him in a hug.

"As good as new. Where are the others?"

"Returned to the Chase. No point in us all waiting around in York for the sheriff to discover us."

"You remained alone?"

"Aye, I wouldn't dare return to Stannington Hall. Not now you're on the run. I don't know how your father is going to react to all this but I doubt he'll want me around at the moment."

"I'll explain things to him."

John raised an eyebrow. "You're thinking of returning to Stannington?"

"Just until I figure out what I'm going to do next. Come on, I've imposed on the hospitality of these fine people long enough. It's time we went home."

"Goodbye, Dickon," said Rebecca. "God be with you."

"And with you, Rebecca," said Simon. "May he bless you and your father for your kindness."

As they left the house and walked down the street, John gave Simon a funny look. "You needn't think those Jews looked after you out of the goodness of their own hearts," he said. "We paid them well enough to keep you."

"I know," said Simon. "But they've been more than good enough to me."

"I was against the idea of leaving you with unbelievers but we were desperate and were told that the Jewess is the best healer in York."

"I know. Let's not talk about them anymore."

With the silver Isaac had given him, Simon was able to purchase a horse and they made good time, reaching the northern fringes of Locksley Chase before dark. They headed straight for Stannington Hall.

The hall was quiet and the fire burned low in the Great Hall. Simon lowered his hood and looked around at his childhood home, wondering how much of it he was going to see in the future.

"You dare to come here?" said his father from the doorway. "You flee from justice and think to find shelter with us? Haven't you done enough to this family?"

"Father," said Simon, turning around to face him. "I know what you think. It's not how it seems."

"How is it, then? Is my son not an associate of thieves and an accomplice to their villainy?"

Simon didn't know what to say, or what to do to make any of this better.

"Maud de Lovetot will marry Gerard de Furnival upon the king's return," his father continued. "Your actions have shamed this family and ruined my plans. I even hear that you dragged Rowena of Rotherwood into your schemes. Now she is shamed too. You couldn't just play the part of a dutiful son, could you? You had to ruin everything with your selfish actions, always thinking of yourself and never your family."

"Father, please …"

"You are no longer welcome in my hall and you are no longer part of this family. I hereby disinherit you. I will not inform the sheriff that you were here – my fatherly duty extends that far, but no further. From now on, you are on your own and without my protection."

Robert and Hugh had appeared in the doorway behind his father. On the steps behind them, Simon could see their mother. There were tears in her eyes but she seemed unwilling to speak up.

"I am sorry," he told them. "One day you may forgive me but until then, I will no longer be a burden to you. Goodbye."

He turned from them and, with John in tow, left the manor hall and headed towards the stables.

"I'm glad that you are with me, John," he said. "Whatever the future holds, I feel I have the courage to face it with you at my side."

"What will you do now?" John asked him.

"There is but one place left that I call home," said Simon, as they rode out of Stannington Hall for the last time. "Simon of Stannington is dead. But Hob of Locksley is alive and well."

The camp at Harthill Walk seemed even larger to Simon than the last time he had seen it. Its inhabitants were hard at work forging a small kingdom from the greenwood: some hanging up newly shot game to cure, others cooking pottage and roasting meat over the campfires, some fletching arrows and others shoeing horses. A blacksmith hammered on his anvil and two women were thatching a newly built shelter. All of them looked up from their work as Simon and John rode into the clearing.

Simon smiled as he saw his comrades, the very men who had risked life and limb to rescue him from the gallows at York: Thomas the miller, William of Studley, Ralph and Ulrich. There were some new faces he didn't even recognise but they looked to him with the same expression of pride as the others.

"The robber chief returns," said a jovial voice and Simon turned to see Brother Broch leaning against a tree trunk with his two hounds at his feet. "For good this time, perhaps? You'll be outlawed, you know?"

"I'm not the first, nor will I be the last," said Simon, as he dismounted. "And you, Brother Tuck? What brings you here? Do you think to join us?"

"Aye, if only to save your villainous souls. Besides, I am no longer a monk of Fountains Abbey, the good Prior Aymer saw to that. He has powerful friends unfortunately, too powerful for my dear Abbot Ralph to stand up to. I felt it was best for all if I left and gave my life over to solitary work. The grange at Copmanhurst will undoubtedly pass to some other monk of my order but I do hope to continue the refurbishment of Saint Dunstan's chapel. I will live in my hermitage there but will offer you and your band whatever help I can."

"Now we can add a defrocked monk to our number," said Simon with a grin. "God help us, has there ever been such a band of rogues!"

"You started something here, Hob of Locksley," said the former monk. "And God will just have to think charitably on the sins of those who perform good deeds in his name."

"We're with you, Simon," said Thomas the miller. "Right until the end, whatever and whenever that will be."

"My loyal followers," said Simon, feeling a little damp-eyed. "I could not ask for better company than you fellows. The sheriff may outlaw us all in due course but what is outlawry here in the greenwood? Here, where there is no tax or starvation, it is the sheriff and his like that are the outlaws. And we, brave men of Locksley Chase, we are the lords of the greenwood!"

CHAPTER XVII
The Road to Rotherwood, March 1194

As dusk settled over the splayed treetops of Locksley Chase, the wandering pilgrim glanced up at the leaden sky that peeked between the gnarled oak branches. He frowned at the boiling grey clouds that were shot through with the red rays of the setting sun. Soon it would rain.

He had wandered for many days, having no horse to carry him, and he was tired and hungry. He had used up the last of his coin and survived only on the charity of those who were pleased to see a palmer returning from the Holy Land. They were eager for stories of the places he had seen and an account of the king's failed quest to reclaim Jerusalem.

Failed? Was that what they were saying in England of all they had achieved in the Holy Land? Perhaps it was the lies of the king's brother that lay at the root of such opinions but despite it all, the pilgrim could see that the people were in high spirits for news of the king's release had swept the country ahead of him. Only one question remained; where was the king now? When would he return?

In fact, the king and his entourage had landed at Sandwich on the 14th of March after a month-long journey through Europe that had taken them through Cologne and Antwerp, finally crossing the English Channel with favourable winds on the 12th.

The plan was to ride to Canterbury, make their devotions at the shrine of Thomas Becket and then move on to Rochester Castle where the lengthy process of setting England to rights could begin. While the ships were still being unloaded, Wilfred had approached the king and asked for a private word.

"Good to have your feet back on English soil, eh, Ivanhoe?" said King Richard.

"Indeed, sire. We are out of danger at last and so too is the relic you entrusted me with." Nothing had been said on the journey home of the piece of the true cross Wilfred had carried around his neck since Acre and he had assumed the king still wished him to safeguard it until they were back in England. He looped the silver chain over his head and pulled out the reliquary, holding it out for the king. "It has been an honour to guard it for you, sire."

"Put it back around your neck, Ivanhoe," said the king.

"You wish me to keep it still?"

"Until your dying day."

"Sire? I don't quite understand."

Richard sighed and patted Wilfred on the shoulder. "Few kings are lucky enough to have such fine knights in their service. And fewer still have such loyal men they can call friends. You never failed me, Ivanhoe. Had I known the full extent of your persistence and devotion to me while I was caged at Dürnstein, my nights would have been a deal less lonely. Thank you, Ivanhoe, from the bottom of my heart. Take this reliquary as my gift to you for your trueness."

"Sire, I don't know what to say …"

"Then say nothing. Now, I suspect you have a desire to continue to your home in the north and see how things have fared in your absence. I have little I can give you to help you on your way for my own finances have been somewhat ruined of late, but I can give you a horse. Poor recompense for your fine Jago of course, but it should get you there."

"You wish me to leave now?"

"I would take you to Rochester with me but it will take me some time to learn the full extent of my brother's treachery. I will have need of your service again, Ivanhoe, but until that day comes, I order you to go home, find that maiden of yours and make her your wife."

It was a strange feeling to leave the service of the one Wilfred had fought tooth and nail to be reunited with. He had grown to love his king dearly over the past four years and it was with some trepidation that he left his side to pursue a more personal quest.

But Rowena was waiting for him, he knew it, and the king's blessing was an unexpected godsend he could not pass up. He mounted his horse just as the king's camp at Sandwich was being struck and took the road west that would take him to London where he could join the Great North Road.

It was when he passed through Grantham after several days' travelling, that Wilfred spotted Brian de Bois-Guilbert and his two Saracen servants at an inn. His heart caught in his mouth as he failed to dismiss the vision as some trick of the light on his tired mind. No, it was the Templar, there was no mistaking it.

What evil business had he here in England with the king so recently returned?

Wilfred remembered that Bois-Guilbert was a friend of Reginald Front-de-Boeuf. He would undoubtedly be riding towards his castle of Torquilstone which lay but a few leagues from Rotherwood. Could fate be so cruel as to put them both on the same road now, after all that had passed?

He touched the reliquary around his neck as he made his plans. He couldn't risk being recognised by the Templar on the road. Not until he was able to take the man to task for his many crimes. The Templar had powerful friends and Wilfred needed to tread cautiously as he planned his enemy's downfall.

He sold the horse the king had given him and traded his riding clothes and mail for a black cloak and sandals. He purchased a long staff capped with iron to which he affixed one of the dried palm leaves folded into a cross that he had brought back from the Holy Land. A broad-brimmed hat embroidered with cockle shells completed his disguise as a returning palmer. Leaving Grantham on foot without being spotted by his enemy, Wilfred headed north.

It was slow going as he followed the Great North Road through Newark and into Nottinghamshire, across the moors that then dipped down into Sherwood Forest. Near Worksop he veered west and entered Locksley Chase, the familiar sights and smells of home so long denied him now flowering in his breast.

Thunder rumbled overhead as the returning pilgrim approached the sunken stone cross that marked the meeting point of four roads; a marker he had last passed when he had been a far younger, more innocent man an impossibly long time ago. The pilgrim gazed at the cross, weathered and mossy with age and then at the road ahead, hearty in the knowledge that still, after all this time, it would lead him home, to Rotherwood.

Printed in Great Britain
by Amazon

12106679R00203